EMMA AND THE CITY

AMY HILLIGES

red
envelope
press

Cover design by germancreative
Author photo © Cloudia Chen

First paperback edition September 2018

ISBN 978-3-9525016-1-0 (paperback)
ISBN 978-3-9525016-0-3 (ebook)

Published by Red Envelope Press

www.amyhilliges.com

In loving memory of my father,
who always wanted the best for me.

And to my husband,
who has always believed in me.

The real evils, indeed, of Emma's situation were the power of having rather too much her own way, and a disposition to think a little too well of herself.

— JANE AUSTEN, EMMA

"Badly done, Emma!"

— MR. KNIGHTLEY IN EMMA

CHAPTER ONE

E mma wished she could freeze the moment.
    She felt like the proud director, producer and screen-writer. (Mentioning casting director, set designer and costume designer would be going overboard.) Everyone was in their places. The beautiful setting showcased the action to perfection. All was as it should be.

Center stage was the leading lady: a pretty, petite brunette clad in yards of bridal white (light ivory silk faille, if you wanted to get technical). Twirling her on the dance floor was the hand-some male lead.

This could have been a non-story of two ships passing in the night. But Emma had made some waves—shifting the course—so the ships would meet. The journey had been rocky but, again thanks to Emma, storms had been weathered and now here they were, sailing—or what was that move? *Shimmying*—off together into the sunset.

Emma whooped along with the other guests. Annalisa and Tom were such hams; they were perfect together.

"How's the cream?"

"Excuse me?" Emma asked, blinking up at her neighbor Adam

Knightley, who had sidled up next to her. He did look good cleaned-up, she had to admit. Most of the time she saw him in sweaty running clothes or the jeans and T-shirts he wore working from home.

"You look like the cat that got it."

Ha, thought Emma.

"In that case, it's delicious." She purred, slanted her green eyes up at him and pretended to lick her right hand, fingers folded down like a paw.

Appreciative laughter rumbled from him as he slung an arm around her shoulders.

Grinning, Emma said, "You cannot tell me, Adam Knightley, that the wedding's not perfect."

"No, I can't," he said. "You've done an incredible job. You've been a true friend to Annalisa."

Emma's chest swelled. Yes, all the sacrifices she'd made, the strings she'd pulled, even talking to her father again so that they could hold the wedding here, at her childhood home, had been worth it. After all, Annalisa was her best friend, her partner in crime since forever.

She could already anticipate flipping through an issue of *The Knot* and seeing the wedding captured in glorious detail by the talented but pain-in-the-ass photographer she'd hired.

"It's almost *too* perfect and polished, though," Adam interrupted her thoughts. "It's like something out of a wedding magazine. I'd imagined something a bit crazier, more colorful, more *Annalisa*."

Emma mentally slapped shut the issue of *The Knot*. What was Adam talking about? "Annalisa gave me carte blanche. She *loves* the wedding!"

It was true. Annalisa didn't care about what she considered frivolous details and had been more than happy to leave the planning of the wedding to Emma.

A conversation Emma had overheard earlier popped into her head:

"—*beautiful, of course, but not at all what I was expecting.*"

"*No, me neither. Apparently, if there's a Bridezilla at this wedding, it's the maid of honor. From what I've heard, you'd think she was the one getting married!*"

"*You mean the redhead with her nose in the air? She sounds worse than my mother-in-law!*"

Emma had dismissed the women's talk as jealousy and petty bitchiness. But . . . ? A pair of vertical lines marred Emma's smooth forehead.

Adam continued, "But regardless of how great a wedding is, a wedding is not the same as happily ever after so don't pat yourself on the back too hard just yet. This is where the hard work for Annalisa and Tom begins."

Emma whirled to face him, flinging off his arm with the motion. "I can't believe you just said that! That was so, so . . . mean and unromantic. We're at their wedding, for Christ's sake! Just because *you* had a failed marriage doesn't mean everyone else will."

Adam held up his hands. "Whoa, okay, maybe that wasn't appropriate. I'm just being realistic here and—"

"—trying to pop my bubble," said Emma.

He seemed to enjoy making a habit of it.

"I'm only doing it for your own good. Otherwise you might fly away."

Despite the joking warmth in his whiskey-brown eyes, Emma felt her heart deflating.

Today was her day—okay, it was actually Annalisa's; she was "only" the matchmaker, best friend, wedding planner, hostess and maid of honor—and she wasn't going to let Adam or anyone else diminish her enjoyment of it by even one tiny bit.

She made some excuse about needing to talk to the photographer and stalked off.

The first dance concluded to wild applause. On cue, Annalisa's dad tapped Tom on the shoulder, cutting in for the father-daughter dance. Soon other father-daughter and mother-son pairs joined them on the dance floor.

A cough sounded near Emma: her father.

Morley Worth offered her his hand. Emma wavered, looking at his upturned palm. Then her heart hardened. Just because they were on speaking terms again, it didn't forgive the past.

"Isabel's over there," said Emma, pointing to her half-sister, who was seated near the bar. "I'm sure she'd love to dance with you."

Emma pretended not to see the way her father's face had fallen before he left.

Instead she surveyed the scene around her: guests laughing and chatting under the enormous airy tent or spilled out onto Hartfield's manicured lawns. Lush greenery and draping fabrics added a touch of refined luxury. Dripping crystal chandeliers and tall centerpieces filled with white hydrangeas and pale peonies upped the glam factor. Here was Emma's vision manifested with a little help from a friend who ran one of New York's most in-demand event-planning agencies.

But something unpleasant gnawed at Emma, preventing her from basking in the moment.

Damn her father.

And damn Adam.

Emma's green satin Manolos clacked on the parquet as she navigated around the dancing pairs until she was at her father and Isabel's side. "It's my turn to dance with Dad now," said Emma. Isabel gave their dad a peck on the cheek and let Emma cut in.

Emma fitted herself in the crook of Morley's right arm, grasped his left hand. A light seemed to turn on and shine through the thin, wrinkled skin of her father's face as he looked at her.

When had he gotten so old?

"Thank you, Emma," he said.

Shame washed over her. "Thank you again for letting us hold the wedding here," Emma said. The words sounded so formal, yet how close she and her father had been when she was little. They had been everything to each other. How had that changed? When had it changed?

"Emma, Hartfield is your home. You're welcome here anytime. You know that."

Yes, thought Emma, but what about Worth Papers & Stationery? I'm never going to be good enough for the family business, am I?

ALL THE TOASTS had been made. The delectable, three-tiered cake had been reduced to a pile of sticky crumbs. And the bridal bouquet had landed in the eager hands of one of Annalisa's cousins. It had all gone off without a hitch. Not that Emma had expected anything else.

For the first time all day, maybe all week, Emma had nothing to do. It was a strange and not entirely welcome feeling.

Needing to catch a breath before the afterparty, Emma gravitated to a bench under a large oak a few yards from the tent.

Now that the night was drawing to a close, the reality of Annalisa's marriage and impending move across the country—and what that would mean for Emma—was beginning to sink in.

"Mind if I join you?" she heard Adam say.

She shook her head, longing to release her long hair from its complicated updo, which had taken what seemed like a hundred bobby pins and half a can of hairspray to secure. Maybe then her head would hurt less.

"Sorry about before," he said, sitting down next to her.

"It's alright." Emma leaned against him, liking his warmth and the smooth cotton of his shirt against her bare shoulder.

Annalisa's laughter carried over from the edge of the tent, where she was talking with Tom and a group of his friends.

"It's going to be strange having her gone, isn't it?"

He did have an uncanny way of reading her mind.

Emma nodded, not wanting to think about how quiet and empty her apartment would be without Annalisa. She suddenly felt like crying. She supposed the exhaustion was catching up to her.

"What was that about earlier?" Adam asked after a few moments. "You were holding court like, like . . . a red-headed Scarlett O'Hara among all the single guys."

"Oh, that." Emma laughed and tossed said head of hair. The effect she'd been going for was ruined by her updo; she wished again her hair was loose. "It wasn't just the single guys, or guys for that matter. They all wanted to hear how Tom and Annalisa met. People just love a good love story."

"And I'm sure you didn't mention, not even once, the role you played in getting them together?" He cocked an eyebrow at her.

"What? And ruin a perfectly good story! What do you take me for?" Emma was beginning to enjoy herself.

"If you want to know the truth . . . " said Adam.

She narrowed her eyes at him. "Don't answer that."

Adam laughed. "Well, you made a lucky guess, and it's paid off. I suppose you're allowed to gloat a little."

"I'll have you know, it was neither luck nor a guess. It was all due to my matchmaking skills."

"Is that what you marketing people call it these days?" said Adam. "In my grandma's day, they called it 'meddling.'"

"That must have been a very, very long time ago," Emma retorted, "when dinosaurs roamed the earth."

Teasing Adam about his age was one of their ongoing jokes.

"I suppose I left myself open to that one," he conceded.

Getting back on topic, Emma said, "Anyway, what would you call me getting your brother and Isabel together?"

"You didn't have anything to do with that," said Adam.

"There you go. I was so subtle, you didn't even notice. That's talent. Admittedly, I didn't have to do *that* much because with the two of them it just clicked."

Adam did not look convinced. "But you didn't even know Garrett then."

"I'd met him that one time in passing."

"Exactly my point—it was just a lucky guess."

Before Emma could reply, a female voice exclaimed, "There you are!"

Brooke, Adam's girlfriend, was striding across the lawn toward them.

"You promised you'd dance with me tonight, Adam. The wedding's almost over. It's now or never."

"He doesn't dance," Emma couldn't help saying.

"Adam, you promised!" said Brooke, scowling at Emma as she pulled at Adam's hand.

"Duty calls," Adam mouthed as he was led away.

Emma followed them back to the party and stopped next to Isabel at the edge of the dance floor.

"What was that about?" Isabel asked, indicating Adam and Brooke's retreating forms with raised eyebrows.

"Trouble in paradise," quipped Emma. "I don't know why he's with her. It's not like he even *likes* her that much."

"You think? I thought they were getting serious. It certainly looked that way at her birthday party a couple of weeks ago. Even Garrett said he thought she was good for Adam."

"*Seriously?*" said Emma. This was the first she'd heard of a birthday party for Brooke, let alone been invited to one. Not that she would have gone, of course, had she been invited. "You and Garrett actually *like* her? She's so possessive and insecure. Not to mention a gold digger."

"Gold digger? I never got that vibe from her."

"Well, I doubt she'll be in the picture for much longer," pronounced Emma with as much certainty as she'd told her audience earlier that she'd just *known* that Annalisa and Tom were *perfect* for each other.

"I guess we'll see." Isabel shrugged. "Though it would be wonderful if Adam found someone to settle down with. He's so good with the kids; he'd make a great dad."

Emma didn't respond. She didn't want to think about the possibility of losing a good friend like Adam to someone like Brooke and their future children today of all days. As if it wasn't bad enough that she was losing her best friend and roommate.

"Speaking of Dad," continued Isabel, "look who he's dancing with."

It was Belinda Bates, Emma's annoying first-floor neighbor. Emma wrinkled her nose. Even from a distance, Emma thought she could see Belinda's mouth moving, her chatter no doubt boring her father to tears.

The DJ announced the last song. Emma let a groomsman drag her onto the dance floor to the opening strains of James Blunt's "You're Beautiful," possibly that spring's most overplayed song. Catching sight of Brooke resting her head on Adam's shoulder, Emma wondered if, at some point, she might need to step in to ensure Adam didn't make another mistake with someone completely wrong for him.

Her dance partner, one of Tom's college friends, said something to her about the afterparty. She dragged her eyes away from Brooke and Adam and rested them on him. He was very good-looking and had been flirting with her all night; Annalisa had already told her what a catch he was. He wasn't a bad dancer, either. After she complimented him on his moves, he whispered something to her about other "moves" he could show her later. If everyone was going to be pairing off, then so could she . . .

Annalisa and Tom rocked up next to them. Annalisa,

animated as always and fueled by attention, adrenaline and alcohol, gave Emma a double thumbs-up behind Tom's back. This she followed with an exaggerated wink and a raised and splayed left hand to display the platinum wedding band nestled under her rock of an engagement ring. Playing along, Tom did a facepalm and shook his head but couldn't disguise the adoring way he was looking at his new wife.

Emma laughed, happiness for her best friend overriding any twinges of sadness and self-pity.

Despite what Adam thought, she was a damned good matchmaker.

CHAPTER TWO

Emma turned from watching the two men carrying cardboard boxes out her front door to the blinking cursor on her otherwise blank computer screen. It was pointless. She sighed and shut her laptop. She'd work when the movers were gone. They wouldn't take long anyway; most of the furniture in the apartment was hers, not Annalisa's.

She yawned, still not fully awake from the movers' godforsaken 6:53 a.m. wake-up call. It figured they weren't from New York. She rose from the dining table, stretched and entered the small kitchen.

From her kitchen, Emma saw the movers carrying Annalisa's antique maple bureau of drawers, inherited from her *nonna*, out the front door.

Unbidden, an image arose in Emma's mind: A skinny, scraped-kneed girl, a tangled nest of red framing her pale, freckled face, watching movers putting into boxes all of her mother's treasured dresses, furs, boots and platforms.

That was the moment when a 4-year-old Emma had realized her mother wasn't coming back—even if she'd put away all her toys every evening and uncomplainingly put on the uncomfortable dresses her mother always insisted she wear.

An excruciating emptiness pushed in on Emma, threatening to suffocate her. She took a few deep, cleansing breaths and focused on the drip-drip-drip of the thin brown liquid into the carafe below.

When the coffee was ready, she poured three mugs, bringing two into the room where the movers were dismantling the dresser's matching four-poster bed. The men gratefully accepted her offering.

Looking around the room, which was empty except for the bedframe, Emma felt a lump in her throat.

"Nice place you've got here. Getting a new roommate?" the one with a Phillies baseball cap and graying beard asked.

Emma shook her head. "I'm going to turn this room into my office." She'd had a roommate after Isabel and before Annalisa. That had ended in disaster; she wasn't about to make that mistake again. "It'll be good not to have to work at the dining table," she added.

"Living on your own is the pits," the other mover, who'd introduced himself as Greg, muttered as he set down his mug and picked up the power drill. "It was hell after my ex-wife left and took the kids. I hated coming home to an empty place. Still do. That's why I'm on the road all the time."

Emma gulped, remembering the sag of her father's shoulders and the dark crescents under his eyes when she'd catch him in the mornings before he'd leave for work.

As if it wasn't bad enough watching all traces of Annalisa disappearing from her home, now she had to listen to some stranger's sob story? And be reminded of her own? Give me a break!

"Yoo-hoo? Morning, Emma!" Her neighbor Belinda's voice.

Emma sighed. That wasn't what she'd had in mind.

Belinda Bates was *that* neighbor, the one who was always

poking her nose into everyone's business. Emma entered her living room to see Belinda holding a round Tupperware container, which she immediately thrust into Emma's hands.

"I just wanted to drop off some cookies—oatmeal raisin, your favorite. Off to work now. I was going to leave them outside your door, but since the door was open . . . We'll all miss Annalisa terribly, won't we? Such a lively girl. The building won't be the same without her. But the wedding, Emma. Oh!" The waterfall of Belinda's words flowed as she gushed about how beautiful Annalisa had looked! the decor! the food! what everyone was wearing! before getting to the point, which was that she'd baked some cookies because she suspected Emma might need some today.

Emma did not know oatmeal raisin cookies were her favorite but decided to take Belinda's word for it. For Belinda, food was the world's best medicine, and she was always making and giving it to her neighbors and coworkers at the hospital. Had Belinda been a better cook, Emma had once remarked to Adam, then maybe her medicine would go down better. Adam had chided her for making fun of Belinda's kind-heartedness. In any case, Emma doubted cookies were going to make her feel better.

After Belinda left, Emma emptied the Tupperware container into a paper bag and gave it to the movers to take with them.

Finally, she had the place to herself. No, that mover was wrong, Emma told herself. Living by herself was going to be glorious. She adored her West Village apartment; it was her sanctuary from the noise and crowds and chaos of the city. As much as she loved Annalisa, Emma had sometimes been annoyed that Annalisa hadn't picked up after herself or was squawking on the phone to her mother again. For a few months, after Monique had moved out and before Annalisa had moved in, Emma had had the two-bedroom, third-floor walk-up all to herself. It'd been wonderful. Just like it would be now.

Tomorrow she would go shopping for a gorgeous desk for her new office. But now, she had work to do.

Emma opened her PowerBook and looked at her to-do list: Comments and e-mails to reply to, research to do, articles to write and edit. And the post about the wedding needed to go up by the end of the day.

Sometimes Emma wondered what the point of it all was.

Her blog, *Worth It*—an online guide to the best places in New York to eat, shop, see and be seen—had started as something to keep her busy after she'd quit her job at the fashion e-commerce site Luxe.

For months after she'd left Luxe (and who could blame her? the marketing director position had her name all over it, not brown-nosing Bridget's), Emma had floundered, not sure what to do with herself. She did not want to subject herself to working for another potentially nasty boss. Even if money wasn't a pressing issue, she minded the amorphous shape of her days. And she hated Adam's harping on her to get involved with Worth Papers & Stationery.

As if that were even an option.

So when she'd hit upon the idea for *Worth It*, she'd grasped it. Now, a year and a half later, she had a steadily growing stream of readers and plenty of experience conceptualizing, launching and running a blog. She enjoyed being her own boss, turning her blog into a money-making venture, and marketing the hell out of it. But ...

But frankly, she was bored. Writing about another much-hyped restaurant, amazing Pilates studio, or talented designer with a new boutique wasn't doing it for her anymore. There was no more challenge; anyone could write reviews. (In fact, it seemed these days, everyone was, what with sites like Yelp soaring in popularity.) Not with her special brand of sass, not with her discerning tastes, not with her unique voice, obviously. But ...

But she had so much more to offer, unique talents that not every Tammy, Dixie and Harriet had. Take, for example, her getting Annalisa and Tom together. Despite what Adam thought, not *anyone* could see the potential between two people and have the ingenuity and industriousness to bring them together. It took someone with imagination (thanks to her lonely childhood, she had plenty of that). Someone with vision.

Emma smiled, remembering how reluctant Annalisa had been to take a chance on Tom after her ex-boyfriend had broken her heart. And Tom, who was based in the San Francisco Bay Area, had no interest in a long-distance relationship. How Emma had had to plot, the little white lies she'd told, to get them together.

And everyone had seen on Saturday how well that had turned out. Better than well. It'd had a fairy-tale ending.

What she craved now was that same sense of satisfaction.

Surely, there must be some way she could bring together her experience, skills and unique talents? Something that could give her the thrill of a challenge and the satisfaction of a job well done?

CHAPTER THREE

Emma descended the stoop of her prewar brownstone. The chill in the air made her cross her arms and shiver. Dammit, she'd underdressed, having been lulled by the glorious weather at Annalisa's wedding to think summer had arrived. Emma considered running back upstairs to grab a cardigan. A glance at her wrist told her she was already late for her lunch appointment. Annoyed, she turned up her street, increased her pace and hoped the clouds would scatter soon.

Yesterday, after posting her article about the wedding, Emma had stood in her dusk-darkened apartment and felt the emptiness and quiet pressing in. She'd reached for the phone to call Annalisa. But Annalisa was on her honeymoon, and it was after midnight in Tuscany. Adam was on a business trip. She dialed Isabel's number.

"Hey, can I call you back?" A baby wailed in the background. "Mila, please take that crown—tiara, *whatever*—off your brother's head. *Right now.* Sorry, Emma. As you can tell, it's chaos here."

Emma had snapped her Motorola RAZR closed.

After a minute of deep, slow breathing, Emma had flipped on the light switches, turned on the stereo, double-checked the schedule for her Pilates studio, and changed into workout clothes. Emma had learned a long time ago not to feel sorry for herself and she wasn't about to start.

But now, marching up heaving Broadway flanked by speed-walking workers in search of lunch, consumers and their colorful shopping bags, and bewildered tourists, Emma felt not unlike a deflated balloon adrift in a sea of people.

Across the street, Emma spotted the restaurant's distinctive striped awning. She wove between the rows of honking yellow taxis stalled by traffic. Only 20 minutes late, she thought, checking her wrist again as she entered the hip, but not-too-hip, restaurant she'd chosen for the occasion.

After adjusting to the comparative darkness inside, Emma's eyes swept over the suited men, well-groomed women and slouching hipsters before settling on the pretty young woman whose fresh-scrubbed face, Roxy T-shirt and wide-eyed stare screamed "not from here."

As a favor to her old nanny, Cynthia Weston, Emma had agreed to meet Cynthia's niece, Hailey Smith, who had just moved to the city.

"Thank you so much for meeting me," said Hailey after Emma had introduced herself. "I read about this place on your blog, which, by the way, is awesome! I can't believe I'm here, in New York, and meeting you and everything. It's so exciting!"

Maybe this wouldn't be so bad.

After they had placed their orders, Hailey explained that she'd just graduated from SUNY Brockport in upstate New York, she'd been in New York City for just over a week, and she had a summer sublet in Brooklyn.

Hailey, however, seemed more eager to hear about Emma and her life in New York than she was to talk about herself.

Everything Emma chose to tell Hailey, from how much fun it had been to attend NYU, to how exciting it had been to work at a fashion e-commerce startup, to what it was like to party at some of the hottest places in the city was met with oohs and aahs from Hailey.

Gratified by Hailey's enthusiasm, Emma told Hailey more: About how her marketing campaign had brought Luxe tons of awareness and new customers. About how her event-planner friend, Sasha, could always be counted on to put her on some list for some party somewhere. About how cool it was to blog for a living.

"You're just like Carrie from *Sex and the City*!" Hailey sighed.

When she told Hailey about setting up Annalisa and Tom and planning their wedding, she got the desired response:

"That is sooo romantic! You're such a gifted matchmaker, Emma! You're like a modern-day Cupid."

Flattered, Emma pushed aside the remainder of her grilled asparagus, baby arugula and burrata salad and leaned forward, ready to give back. "So, what kind of a job are you looking for?"

"Just a server job for now so I can pay the bills while I figure out what I want to do with my life," said Hailey with a self-conscious laugh.

"You have no idea what you want to do?"

Hailey shook her head, her messy ponytail swishing from side to side.

When she'd been Hailey's age, Emma had also not known what to do. She'd always assumed she'd follow her dad into the successful business her grandfather had built from nothing. She'd been blindsided, then, when shortly before she'd finished her business degree, her dad had told her he would not condone her working at Worth Papers & Stationery and she should just go find a job in "fashion or something." How that had killed her.

"I take it you have waitressing experience?" asked Emma.

"Yes, I waitressed all through college. So far, I've replied to a few Craigslist ads and went to two open interviews, but nobody's gotten back to me yet." Hailey's shoulders dropped. "Maybe it's harder to find restaurant work here than I thought."

Emma considered the girl across from her and made up her mind. "There's this cute French place near my apartment in the West Village. I think a couple of the servers are leaving. I could introduce you to the owner."

"Oh, but I couldn't. It was already so nice of you to meet me for lunch today. I told my aunt it wasn't necessary. I know how busy you must be."

Emma smiled. "Lesson number one, Hailey: Connections and who you know is everything in this city."

"Oh, okay," said Hailey, looking down. Then Emma noticed how Hailey pulled back her shoulders and raised her eyes. "Yes, in that case, Emma, I accept your offer . . . if it's not too late. In fact, that would be amazing. But only if it's not any trouble for you."

"That a girl," said Emma. With the right person to guide her, Hailey might make it in this city after all.

After lunch, she took Hailey to Café Bisou and introduced Hailey to the owner, Helene.

When Helene asked Hailey to come back to trail, Hailey was elated. But then Emma saw the self-doubt creep in as Hailey frowned and said, "Hopefully they'll like me, and I won't do something to mess up."

"Lesson number two," Emma said. "If you don't feel confident, fake it until you are."

Emma had been faking it for so long she didn't know where the insecure girl she had been ended and the confident young woman began.

Emma also secured an appointment for Hailey with her hair-stylist, Marcello, because, if Hailey was going to become a New Yorker, she needed to look the part. And her curly, frizzy hair wasn't going to cut it.

One of Emma's first memories was of her mom sighing as she'd tried to untangle Emma's carrot-red curls, pulling the comb through so hard Emma's eyes had smarted. Her mother, with her silky, straight blond hair, was the most beautiful woman Emma had ever seen. So when her mother had muttered over her head about how different Emma was from her, Emma had known that different meant ugly.

No wonder her mother had left.

As soon as she could, Emma had started straightening her hair and to this day still wore her hair straight.

"Wow," Hailey said as they parted with plans to meet again soon, "I feel like the luckiest girl ever, like you're my fairy godmother!"

By the time Emma walked back to her apartment, the sun had crept out from behind the clouds and its rays warmed her bare arms and legs. All in all, she was very pleased with her afternoon's efforts.

As she entered her building, Emma felt less adrift and more afloat. Yes, she would turn Hailey into a sleek, confident New Yorker. She'd introduce her to people worth knowing, find someone who'd fall for the new and improved Hailey, and help her get into the career of her dreams.

Surely, even Adam couldn't find fault with her for helping a shy, sweet girl like Hailey, could he?

CHAPTER FOUR

A dam knocked on the door then leaned against Emma's doorframe, hoping she was in. When she opened the door, he waved the menu from their favorite Chinese takeout.

"Adam!" Emma squealed and launched herself at him. "Did you just get back?"

"Yeah, a couple of hours ago," he said, returning her hug. Brooke had wanted to see him tonight. He'd told her he was too tired. Brooke had then offered to bring takeout. He'd said he needed an early start because of the piled-up work that would be waiting for him tomorrow. She'd relented when he'd promised to take her to dinner tomorrow night. Going one floor up and seeing if Emma might be interested in ordering Chinese with him was a different matter entirely, he told himself.

Emma pointed to the couch, then went to the fridge and pulled out two bottles of Stella.

"Aww, what a nice welcome back," Adam said, making himself comfortable on her low, designer sofa and accepting a beer.

Adam tapped his green bottle against Emma's and took a swallow. Looking around the room, he noted the missing items: the reading chair, the colorful owl cushion, which Annalisa's *nonna* had knitted her that always occupied the chair, and the legal textbooks that were usually piled around the chair. "When did the movers come?"

"Monday."

"And T and A got off to Italy without a hitch?"

Emma nodded, her lips quirking a little at the corners.

He'd thrown in the silly nickname to elicit a smile from Emma. He'd anticipated how'd she'd feel when the wedding was over and the fairy dust had settled. His ex-wife, Caroline, who'd used the planning of their wedding to avoid dealing with other issues, had come down with a thud after the honeymoon. Granted, Emma wasn't the bride and Caroline hadn't lost a best friend, but he was sure there was some parallel there.

Which meant Emma could use a friend now. In the last year, between Emma's blog, Annalisa's wedding and Brooke, he and Emma hadn't seen much of each other. He hoped to remedy that now; he knew that, despite her knowing a lot of people, Emma had few close friends. "And Emma, feel free to come find me if you ever get bored, lonely or just want someone to share takeout with, okay?"

"Thanks," said Emma. Her smile of appreciation changed into the teasing one he was more familiar with. "Sure about that? What would Brooke say?"

There was definitely no love lost between his girlfriend and his neighbor, another reason why he and Emma had spent so little time together recently. Brooke had, more than once, accused him of being interested in Emma. (And Emma, damn her, seemed to take pleasure in flirting with him when Brooke was around.) Despite his claims that Emma was just a friend, Adam had to admit that Brooke was not completely off the mark.

When he'd first moved into Emma's building eight years ago, he had found himself attracted to his neighbor and entertained the idea of her as a rebound. On second and third thought, he knew it would have been a terrible idea because: 1) She had never shown any signs of being interested in him; 2) she was a junior in college, not even the legal drinking age, and he was getting divorced and on the verge of 30; and 3) having a casual rebound with someone who lived one floor above you just couldn't be a good idea.

A few months later, when his brother had hit it off with Emma's half-sister and roommate, anything casual would have been doubly awkward.

"When did Emma Worth care what others thought?" Adam took a long swallow. "Anyway, it's not like Brooke and I are *that* serious."

"Ha, that's what I told Isabel," said Emma, looking pleased.

"I'm flattered my love life is of such interest to you," said Adam, not understanding why women, particularly Emma, were always so obsessed with other people's love lives.

"You wish, Knightley," said Emma. They exchanged smirks and took swigs from their bottles.

"How was the afterparty? You and that one groomsman looked pretty cozy there at the end of the wedding."

He wasn't fishing for details. Of course, he wasn't.

"You mean Garver? Yes, we had a lot of . . . fun . . . afterward," said Emma, her eyes taking on a faraway look, a little smile tugging at her lips.

He so didn't need to know that. And what the hell kind of name was Garver, anyway? "Are you going to see him again?"

"No, I doubt it. It was just a, you know, wedding hookup. Though I will say, I'm flattered that my love life is of such interest to *you*." Emma gave him an impish smile.

Okay, she'd called him on it. "Touché."

~

"So, I've been thinking about my blog . . . " said Emma before putting a mouthful of mapo tofu and steamed brown rice into her mouth. She was eager to share with Adam the brain wave she'd gotten after leaving Hailey on Tuesday.

When she'd arrived home, she'd thought about what Hailey had called her: fairy godmother, Cupid, Carrie Bradshaw. Roll them all into one and you get some sort of lifestyle and dating guru, right?

With *Worth It*, she'd positioned herself as a stylish, savvy, modern New York woman; that was her brand. Maybe there was some way to extend that brand to accommodate this?

The more she'd thought about it, the more excited she'd gotten.

"I'd position myself as a lifestyle expert, not just an expert on things to do and places to go in New York," Emma explained. "This would increase my reach, and the blog could be a launching-off point for a book deal or coaching business."

She looked expectantly at Adam.

"What's brought this on?" he asked.

Emma didn't want to tell him she was feeling unchallenged, stagnant, bored. He would only bring up Worth Papers again.

The last time they'd had that argument was nearly two years ago, when she'd left Luxe and around the time her father was retiring. "Not all of us are workaholics who're meant to be running multimillion-dollar companies," she'd flung at him when he'd asked if she was really so ready to give up claims to her family's business. That hadn't actually been fair, she knew. Adam was pretty good about balancing his work and his life. It was her father who'd been the workaholic, who'd practically vanished after her grandfather had died, leaving her all alone.

"I really enjoy helping people," Emma told Adam now.

"Meddling."

She ignored him. "And readers really seemed to respond to my articles about wedding planning—you know how-to rather than where-to-go articles. So, what do you think?"

She didn't know why it was so important that she got Adam's

thumbs-up. She supposed his professional opinion mattered to her. After all, Adam's B2B startup had not only survived when the Internet bubble had burst, it had thrived; now he was scaling up his second startup.

She also knew firsthand that he was a good mentor. During her senior year at NYU, when she'd had the falling out with her dad—she'd wanted to do her final research project on Worth Papers & Stationery and he'd forbade it—Adam had stepped in. He'd let her do her project, a strategic marketing plan, on his company. He'd even implemented a few of her ideas, much to her pleasure.

"From a business and growth standpoint, I can see the merits," Adam said. "What kinds of articles or advice are we talking here?"

"Style, career, dating, confidence . . . like what would be covered in a typical women's magazine. But I would give it more of a New York spin and perhaps narrow the focus to young women finding their feet in the city."

Adam looked thoughtful.

"I don't know, Emma. Clearly, you have great style and fashion-sense but—"

"But what?"

"What qualifies you for the other stuff?"

Ouch!

"What I mean is . . . "

Let's see how you dig yourself out of this one, Knightley.

" . . . you're great at projecting this image of yourself that's polished and perfect, but that's not the real you, Emma."

Emma slammed her beer bottle down on the table. A bit of foam frothed over the top.

"Emma, we've been friends and neighbors for a long time," Adam continued. "We're also technically family. I know you're not who your blog persona is. I *prefer* the you *I* know. That wasn't meant to be a criticism."

She felt a teensy bit mollified. "So what's that got to do with the blog?"

"Maybe you should work on figuring some stuff out for yourself before you start dishing out advice."

The nerve!

"Forget I said anything," said Emma, pushing away her half-eaten takeout carton; her appetite had vanished. She got up to get a rag to wipe up the beer.

"Stop, Emma," said Adam, laying a hand on her arm. She shook it off. He followed her into the kitchen. "It's great that you're taking your blog in new directions and thinking of ways to spin it off into other things."

Her arms crossed, she let him continue.

"You've got a good mind for business, and I've no doubt you can be successful. Who am I to judge, anyway? I don't read women's magazines and the web is full of people—qualified or not—giving advice."

You've got that right, Knightley.

"You have a loyal following who like your voice and believe in you. I believe in you. Always have."

Emma let her arms drop to her side.

"Friends?"

Emma looked at Adam's familiar face. She was glad he'd come around to her point of view—he always did, sooner or later—not that it would have stopped her. She nodded and watched the smile she could never resist light up his face.

After a beat she rubbed her hands together and said, "Fortune cookie time!" Rag in hand, she dashed back to the dining area. She heard Adam's laugh following her.

"Alright, you go first," she said, holding up the two fortune cookies for him to choose from.

After extricating the little strip from one, he read, "'Everyone feels lucky for having you as a friend.'"

"In bed," they chimed in unison.

"Okay, now me," said Emma. "'There is no mistake so great as that of being always right.'"

"Now that's what I'd call a bull's-eye," said Adam, laughing.

"Not funny," said Emma, punching him in the arm.

"You're right, as always."

That earned him another punch, but she couldn't help grinning. Yes, despite their little tiffs, she did feel lucky to have him as a friend.

CHAPTER FIVE

The following week, Hailey arrived at Emma's apartment alert and ready to submit to Emma's will, Emma's will being to give Hailey a complete wardrobe revamp, a key component of Project Hailey: Phase One.

While Hailey admired Emma's apartment and the view from her private rooftop terrace, Emma was no-nonsense, saying they had a lot of work to do before Hailey's afternoon shift started.

First they looked through the clothes Emma had asked Hailey to bring. All but a pair of jeans and a couple of tops met Emma's approval.

Next they delved through a pile of clothing destined for Goodwill and vintage stores. Emma held up various items in front of Hailey, who was curvier and about three inches shorter than Emma but had the same shoe size.

"You're not going to wear any of this stuff anymore?" asked Hailey, fingering a cashmere T-shirt in a warm coral shade and taking a peek at the label. "This is like really expensive designer stuff."

"A lot of it I got for free from Luxe. Some were Annalisa's, which is lucky for you, since you're about the same size."

They spent the better part of the morning rummaging through the castoffs, Emma telling Hailey to try various things on, Hailey gingerly pulling on, up and off pieces with labels that said Theory, Plein Sud, Sass & Bide and many others that Hailey had never heard of before.

In additional to getting a sense of what colors, cuts and styles suited Hailey, Emma also learned that Hailey was in New York because of a boy.

Typical.

Hailey's college boyfriend, Chris, her only "real" boyfriend, had dumped her a few months before graduation.

"You know, we'd been talking about moving in together when we graduated," sniffed Hailey, "so I totally wasn't expecting it. He said we were too young to tie ourselves down with each other for the rest of our lives before we'd seen the world."

"So basically, he just wanted to screw other girls," concluded Emma.

Hailey nodded, biting her lips. Emma handed her a tissue and Hailey told Emma, between inelegant honks into the tissue, how he'd gone to the Bahamas on spring break with people from his major and had slept with one of the girls in the group. "I think they're still hooking up," Hailey wailed. "When I found out, I was just devastated; that's when I knew we were really over. I decided right then and there to move to the city as soon as I graduated."

Emma said something to Hailey about being brave and making the right decision. Hailey nodded, but she seemed to have lost all enthusiasm for the task at hand. Seeing that Hailey's mind was clearly elsewhere, Emma announced that she was satisfied with their morning's work and was now famished.

But like a puppy dog who'd just been shown a new toy, Hailey couldn't let go of the topic of boys in general and her ex in particular.

"Part of me thinks he was right, that I should see the world. I mean, I guess that's why I'm here," Hailey remarked on the way to the restaurant.

As they waited for the waitress, Hailey said, "It makes me want to throw up to think that maybe he was already into Angie —that's the girl he slept with—while we were still together. That maybe he had even been thinking about *her* while we were, you know, *together*."

After placing their orders: "I wonder when the hurt will go away and I'll be ready to be with someone else?"

Over their cold soba noodles, Hailey asked Emma if she was seeing anyone. Emma saw this as a sign of progress but didn't exactly welcome talking about her own love life.

"No," replied Emma, stabbing her straw at the ice cubes in her glass before draining the last of her pomegranate iced green tea. "I'm taking a break from dating. I don't want to sound egotistical, but I find most guys aren't up to my standards. And I certainly wouldn't want to be with *just anyone*."

"Oh really? Okay," said Hailey, appearing to digest this. "But don't you get lonely? Don't you want to be with someone?"

"Of course it would be nice. But I'm not convinced it's worth the trouble," said Emma. And it was true. The guys she met tended to want more from her than she was willing to give.

Take Garver from the wedding, for example. She'd happily flirted with him at the afterparty, had even kissed him. But she hadn't been interested in more than that and she certainly hadn't slept with him as she'd led Adam to believe. But Garver hadn't wanted only to sleep with her; he'd wanted to see her again. He'd said he was often in New York for work, that Chicago was only a two-hour flight away, and had insisted she take his number and call him "anytime."

With some of the others, she'd had to be painfully straight when they wouldn't take the hint. The last guy, for example, had threatened to throw himself into the tracks of the oncoming L train when she'd told him she didn't want to see him anymore after a handful of dates. That experience had taught her it was better just not to date at all. Also, it was best not to break up with someone on a subway platform.

"I wouldn't want to share my apartment with some guy and his stuff and have to pick up after him," added Emma. "I have some good friends, an adorable niece and nephew. I don't have to worry about money. My life is perfect as it is. I don't need a guy to clutter it up."

Hailey didn't look convinced. "So how come you're into matchmaking if you don't believe in love?" she asked.

"I didn't say I don't believe in love," said Emma. It was just that everyone she'd ever loved had chosen something else over her: her mom had chosen a glamorous jet-setting lifestyle, her dad had chosen work. "Maybe it's just not for me. But I'm all for helping my friends find love. That's more rewarding for me, anyway."

Emma continued, "And what's clear to me is that you need to forget about your ex. You're here now, far away, in the big city. I think you're ready for someone new. And I'm just the person to help you navigate the New York dating scene."

CHAPTER SIX

Returning from the gym a couple of mornings later, Emma's heart stopped. Parked in front of her building was an ambulance. Belinda Bates was flapping on the sidewalk next to a paramedic, who looked like he was trying to calm her. Near them, at the bottom of the stoop, was Zak Elton, the new tenant in the basement apartment. Heart palpitating now, she thought about Adam, who sometimes worked from home.

Running to Zak, Emma demanded, "What's happened?"

"It's Belinda's mom. A stroke or something. The paramedics have just put her in the ambulance."

Emma's initial relief that it wasn't Adam turned to guilt. Mrs. Bates was all the family Belinda had other than her niece, Juliette Fairfax, who lived in L.A..

The paramedics ushered Belinda into the back of the ambulance and drove off. When the siren became distant enough that conversation was possible, Emma pumped Zak for details.

He told her he'd heard Belinda screaming. "Holy shit, the way she was yelling, I thought it was 9/11 all over again. That was some wake-up call. I rushed upstairs. Belinda's door was open.

She was on the phone to 911. Her mom was on the floor after getting dizzy and falling. She was slurring her words, confused, and she couldn't move."

"Dear God, I hope she's going to be okay. Good thing you were here, Zak."

When there was nothing more that could be said about Mrs. Bate's stroke, Emma told Zak that Belinda and her mother had lived in the first-floor unit for nearly four decades. Emma's grandfather had offered the two-bedroom apartment to the widow and daughters of Gerald Bates, a loyal, high-ranking employee at Worth Papers & Stationery for what, even in the 1960s, was an incredible deal. "He promised they could stay in the unit according to NYC rent-control regulations for as long as the building was owned by the family."

"Your family *owns* this place?" Zak asked.

"Yeah. But we leave the running of it to K&M Property Management."

Zak whistled, impressed.

"Have you met all the neighbors yet?" asked Emma.

"Belinda a few times. She even brought me soup once when I had a sore throat."

"I'll bet," laughed Emma. "Any excuse to talk to someone, feed them or give them medicine—preferably all at once—that about sums her up to a T."

Zak continued, "Adam and I had a beer together right when I first moved in."

"Oh, I didn't know that. He's also a fixture here. It's really your apartment where all the changeover takes place."

"Who's the cute chick with the brown hair? Does she live here, too?"

At first, Emma thought he meant Hailey. Realizing he must be referring to Annalisa, Emma broke the news to him about her ex-roommate's recent nuptials.

"That sucks," said Zak. "She was hot."

Emma took a good look at her new neighbor. He appeared to be in his late 20s and was lanky with carefully mussed, dyed black hair. The murky bluish-green of a tattoo on his pale bicep peered out from under the short sleeve of his faded black concert T-shirt. Another tattoo, a large snake, wound up his other arm.

She'd never really noticed him before; he wasn't her type. But now . . . Emma cocked her head and asked, "What do you do, Zak?"

"I'm a musician, the frontman for Broken Extremities."

"Ah, you're in a band," said Emma, able to see his appeal from the perspective of a girl gazing up at him from a sweaty, heady crowd of worshipping fans.

"Yeeah. We're playing Warped Tour later this month—Jacksonville, Tampa, Miami, Orlando, Atlanta. We've also got demos out to the big studios. I think we're totally on the cusp of a breakthrough. You should definitely come to one of our gigs sometime —while we're still doing regular gigs—so you can say you knew Zak Elton way back when," he gave her a lopsided grin.

Hadn't Hailey mentioned wanting to go to some gigs? Didn't Hailey also say she *always* seemed to fall for guys who were engineers or musicians? As an idea began to form in Emma's head, she flashed Zak one of her winningest smiles.

EMMA STEPPED BACK to admire her handiwork. Before her was no longer a nondescript waitress but a pretty young woman, someone who looked polished and sexy enough for New York but also refreshingly innocent.

"So, what do you think?" Emma turned Hailey around to face the mirror.

"Wow," said Hailey leaning forward and tilting her head just so to better peer at her face in the mirror. "I look so . . . different. I hardly recognize myself."

"You look fabulous, Hailey. If I do say so myself," said Emma.

"You don't think the makeup is . . . too much?" asked Hailey, biting her lower lip.

"I know it feels like a lot because you're not used to it but considering the crowd we're going to be hanging out with tonight, it's not. Trust me."

"Okay, Emma, if you say so," said Hailey. "I do love how you've done the smoky eyes on me. Whenever I've tried to do it, I just look like a raccoon."

"And didn't I tell you Marcello was a miracle worker?"

Hailey ran a hand through her hair, which had been cut into long, choppy layers, then blown straight and finished with a spritz of gloss serum. "My hair has never looked so sleek and shiny."

"Are you pleased?"

"Yes, totally!" said Hailey, taking tentative, teetering steps on her borrowed heels and angling her body side to side. "If only Chris could see me now, he might—"

"Tsk-tsk, Hailey," said Emma, wagging a finger. "I don't want to hear another word about Chris. He's in the past now. This is the new you."

"Sorry," said Hailey, her head dropping. "I forgot. I'll try to remember to not talk about him anymore. But sometimes I just can't help it."

Phase Two of Project Hailey, finding her a new boyfriend, needed to go into effect sooner rather than later.

"The best way to forget about someone is to move on," said Emma. "I really think you're ready to meet someone new. Starting tonight."

"You think so, Emma? But I'm not the type of girl who can, you know, just do casual hookups. At least I don't think I am

. . . ?" With uncertainty written across her face, Hailey looked to Emma as if for confirmation.

"Oh no, Hailey. I'm not saying you need to sleep around, if that's what you're concerned about. Any girl in this city can get laid if she wants to. Now scoring a boyfriend, on the other hand, is a competitive sport."

Seeing Hailey's brow furrow in confusion, Emma said, "Don't worry. I know you want something like what you had with Chris, am I right? Think of me as your dating coach. All you have to do is follow my lead."

"Okay," said Hailey, her forehead clearing, a smile returning to her lips.

"Freeze, Hailey," said Emma holding her thumbs and index fingers up to frame Hailey as if in a camera's viewfinder. "You look gorgeous with that small, secretive smile on your lips. Guys will totally fall for it. Which reminds me: We need to take some "after" pictures of you now for the blog. To capture you in all your brand-new New York glory."

As Emma went to get her camera, a knock sounded at the door.

"That's probably Adam from downstairs," said Emma, opening the front door to find not Adam but Zak.

"Zak, how nice to see you!" Emma beamed at her visitor. The timing couldn't be better if she'd planned this herself. "Come on in for a drink and come meet my friend, Hailey."

"Cool. Don't mind if I do. A beer would be great. I came by to tell you I just ran into Belinda."

While Emma grabbed him a cold beer, Zak related that Belinda had returned home to pack some things for the hospital; she would spend the night at her mother's side. Mrs. Bates had, luckily, only suffered a ministroke and her symptoms had cleared.

"That's a relief," said Emma, promising herself she would send flowers the next day before focusing on the more exciting potential developments at hand. "Hailey, Zak's the lead singer in a really hot, up-and-coming band."

"Really?" said Hailey, checking Zak out with what appeared, to Emma, to be interest.

Emma smiled into her glass.

"Yeah, we're called Broken Extremities."

"Wait, I've heard of you! I think I saw that name on some flyers."

"Awesome. Yeah, that would be us. We play a couple of regular gigs around the city. I was telling Emma that she should come check us out," said Zak, piercing Emma with his striking pale blue eyes, before turning his gaze back on Hailey. "You both should."

"I'd love to! I've been wanting to see some bands. What kind of music do you play?"

Emma excused herself to get her camera while Zak answered Hailey, throwing out terms like "diverse influences," "garage rock," "progressive." After a couple of hesitant questions from Hailey, the conversation lagged.

Emma saw that she was going to have to help Hailey and Zak along. Recalling the concert T-shirt Zak had been wearing earlier, Emma said, "Zak, Hailey's a big fan of Coheed and Cambria."

"No shit?" said Zak.

"Uh, I don't really know—" Hailey looked like she was going to protest.

Emma cut her off. "Remember you said you would love to see them live?"

"Right . . . " said Hailey nodding along with Emma. "Yeah, they're . . . great. I'd love to see them live . . . "

"They play a fucking great show. I saw them when they played Warped Tour in 2003," said Zak, recounting how the show had "rocked" and how "inspiring" the band was.

"Oh, cool, Warped Tour," said Hailey, looking relieved.

"Yeah, in fact, we're playing Warped this summer. I'm so amped. It's gonna be epic!"

As Hailey began to say something, Zak turned to Emma and said, "So where are you two all dressed up and going tonight?"

"I'm taking Hailey out on the town. It's the opening of Allegra Alessi's new boutique in Nolita."

Zak whistled. "You're certainly well connected."

"I do my best," said Emma, pleased. "Hailey's new to New York. I'm going to show her some of the glitter and glam of the city. She's also single and certain to break some hearts."

Hailey opened her mouth.

Zak slid his gaze up and down Hailey's body. "Without a doubt."

Hailey blushed and shut her mouth. Zak looked at Emma as if for approval. She rewarded him with a smile.

Holding up her sleek little Canon, Emma began, "Zak, would you be so kind as to—"

"Take some pictures of you?" he asked. "I've got a good eye, used to be a photographer's assistant to this bud of mine. He's now a fashion photographer. He's shot Gisele, Tyra Banks and that hot Frenchie with the teeth and tits."

"Laetitia Casta. Yes, that would be great," said Emma, handing the camera to Zak while she posed Hailey and smoothed her hair.

As Zak clicked away, Emma adjusted Hailey and instructed her on how to look for the camera before being urged to join in by Zak and Hailey.

After a handful of shots, Emma took the camera from Zak to scroll through the pictures. "Look, Zak, this one of Hailey is great. Hailey, come check this one out. You look fabulous."

"You think so?" said Hailey, scrutinizing the picture on the screen. "Yeah, I suppose it's not too bad . . . "

"Not bad? You look phenomenal. Doesn't she, Zak?"

"Yeah, hot. My favorite, though, is this one of the two of you," said Zak, scrolling forward to one of the last pictures. "Shoot me over the pictures and I'll touch it up for you, drop out the background, whatever you need. I'm pretty skilled at Photoshop. I do all our flyers and stuff."

"Thank you, Zak," said Emma. "What a thoughtful offer. I'll do that."

CHAPTER SEVEN

"What do you think of our new neighbor?" asked Emma. It was Saturday morning and for some reason she had agreed to go on a jog with Adam.

"Zak Elton? I got the sense that he was a bit full of himself," replied Adam as they navigated the traffic around Eighth Avenue.

"Really? He seems like a good catch to me."

"Why? Are you interested?"

"Me? God no! I was thinking of him for a friend of mine."

"Ah, I see; you're matchmaking again."

"What if I am? So this friend, Hailey, she's new in town and super sweet. Her boyfriend dumped her and she's really into musicians. I'm pretty sure Zak is single based on what he said about Annalisa. I think they'd be perfect for each other."

"On what basis? Because they're both single? Give me a break, Emma."

Adam was a man. He didn't understand.

"No, of course not, Adam, that would be silly," Emma gave a little laugh. "I felt the sparks radiating off of them when they met."

"I suppose nothing I say is going to make a difference," he said. "So I'd best keep my mouth shut."

"Good, agreed."

They jogged across the cobblestoned alleys of the Meat-packing District, the empty, quiet streets an about turn from the crowds that thronged the trendy area when the sun went down.

"Who is this Hailey, anyway? You never said anything about a friend moving here," said Adam.

"She's the niece of my ex-nanny, Cynthia. As a favor to Cynthia, I'm keeping an eye on Hailey, showing her around a bit. I got her a job waitressing at Café Bisou."

"That's good of you."

"She's nice, young, just out of college and figuring out who she is. I think she's really starting to blossom. On Thursday night I took her to one of Sasha's boutique opening parties. She seemed way more self-assured. Maybe it was the new haircut and the makeup and outfit. The guys were definitely checking her out."

"I'm sure they were with you as her companion," said Adam, eyeing Emma's outfit, a pair of short purple running shorts from adidas by Stella McCartney and a wide-shouldered hot pink Nike top over a black sports bra.

Ignoring whatever Adam meant by that, Emma continued, "And she managed not to talk too much about her ex-boyfriend and even flirted with a couple of the guys."

"And what did the lovely Sasha make of Hailey? Was she as enthusiastic as the guys?"

"You know how Sasha is: The moment she realized Hailey had no connections and was not a threat to her, she lost interest," said Emma.

"Sounds like Sasha. A word to the wise, Emma: This girl, Hailey, by the sounds of it, is innocent and impressionable. I'd be cautious about trying to set her up with someone like Zak. I don't know him well, but I know the type. Also, by the sounds of it,

Sasha's parties can be quite a scene. Be careful that she doesn't get in way over her head."

"I'm meant to be watching out for her, and that's exactly what I'm doing," Emma snapped, jogging ahead of Adam. "You don't even know her."

Emma cast her mind back to when her relationship with Adam had taken on this big brother-little sister dynamic. No, that wasn't the right way to define their relationship. Whatever it was, she supposed the dynamic had been there from the first time they'd met, long before they'd become half siblings-in-law.

She'd been a junior and had talked Isabel into throwing a party. Isabel had invited a handful of friends. Emma had invited her friends, friends of friends, and many of her NYU Stern classmates, believing then that a party wasn't a party without an apartment full of people.

Being underage, Emma had sent Isabel to the liquor store to buy the hard stuff and had handed Jim and Maurice, the Ph.D. students living in the basement of the brownstone, a wad of cash to buy beer. Not surprisingly, the promise of free beer and a house party had spread like rumors of a professor whose class was easy or a coed who was, likewise, easy.

The girls managed to funnel most of the partygoers onto the roof terrace, despite the coolness of the October night. The apartment was, nevertheless, raucous as the overflow mixed drinks in the kitchen, played drinking games in the dining area, and danced in the living room.

"Emma, this guy's been looking for you," said one of her guests, indicating a man she'd never met before.

"Are you the one responsible for this party?" he demanded.

"Yeah," she said, looking him up and down. Prone to judging people by their appearance, Emma decided he wouldn't necessarily turn heads, but he was pleasant enough to look at, possessing a good height and build, regular features, brown hair cut short. Of course, he'd need to wipe that awful expression off his face and he definitely needed to lighten up. But then, he was old; in the neighborhood of 30, she guessed. "What's it to you?"

"I'm your new neighbor. One floor down. I didn't realize I'd moved into a frat house!"

A tinkling sound emerged from Emma's mouth. "That's funny."

This only seemed to irritate him more. "Seriously. It's way too loud. I'm exhausted and would really like to sleep in my new apartment without fear that the ceiling is going to cave in on me."

"What you need to do is relax, loosen up. Come, have a drink; you're here anyway."

Adam only shook his head. "What I would really like is for you to turn down the music and tell your guests to go home."

"As if!" Emma laughed again. Then she cocked her head to one side. "You're not from around here, are you? If you have a problem with noise, then you've moved to the wrong place. Whoever thought New York would be quiet."

"I'm not joking! If you don't turn down the music and control your guests, I'm going to call the cops."

Emma smiled to remember how annoyed Adam had been. She had probably been too drunk to realize how upset he was or too drunk to care.

"Here," she'd said, grabbing one of the full cans of beer that Jim was walking by with and thrusting it into Adam's hand. "By the way, Jim, this surly guy here is our new neighbor. He's threatening to call the cops. We can't let him do that, can we?"

Jim stuck out a hand, and Adam could do nothing but grasp it. "Welcome to the building. I'm Jim. I live in the basement unit."

"Adam Knightley," said Adam, shaking Jim's hand. With Jim distracting him, Emma fled the scene. She'd send Isabel over to placate him.

A little while later, Emma spied on Adam from afar, gleeful when she saw him sipping from the can of Heineken she'd shoved in his hand and chatting with a couple of her business-school classmates.

Later, when most of the guests had left, Emma found Adam standing before her.

"Sorry about earlier. I was super cranky and tired. I'd just flown in from Frankfurt and was deep asleep when my ceiling started to shake."

Emma nodded and waited for him to continue.

"But it was a fun party," he conceded, much to her delight. "I just hope it's not a regular occurrence."

"Every Friday night," she'd said with a straight face. Then her face had broken into a wide grin.

"Phew, you had me there for a second," he'd said, and returned her smile. His smile, Emma had decided, changed his face from passably pleasing to decidedly good looking.

Over the years, reflected Emma, as friends and neighbors, the third and fourth wheels to Garrett and Isabel, and as godparents to Mila, they had developed a familiarity that was as comfortable as it was trying at times. She couldn't count the number of times when Adam was displeased with her, the times they had bickered over something or other. But she usually managed to have him see her side of it or at least squeeze an apology out of him.

"Alright, Emma," Adam said now, breaking into her thoughts. "You're right, I don't even know her. That was maybe out of line."

Case in point.

"It's just, I know how enthusiastic you can get when you have a new project," he said. "That's one of the things I love about you, but sometimes you get carried away, which isn't a bad thing if it's being channeled in the right direction."

After the run, breathless and high from the physical exertion, they continued chatting on the landing outside Adam's apartment. Emma was about to suggest that Adam make her one of his amazing cappuccinos when Adam's front door opened.

"I thought I heard your voices," said Brooke. She was wearing one of Adam's button-down shirts; her legs were bare. She leaned into Adam for a kiss. "I didn't know you ran, Emma."

Emma couldn't miss the accusing tone in Brooke's voice or the possessive way she had placed a hand on Adam's sweaty chest.

"Oh, I'm not much of a runner. I only go with Adam." Then turning to Adam, Emma pulled out the rubber band from around her ponytail, shook out her long hair and said, "It was a lot of fun; we should definitely do it more often."

The way Brooke's face pinched up made Emma want to laugh.

CHAPTER EIGHT

"So how did it go with this Rob guy? Are you going to hire him?" asked Emma. It was the following Thursday night, and she was in Adam's apartment, her laptop open before her.

She loved his open-plan apartment, which was decorated in a mix of modern and vintage, wood and leather; definitely a guy's place. She was sitting at a bar that had been scrounged from a real, old-fashioned saloon. It fronted his tiny galley-style kitchen. Above it, two industrial metal lampshades illuminated the notebook in which she'd been scribbling notes. On the wall opposite, a large gilt mirror reflected her and Adam.

Over Thai takeout, they'd gone through the beta version of her redesigned blog with Adam offering suggestions for improvement. Pleased with her progress and his input, she closed her notebook and laptop and slid them aside.

"Yeah, he's a solid programmer and seems to have a lot of drive and good ideas," said Adam. "Exactly the kind of guy I need for the role. Heads and shoulders above the other two I'd interviewed."

Emma didn't welcome the news. She'd met Rob Caumartin when Adam had brought him into Café Bisou for lunch earlier in the week. She'd been there working on her blog and had taken the opportunity to introduce Hailey to Adam.

Normally, Emma wouldn't have paid much attention to someone like Rob, who checked all of her boxes for geek: An ill-fitting, checked shirt. Baggy khakis. Hiking boots to an interview —*Who does that?* However, she suspected this Rob dude had his eyes on Hailey, and therefore required some watching out for.

"That's great," she said, "except there seems to be something a bit off about him."

"What do you mean?" asked Adam.

"I can't quite put my finger on it. He seemed too eager to please somehow."

Adam laughed. "Phew, I thought you were going so say, psycho-stalker off, like that guy you dated."

"Now that you mention it," said Emma, "he was in Café Bisou the very next day, you know. He was bothering Hailey while she was trying to work. And then he started asking me all kinds of questions about you, about Hailey, about what I was doing, about my blog. Then he started spouting off to me about CSS and SEO and plugins and widgets and God knows what else. At the time I thought he was just brown-nosing, like he might get me to put in a good word for him. But now . . . maybe he was trying to worm his way into my trust and get information out of me."

"I think someone has an overactive imagination," said Adam, walking around the bar to the fridge.

"Don't laugh at me," said Emma. "I'm worried about Hailey, actually. I think she might be his target."

"Or maybe," said Adam, pouring a bottle of craft beer into two glasses and handing one to Emma, "he's just a normal, young guy —someone who's perhaps a bit awkward when he's around pretty girls—who might be interested in Hailey. I wouldn't blame him if he were; she's a really sweet girl."

Emma took a sip of her beer, pleased by Adam's approval of her prodigy.

He continued, "I'm happy to see you take an interest in someone like Hailey, but I'm kind of surprised."

"Why?"

"She's very different from the women you normally hang out with, Annalisa and Isabel excepted. They're usually catty, self-centered and ambitious."

"That's not true!" was Emma's automatic response. Racking her brain, Emma thought of Sasha, her friend Lauren from Luxe who now worked on a celebrity gossip magazine, and a couple of the women she sometimes socialized with. Unable to come up with anyone who didn't fit the bill, she said, "Hailey *is* sweet. When I think of my ideal blog reader, I think of Hailey and that helps me gear the content and tone."

"I hope you're not just using Hailey for the sake of your blog."

"Of course not. I like her. I'm helping her: introducing her to the city, helping her find her place in it."

"Are you sure, Emma? Just make sure you let her live her own life, okay?"

"What's that supposed to mean?"

"You know what I mean. I don't want to see someone like her get hurt."

"She won't," said Emma. "I only have Hailey's best interest at heart. Honest."

And Hailey's best interest wasn't to date a weirdo geek like Rob, it was to be with a hot rock star like Zak.

"WHAT DO YOU WANT TO DRINK?" Adam asked Emma and Hailey over the cacophony created by the pop punk band currently on stage. They were on the Lower East Side, in a dark basement club filled with a mix of hipsters and rockers.

The pop punk band left the stage followed by a smattering of applause. Drinks in hand, Emma, Hailey and Adam found a spot near the front. Zak and his bandmates, two guys in similar costumes of tight jeans and scruffy, vintage-store button-downs, were tuning instruments and performing sound checks.

Tonight, both Emma and Hailey were dressed in jeans. Emma had paired hers with a deconstructed black "I Love NY" T-shirt that was ripped at the neck and shoulders then safety pinned back together at the shoulders. Hailey was in a simple black tank top with a scooped neckline.

After several more minutes, the stage darkened and spotlights fell on the three Broken Extremities bandmates poised for action. The crowd, which had thickened since their arrival, grew quiet, the hush broken by the sound of guitar chords and then a raspy voice. Apparently, many in the crowd had come especially for this band and were rocking along with the songs, some even singing along.

Emma swayed along with the crowd and enjoyed the rush of watching a band perform live. They weren't bad, she decided, and noticed the effect Zak was having on some of the girls in the crowd.

Hailey's gaze was transfixed on the boys onstage. Hailey seemed a lot more comfortable in this environment than she had last week at Sasha's party.

Bumping Hailey with her elbow, Emma said in a loud whisper, "Did you see that? Zak was showing off for you when he did that riff thing with the guitar."

"Me, really?"

"Yeah, when he was singing 'I want you' earlier, he was looking right at you."

"Are you sure, Emma?"

"Pretty sure."

"Really?" giggled Hailey, entranced by the trio, whose mouths were pressed close to the mikes, their hands moving in a blur over their instruments.

"Adam, what do you think of them?" asked Emma, after the band had finished.

"I think there's potential but not a lot of originality. I feel like I've heard them before, or a band like them."

"But that's not necessarily a bad thing?" interjected Emma.

"True, it could be what listeners want. But personally, there was too much primping and affectation for my taste."

"I think they're good and have the right kind of look and sound to be stars, don't you think, Hailey?"

"Yes, definitely," said Hailey. "I felt all tingly watching them."

"Are you planning to stick around?" asked Adam.

"Yeah, the night is still young. We'd like to chat with Zak and his bandmates a bit, see what they're up to later," said Emma, looking to Hailey for agreement. She was met by Hailey's enthusiastic nodding.

"Then I shall leave you ladies to it," said Adam, downing the rest of his beer. "Brooke's planned a weekend trip away. Early start in the morning. Give my best to Zak and the band."

Emma's spirits dropped. She was about to protest Adam's early defection when it occurred to her that Adam's presence might, if not sabotage her mission, impede its smooth and successful deployment.

In leaving, Adam leaned in close to Emma's ear. "Take care of her. She's a good girl." Her ear tickled with the warmth of his breath.

After Broken Extremities had broken down their equipment, Zak came over to Emma and Hailey.

"I'm so stoked you two came," he said, giving them sweaty cheek kisses.

"We wouldn't have missed it for the world, would we have, Hailey?" said Emma.

"No. You were great up there!" said Hailey. "Thanks for inviting us."

"The guys and I are heading over to Dark 89 for a drink. Wanna join us?"

Soon after, after descending into the cave-like lounge, Emma maneuvered herself so that Hailey would be seated next to Zak. She herself ended up between Lance, the drummer, and a girl who was with the bassist, Stuey. Lance seemed to be totally high and barely said anything, except for some chuckling to himself and the occasional, "Yeah, man." Stuey and the girl mostly sucked face (there may have been some petting involved), leaving Emma free to watch progress between Hailey and Zak.

Though she couldn't hear what was being said between them above the music, Emma was enough of an expert in body language to catch the drift. Zak appeared animated and loquacious, probably high from the performance and eager to impress Hailey, who, Emma knew, was starstruck and tipsy. Zak had his arm around the back of the banquette around Hailey's back, another good sign. When he started to play absently with Hailey's hair, Emma did a little mental victory dance. Every so often, Zak would look over at Emma and smile. She smiled back encouragingly, feeling like she was witnessing the beginning of another successful match. She imagined being featured in a magazine article in *Vanity Fair*, a glowing reportage titled "The Cupid of New York," "Emma the Enchanted," or the like.

Shortly after 2 a.m., Emma had had enough. Hailey's head lolled against the back of the red vinyl banquette, her makeup-smeared eyes were shut, and Emma detected the subtle rising and falling of her chest. Zak was talking to a girl on his other side. There was no more to be gained tonight but, Emma decided, the seeds to this romance had been successfully planted.

Already plotting how she would bring them together the next time, she nudged Hailey awake and they said their goodbyes.

CHAPTER NINE

At 5:30 p.m. a few days later, Emma met Hailey amid the students, shoppers, locals and tourists basking in the warmth of a perfect June day in bustling Union Square.

"Omigod, omigod, Emma," squealed Hailey upon seeing her.

"Hailey, what is it?" asked Emma. She'd received an urgent text from Hailey asking her to meet her after Hailey's shift.

"He's asked me out!"

"Who, Zak? He doesn't waste time . . . I like that."

"Zak? No, not Zak, Rob!"

"Rob, Rob . . . ?"

"The guy Adam was interviewing."

"Oh, him. Him, Hailey? But he's like a student, and so not cool!"

"He just got his master's. Wait, so you think I shouldn't accept?"

"I didn't say that, Hailey. You have to decide for yourself. How did he ask you? What did he say exactly?"

"Well, he didn't actually *ask* me. He slipped this to me when he was leaving today," said Hailey, withdrawing from the back pocket of her jeans a carefully folded white square with the fleur-de-lis logo from Café Bisou on the front. Hailey turned it around, smoothed it out, and handed it to Emma. "Here, look."

"What's this? He asked you out on a napkin!" said Emma, clucking her tongue.

Dear Hailey,
Wanted to ask you in person, but you're super busy.

"It was during the lunch rush," explained Hailey.

You caught my eye when we met. That's why I'm haunting the café—hope you're not creeped out. (J/K) I really enjoyed chatting with you and would love to take you out sometime and get to know you better. Let me know.

Hope to hear from you soon!
Rob
917-555-5555

"It's a nice note, right?" asked Hailey the moment Emma lowered the napkin. "Cute, like he is?"

"More like cheesy and creepy," said Emma. "Who writes 'just kidding' like that anymore? It's so 1985! Has he been, like, stalking you at work?"

"No! I mean, he's come in a few times since that time Adam brought him in. We don't really get to speak much besides, you know, the usual, 'Hi, how's it going?—Good—Good—What can I bring you?' I have caught him looking at me while I worked, though, but he'd always look away really embarrassed at getting caught, and I'd get really embarrassed at catching him catching me catching him."

When Emma didn't say anything, Hailey demanded, "So, what should I do?"

"I can't tell you what to do. Go with your feelings."

"I feel like . . . he'd be someone fun to—" began Hailey.

"It sounds to me like you always feel a little uncomfortable and awkward when you're around each other and you don't have a whole lot to say to one other. That's not a good sign. Go out with him if you want, but I think someone very hot and worthy is really into you. In fact, he's going to come meet us for a drink in —" Emma checked the Cartier on her wrist, "10 minutes."

Hailey looked confused. "Who?"

"Zak, of course," sighed Emma. Hailey could be quite dense sometimes. "Who else?"

"No way. Zak's meeting us now?"

"That's right. He asked me earlier what we were up to this evening. I told him to meet us at Coffee Shop at 6."

"Okay, but what about Rob?" wailed Hailey.

"If you want to go out with him, go for it. It's normal to date around in New York. But I get the feeling Zak is looking for a girlfriend, not someone who just wants to play around. So he might not be interested in you anymore if he knew about Rob."

She was only stretching the truth a little. Zak had, after all, complained about how difficult it was to meet anyone when he was working, rehearsing or playing gigs all the time. And he did say it got old with groupies constantly throwing themselves at him. So that must mean he was looking for someone serious, right?

"You really think Zak is that interested in me? That he might want me as a girlfriend?"

Emma nodded.

"But what should I do about Rob? Text him 'No, thank you' or something?"

"Uh-uh, that might be awkward. Best just not to reply at all. You don't want him to start phone-stalking you, too. Hopefully, he'll get the message and be so embarrassed, he'll stop coming to the café."

"If you think so. Thanks so much for your advice. I'm so bad with this whole dating and relationship stuff. I don't know what I'd do without you!"

CHAPTER TEN

Emma was feeling good. She'd gone live with her redesigned blog, e-mailed the link to her network of friends and acquaintances, and was gratified by the mostly positive response.

She pictured her audience like a field full of Haileys: young, green and full of potential, all looking up to her.

You wouldn't know it to look at her today, but Emma had spent much of her youth unsure of herself, gawky and lost.

If high school for Emma was like New York for these girls, then Emma could relate to going to a new place scared, friendless and alone. Her nanny, Cynthia, had just moved away. And she'd finally realized that her father was too wedded to his job to bother with her. Enter Annalisa, who was loud, outgoing and fun. To ensure that Annalisa would like her, Emma had pushed her boundaries and copied what Annalisa did.

And it had paid off, hadn't it? By the time she'd graduated, Emma had served on student government, been on the cheer-leading squad, played on the tennis team, acted in school productions. Anything to stay friends with Annalisa and avoid going home to a large, empty house.

Her friendship with Annalisa had changed and equalized over

the years. (Emma supposed hers with Hailey had the potential to do so, too. Yet, looking over to where Hailey was bussing a table, she just couldn't imagine it.) And her popularity and self-confidence had skyrocketed.

And now, through her blog, Emma intended to take on Annalisa's role for her readers. And one by one, post by post, she'd turn these shy, insecure girls into stylish, sassy and confident New Yorkers.

She imagined how thankful they would be, when, thanks to Emma's advice, they would find their soulmates. And look fashionable doing it. And rise up the career ladder at the same time.

She imagined receiving hundreds of fan e-mails, letters and cards filled with before and after pictures, wedding pictures, and baby announcements, the girls all named Emma.

She imagined women who'd conquered their small-town fears to become successful New Yorkers working in the industry of their dreams. Creating cocktails and dishes called the Emma something or other. Calling pieces from their Autumn/Winter collection after her or a bag, the "Emma," being the new "Kelly."

She imagined books dedicated to her and acceptance speeches where her name would make an appearance.

Lost in these daydreams, she didn't notice Adam until he'd landed in the empty chair across from her.

"Daydreaming about me again?" teased Adam.

"You wish," said Emma. "As a matter of fact, I was thinking about *Worth It*." She detailed the number of page views she'd already gotten that day and since the relaunch of her blog with the pictures of Hailey before and after her makeover.

"That's great, Emma. How's Hailey enjoying the attention?" asked Adam.

"She says she feels like a celebrity. She e-mailed the link to a bunch of her friends back home. According to Hailey, they were totally in awe."

"She did look very striking in those pictures you posted. But somehow," said Adam, looking toward Hailey who was taking an order at a neighboring table, "I like her more natural."

"Zak actually took and Photoshopped those pictures for us."

"You seem to have gotten quite cozy with him," observed Adam.

"Just being neighborly. Nothing wrong with that, is there?" she said with a raised eyebrow, daring him to disagree. "Hailey and I have hung out with him a couple of times. He's been good company."

"You're not still trying to get Hailey and Zak together, are you?" asked Adam under his breath. Presumably so Hailey wouldn't overhear. "Because if you think Zak will fall for someone like Hailey, you're mistaken."

"Whoa, what do you mean by 'someone like Hailey'?"

"That wasn't an insult. I really like Hailey. She's nice, unpretentious. And naive, Emma. Zak isn't. He's pretty sure of himself and making the most of the whole rock-star and picking-up-chicks thing. He isn't looking for someone like Hailey. If anything, he's more likely to be interested in you."

"Me? That's ridiculous. Zak is not like that at all! He's totally sick of all these girls throwing themselves at him, he told me so himself. He wants to find a nice girl to come home to at night."

"I'll bet he does," said Adam with a smirk.

"What's that supposed to mean?"

"Emma, you may be smart enough not to get hurt, but Hailey's young and innocent. She's not from the big city. She's probably not had a lot of experience with men, let alone with guys like Zak and guys in New York. As her friend, you need to watch out for her feelings, not think about how great you'll feel and how much you'll be patted on the back if—and that's a big if—they get together."

"Thanks for this week's lecture, Professor Knightley," said Emma, squirming at Adam's far-too-accurate reading of her thoughts. "For your information, I'm almost certain, based on the hints Zak has been dropping, that he's going to be dedicating a new song to Hailey tonight."

"Is that right? I expect you and Hailey will be among the screaming groupies in the audience?"

"Absolutely. Would you like to come?"

"No, thanks."

"By the way, how is Brooke? Has she been more and more demanding? Wanting to account for every moment you're away from her? See, I know the type, and I don't think she'll be the type to—"

"Okay, point taken," said Adam. "Have fun tonight, but not too much."

LATER THAT AFTERNOON, Emma arrived home at the same time as Belinda, who was returning from her nursing shift.

"Emma, how are you, honey? You look a little skinny. Are you well? Have you been eating enough? I know how important it is for you young girls to stay skinny, but there is such a thing as taking it too far. Speaking of feeling well, Mother is doing much better, thanks for asking. I mean, I assumed you were going to ask. Everybody has been so kind to us. Where would we be without our friends? Did I tell you Adam brought the biggest bouquet of dahlias and a box of Mother's favorite chocolates when she came home? He's a real catch. That girlfriend of his is one lucky gal. I wonder if we could be expecting wedding bells in this building again sometime soon?"

"No, I don't think that's going to be the case," said Emma, shaking her head. "They haven't been together that long. I doubt they're very serious."

"Well, I for one, would be happy to see him settle down with that nice woman. Perhaps to have a baby again in this building. It's been too—" Belinda stopped herself, gave Emma a funny look, and picked up the previous thread. "Speaking of catches, I think I know someone who has his eyes on *you*."

"Me?" laughed Emma, wondering who Belinda could possibly know who could be interested in her. Outside of the apartment building, it wasn't as if they ran in the same social circles.

"Yes, that nice young man who lives downstairs, who was there to help when Mother had her stroke."

"You mean Zak?"

Oh, Belinda, thought Emma, mentally shaking her head, you have no idea.

"Yes, Zak Elton. What nice people we have in this building! Mother and I are so lucky to live here, in this neighborhood. If it wasn't for your wonderful granddaddy, we would never, in a million years be able to afford to live here. Imagine, being neighbors with a rock star, an entrepreneur, and a star blogger—we count our blessings everyday—it's almost as impressive as our Juliette working for Hollywood stars."

Here we go again, thought Emma, who knew one of Belinda's favorite topics was her niece, Juliette.

"Belinda, it's great to chat, but I'm expecting a very important phone call for work."

"Oh, okay, you go now, honey. Your blog is fabulous, by the way. I read every word of it to Mother yesterday. We can't wait for your next post. Say hi to Mr. Ralph Lauren and Mr. Calvin Klein from me, their old friend, Belinda Bates, will you?" Belinda chuckled at her own joke as Emma escaped up the stairs to her apartment.

CHAPTER ELEVEN

"To end the night, I'd like to debut a new song I've been working on. I want to dedicate it to a very special girl," said Zak, looking over to where Emma and Hailey were standing in the crowd near the stage. "It's called 'Muse.'"

Zak's throaty voice and his words made the skin on Hailey's arms pucker into a million little bumps . . . her insides turned to mush. She'd been waiting for this all night—Emma had been talking it up ever since Zak had made them promise to come to the gig tonight—and now the moment was here. And the surprise was exactly as Emma had predicted!

> *I dream about your lips*
> *And the sexy way you move your hips.*
> *You are bright,*
> *You light up my day.*
> *You are beautiful,*
> *You make me wanna say:*
>
> *Will you be my muse, muse, muse?*
> *Will you be my muse, muse, muse?*

I dream about you and me,
How it seems that we were meant to be.
You inspire me,
You make me feel alive.
You excite me,
With you I'm in overdrive.

Will you be my muse, muse, muse?
Will you be my muse, muse, muse?

"Did you hear those lyrics, Hailey? He wrote them for you! How cool is that?" said Emma when the applause had ended.

"Omigod, omigod, omigod! I can't believe it! He really wrote a song for me?" asked Hailey.

"Not only that, he wants you to be his 'muse,'" said Emma with a giggle and wink.

"I *know!* This is so awesome, Emma, and it's all thanks to you!" said Hailey, wrapping Emma up in a fierce hug. First the job, then the makeover and blog post, and now this. She didn't deserve so much happiness. "Oh God, what am I going to say to him later? How am I going to act?"

Emma gave her some suggestions about taking some calming breaths to relax herself and complimenting Zak. It always sounded so easy coming from Emma, who was naturally so together.

Later, after the band had finished breaking down the equipment, Hailey spotted Zak talking to a group of fans. She'd been keeping an eye out for him, of course. Upon seeing them, Zak thanked the group and came over. He leaned over and gave Emma, who was closer to him, a one-armed hug and a peck on each cheek, then turned to Hailey to kiss her cheeks, too. Hailey felt blood rush to her cheeks.

"My absolute favorite ladies. Thanks so much for coming out tonight. It means a lot to me," he said.

"Zak, we wouldn't have missed it for the world," said Emma. "You guys were great up there. And your new song . . . wow, we were blown away!"

"Yeah, Zak, it was a-maz-ing!" Hailey said, hoping she didn't come off sounding too gushy. How she wished she could be cool like Emma.

"Didn't I tell you you'd fucking love it?" Zak said, looking at Emma.

Emma smiled back and asked, "Are you doing something with your bandmates now? If not, I thought we could go back to my place for a drink; we could hang out on the roof-deck."

"The guys said something about going to another bar," said Zak, flicking his eyes over Hailey before turning back to Emma, "but I prefer your idea."

Now here they were on Emma's roof, and Hailey was sitting next to Zak on the sofa. The whole left side of her body, the side next to Zak, was tingling and alert.

Zak sprinkled a line of weed on a piece of Rizla, tucked in a cardboard filter, and rolled the whole thing lengthwise back and forth between his expert fingers before swiping his tongue across the edge of the paper and sealing it.

What would it feel like to have his fingers on her, his tongue licking her? Hailey felt her nipples tighten; she blushed, glad for the darkness. After taking a long drag, Zak held the joint out to Emma, who waved it away and picked up her beer instead. Zak then offered the joint to her. Hailey accepted, thinking about putting her lips on the spot where Zak's lips had been a moment ago. She sucked in—she'd never quite gotten the hang of this, and it had been a while since the last time she'd done it—and was glad she didn't cough.

Ahh, this was the life.

She wasn't sure how much time had passed when Emma yawn loudly, a hand in front of her open mouth.

"God, am I tired!" said Emma, hopping to her feet. "The late nights this week with the relaunch have really caught up to me. I'm going to crash if I sit here a minute longer." As Zak started to stumble to his feet, Emma said, "No stay where you are, Zak. You're both welcome to hang out for as long as you want. And Hailey, feel free to crash on the sofa in my office, the bedding's in the closet. 'Night you two and be good," she said, her tone insinuating otherwise. With a little wave of her fingers, Emma disappeared through the door that led down to her apartment.

Hailey was too drunk and stoned to know what was happening except that she didn't want it to end. Everything was sooo good. She was on a private rooftop terrace with the lights and noise of Manhattan surrounding her. She had this amazing new friend, who was like Carrie from *Sex and the City*. And sitting on the couch next to her was a bona fide rock star, who'd written a song for her. *Her!* That must mean he wanted her, right? And you know what? She was going to do something about it. For once in her life, she wasn't going to be the "girl" waiting for a guy to make the moves on her. She was a New York girl, and she was going to start acting like one. If there was ever a time in her life to be like Carrie's slutty friend Samantha, it was now.

Hailey turned toward Zak. His neck was just inches away. If she just stuck out her tongue, she could lick that beautiful patch of exposed skin. She closed her eyes, leaned closer, and tasted the saltiness of his sweat with a flick of her tongue before placing her lips on his neck.

For what seemed like a long while, he didn't respond. Then he started to stroke her leg. The rhythmic movement and the idea that it was Zak's hand on her thigh sent quivers of excitement right up to her crotch. That was all the sign she needed. She climbed onto his lap, straddling him, and launched her mouth at his.

Zak's eyes were closed. She felt him getting excited. She

moaned against his lips. His hand, which was up her shirt, grabbed and kneaded her right tit.

"Shall we go down to your place?" Hailey whispered, shocked by her own behavior. "It'll be more private there."

CHAPTER TWELVE

"Just coffee and toast for me, please," said Hailey to the waitress. Hailey clearly looked to be suffering from the effects of the previous night.

"Is it that bad?" asked Emma, after the waitress had left. "How much did you drink?"

"Too much! Plus the pot. I was pretty wasted." Hailey winced. "Oh God, I hope I didn't make a fool of myself."

"No, not that I saw," said Emma. "Now tell all. What happened with Zak?"

"Well, we kind of . . . you know," said Hailey, a dreamy smile flitting at the corners of her mouth. "We did it."

"Oh." This was a good thing, right? Emma had left them alone last night so they could get to know each other better, make out a bit. She'd imagined Hailey would have held back and Zak would have liked her enough to wait. But then, who was she to judge if two people liked each other so much they couldn't wait to get their hands on one another? "Uh, how was it?"

"Good . . . amazing! I think. I was pretty gone, though. After you left, we made out on your roof. Then it started getting really hot and heavy. So we went down to his place. We kept on going and then it was, you know, over, and then he fell asleep. I laid there for a long time just checking him out. He's so hot! I still can't believe it. He has all these tattoos on his chest and back. There's even this one of an eagle on his butt che—"

"You can spare me the details of his body," said Emma. The waitress appeared with their coffees. "How do you feel now?"

"If it wasn't for this splitting headache and feeling like I'll puke if I eat anything, I feel fantastic. Like a real New Yorker now . . . "

It would take a lot more than getting laid to feel that way, thought Emma.

" . . . I can't believe I've only been here a month and I have a job and I'm in love."

"Love! Really, Hailey?"

Wow, she really did have the touch. Was this a done deal already for Zak and Hailey? She'd barely had to do anything; it was almost too easy. She would have preferred a bit more of a challenge, not that she was complaining. Emma squeezed Hailey's hand on the table, feeling that swell of success that she'd come to crave.

Hailey nodded, then winced, then attempted to smile, making Emma laugh at her effort. "I've never felt the way I did last night. Confident and in control and desired. After what happened with Chris, I thought maybe I had gotten too fat and ugly, and no guy would ever want me again."

"Shut up, Hailey! You're beautiful; no one could ever think you were ugly. If they do, they don't deserve you. Remember, you control how you feel about yourself, not other people. You know, I had a bad childhood, so I had to fake being happy and that everything was perfect. Eventually it worked, and I am, and it is."

"I had no idea, Emma." Hailey picked up a slice of warm toast and nibbled on a little corner of it, as if to test its effects on her stomach.

"It's no big deal now; ancient history. Just like Chris is, right?"

Hailey nodded again, slower and more cautiously this time.

"Do you think Zak feels the same way about me as I do about him?" asked Hailey, wrinkling her brow. "I mean, he certainly seemed to be into it last night. And you did say he wanted something serious, right?"

"He did, Hailey. Based on all the signs and hints he's been sending these last few weeks and then The Song—he wouldn't write a song for a girl he wasn't at least falling in love with—he must really be into you, too," said Emma.

And if he's not quite there yet, she thought, I'm sure a little prodding on my part will do the trick.

"That's reassuring. Thank you, Emma . . . for everything," Hailey said, flashing Emma a pained smile.

"Don't mention it, Hailey," said Emma, patting Hailey's hand. "I'm just happy if you're happy; that's enough for me. So how did you leave it?"

Hailey explained to Emma about waking up early, unable to sleep from still being drunk and high on the experience. "My makeup was everywhere. I didn't want him to see me like that. Plus all my liquid courage had evaporated. So I did the walk of shame and came home."

"He was still sleeping when you left?"

"Yeah, but I left him a note. I found some Post-Its on his desk. I wrote that I'd had a really great time and I drew a heart and left my cell number—that wasn't too forward was it?"

"No, Hailey, that was perfect."

"I put it on his nightstand—" Hailey stopped, that look of doubt and furrowing of her brows again.

"And what, Hailey?"

"Uh, nothing, never mind. I just remembered something. I'm sure it wasn't . . . anything," said Hailey, looking on the verge of tears. "Thanks for inviting me to brunch and coming out to Brooklyn . . . but . . . I really need to go back to bed. I have the dinner shift tonight. It's going to be super busy, and I don't feel great at all."

Emma frowned, wondering at Hailey's hasty departure, but put it down to her delicate head and her being worried about working her first Saturday dinner shift.

~

EMMA HAD JUST GOTTEN into the taxi when the text from Zak came:

What ru up 2 now?

It was after 2 a.m.. She suspected Zak hadn't been able to get a hold of Hailey so was trying her in hopes of reaching Hailey.

She tapped back: *Heading home now. Hailey not with me, she's working.*

Great, where ru? Wanna meet 4 drink?

Emma frowned at her screen, not sure why Zak wanted to meet her for a drink when he was obviously booty calling Hailey.

She replied: *In taxi, heading down Lexington. Where are you?*

East Village. 3rd and 15th. I'll wait for you at corner.

Okay then, thought Emma. She supposed she could give him a ride home and use the opportunity to ensure everything was on track with his and Hailey's romance. Get the full story from his side.

"Thanks, Emma," said Zak a few minutes later, squeezing in next to Emma in the back of the cab as it squealed away from the curb. "Wow, you look hot," he slurred, eyes fixed on her chest.

She'd been at Sasha's 35th birthday party. Knowing Sasha and the crowd she ran with, Emma had chosen something more risqué than usual, hence the low-cut, semi-sheer top.

As she was leaving her apartment building earlier, she'd met Adam and Brooke coming in. Brooke had glanced at Emma and snaked her arm around Adam's waist. Stupid, insecure bitch, Emma had thought, pulling back her shoulders and flashing

Adam a dazzling smile to spite Brooke. Adam's look had been inscrutable; she hoped he hadn't thought the top too slutty. Now, once again, she wondered if she might have been better off wearing something that covered up more skin.

"Guess who I had brunch with this morning?" Emma prompted. When Zak said nothing, she said, "Hailey. Too bad she had to work tonight."

"Yeah, too bad," said Zak, putting his arm across the seatback around Emma's shoulders. "Where were you tonight looking smokin' hot like that?"

Ignoring his question, she continued, "She's a sweet girl, isn't she?"

"Yeah, sweet girl," parroted Zak. "But I bet you taste much sweeter."

Before Emma could act, Zak had flung himself on her and fixed his mouth on hers.

"Me?" spluttered Emma, shoving him away, incredulous that Zak was trying to kiss *her*. "What's that supposed to mean? You're in love with Hailey!"

Zak laughed, sounding genuinely amused. "In love with Hailey?"

Emma was sick of him repeating everything she said.

"Why would you think that? 'Cause we fucked last night?"

"Uh, *yeah*!" Emma spat out. "And you've been after her for weeks, inviting her to your gigs, hanging out with us. And you wrote her that song!"

This was beyond comprehension.

"I've been inviting everyone and their grandmothers to my gigs. And Emma, I wrote that song for *you*," said Zak, grabbing Emma's thigh and lunging at her again.

"Get. Off. Of. Me." Emma pushed him off and slapped his face away. "You try that one more time and I'll have the driver stop and kick your sorry ass out," she hissed, meeting the driver's eyes in the rearview mirror.

This couldn't really be happening, could it? Zak, who she'd been trying to set Hailey up with, was interested in *her*? But how was that possible?

"Listen to the lady, my friend," said the driver. "Leave her alone or I do like she says."

"What the fuck, Emma!" said Zak, shooting daggers at the back of the driver's head. "Is this one of you girls' 'playing hard to get' games? You're the one giving me these secret looks and smiles all the time. If you were trying to get my attention, it certainly worked. You have it, and I want you, Emma. So fucking badly!"

Ooh, the nerve of him! Emma laughed in his face. "You and me, Zak! That's ridiculous! I was only trying to get you to go for Hailey."

"Hailey, my ass! Where did you even get the idea that I would be interested in that dumb little whiny . . . nobody. I only tolerated her 'cause she's your friend."

Emma was so enraged she couldn't even look at Zak, much less spend another second enclosed in the back of a taxi with him.

"Driver, this is good right here," said Emma, as soon as the taxi rounded the corner of her street.

"Are you sure, lady? I don't want this jerk giving you no trouble."

"I can handle him," said Emma, handing the driver a few bills that amounted to nearly twice what was on the meter. "Keep the change," she said and climbed out. He thanked her profusely and stayed put, even after Zak had emerged and slammed the door.

"So let me get this straight, Emma," said Zak, joining her on the sidewalk in front of their building. "You're saying you're not into me? You only wanted me to go for Hailey?"

"Yeah, wasn't that obvious? And, and, I mean, you slept with her last night! And now you're telling me you want me. That's plain disgusting! What kind of a guy are you?" demanded Emma, trying not to shout.

"She threw herself at me! I can't help it if she unbuttoned my jeans!"

"But you didn't have to go along with it! What was your excuse? 'Oops, sorry, my dick just fell into your pussy.' And besides, what makes you think, even if I liked you, that I would still want you *after* you'd slept with my friend? You've just made yourself totally no go."

"But I thought about *you* the whole time, Emma. I swear. I'd Photoshopped Hailey out of that picture of the two of you and had it on my nightstand. I was looking at *you* while I was fucking *her*."

"Oh my fucking God!" said Emma, slapping her forehead, incredulous. "How stupid could I have been? Trying to set up my sweet and innocent friend with someone *like you*. Get the hell away from me."

Emma shoved Zak out of her way, ran up the stoop and pushed herself through her building's front door. She collapsed against the back of the door and wiped her mouth with her hands.

She would need all her marketing skills to spin this to Hailey in a way that wasn't going to break her poor little eager heart.

CHAPTER THIRTEEN

There was nothing Emma hated more than being wrong.

As much as she wanted to lift the blame from herself, she could not, in all honesty, do it. Looking back now, it pained her to have to admit that her actions could be construed as interest.

As if watching a highlights reel of the interactions between her, Hailey and Zak, Emma saw herself always doing the talking, accepting invitations and suggesting meetings. She had smiled and looked on at Zak encouragingly when he spoke with Hailey or when she wanted him to make a move on Hailey. She supposed a conceited blockhead like Zak could read it as her sending him signals.

Even Belinda had been right about Zak being interested in her. And she'd completely dismissed it. Adam had hinted at the same thing.

Okay, so she'd been wrong. There was a first time for everything.

But the worst of it was, would Hailey really have gone for Zak and slept with him had she not hinted—okay, if she was going to be honest with herself—blatantly told Hailey that Zak had dedicated the song to Hailey and wanted her for a serious girlfriend?

Of course, it wasn't her fault that Hailey was naive enough to believe everything Emma told her.

Except she couldn't really blame Hailey for being naive, could she? Certainly not when Adam had taken every opportunity to remind her of it.

When it came down to it, she'd screwed up, and she didn't want to have to admit that to anyone, especially not Adam.

The bigger problem, now, was how she was going to break it to Hailey.

Unable to face seeing Hailey on Sunday afternoon, Emma had canceled their plans to go to Central Park Zoo in favor of joining Isabel and her family for a trip to Highbury-on-Hudson, the village where Hartfield was located, for Father's Day lunch.

But she couldn't ignore Hailey and her calls forever.

On her way to meet Hailey on Tuesday, Emma was almost thankful for a brief reprieve in the form of Belinda Bates, who told Emma that Zak had left that morning to go on tour with his band.

Walking around the zoo, Emma listened with a heavy heart to Hailey's manic chatter about Zak, which ping-ponged from elation for how "amazing" the other night had been and how "hot" Zak was to worry as to why Zak hadn't called yet. Even the adorable penguins and puffins in the Polar Circle couldn't cheer Hailey up.

Emma's original resolve to take full responsibility, laying the truth out for Hailey as gently as possible, began to waver. With the knowledge that Zak was out of town, Emma could soften the blow for Hailey. Or at least delay it.

"The reason Zak probably hasn't called, Hailey, is that he left for Florida this morning."

"Oh right," said Hailey. "How could I have been so stupid to forget? They're playing Warped Tour starting this week."

"Exactly," said Emma, nodding. "Zak told me it'd been so hectic with rehearsals and packing and getting everything ready that he had no time to do anything else."

"Did he say anything about . . . *me?*" asked Hailey. Her expression seemed suspended between joy and pain as it waited, no doubt, for Emma's response—the cue that would decide which emotion would earn its rightful place on Hailey's face.

Remembering how Zak had described Hailey during their last encounter, Emma tried to keep from squirming. "Of course he did," Emma finally said.

Seeing the way Hailey's face lit up, Emma continued, "He told me to tell you goodbye; he's sorry he didn't get to see you before he left."

Hailey clapped her hands in joy, like a little girl, making Emma wonder if she'd done the right thing. At some point Hailey's hopes would need to be dashed. But perhaps time and distance would damper the disappointment?

CHAPTER FOURTEEN

"Is that you, Emma?" Belinda Bates' iron-gray head poked out of the doorway of her apartment not two seconds after Emma entered the building. "Just the person I was hoping to see! What great timing."

Resigned, Emma asked, "How are you and your mother?" She gathered her hair into a ponytail and used it to fan the back of her sweaty neck. In the past two weeks, the temperature had been rising steadily.

"As well as can be expected considering this awful heat. Lordy lord, is it hot! And wouldn't you believe it, our air conditioner broke this week. I knew I should have gone for the name brand. Poor Mother. She's resting now; trying to at least. I don't think she slept a wink last night, it was just that stuffy and disgusting. Finally, I opened the windows, but it was so loud—not for Mother, of course, you know, because of her hearing—but then I couldn't sleep because of all the traffic ... "

Belinda droned on, managing to even yawn without interrupting herself. Emma, coated by a thin film of stickiness that she couldn't wait to rinse off, cleared her throat and said, "Was there something important that you wanted to tell me?"

"Oh yes, yes, sorry for getting distracted by this heat. It does have that effect, doesn't it? In fact, I do have something terribly exciting to share with you, Emma. You will be so pleased, I'm sure. It's really the very best news you can possibly imagine. Mother and I are absolutely over the moon. I bet you're dying to know, aren't you?" asked Belinda, looking ready to burst.

Emma nodded. At least she didn't have to fake enthusiasm as she willed Belinda to spit it out already and let her retreat into her own air-conditioned apartment. At this rate, she'd barely have time to shower before heading out to dinner with Adam.

"Juliette is coming back for the summer!" Belinda paused for a second, whether to let the effect of her announcement sink in or to catch a much-needed breath, Emma wasn't sure. "Isn't that just the most fantastic news? Our Juliette's going to spend the whole summer in New York! Right here. With us. We feel so blessed, so, so blessed!"

"How wonderful for you and your mother," said Emma, surprised by the news. "I know how you both dote on Juliette. Is she still working as a nanny for the Dixon-Lanes?"

"Yes. They just adore her, can't possibly do without her. But Juliette wrote that she has the next couple of months off and wanted to spend it in New York with us. Isn't that absolutely the sweetest of her?"

"I would think, with the kids out of school, summer is exactly when Blake and Genevieve would need the most help."

"Juliette only said that they both had a break from filming this summer and they wanted to spend it with the kids. I believe Juliette said the grandparents will be around to help. What was it that Juliette wrote in her e-mail? Something about them 'wanting to be like a normal family.' I printed it out; I can go get it if you give me a second."

"No, no, no, Belinda. I think I get the gist of it," said Emma, waving her hands to stop Belinda from retrieving and then reading word for word yet another one of Juliette's missives. For the ten years that Emma had been living in the building, she'd been listening to Belinda read from Juliette's e-mails, and before Belinda had gotten a computer, to her reading from Juliette's hand-written letters. Thankfully Juliette was as succinct as her aunt was verbose.

"Juliette arrives on Tuesday. Next Tuesday! Already! Can you believe it? I have so much to do to get the apartment ready for her. And I must not forget to call the piano tuner. Juliette will need an instrument to play on right away. Once she's settled in a bit, we can do a little welcome-back party for Juliette. Ooh, maybe a piano recital. Wouldn't that be nice, Emma? You, of course, would be at the top of the guest list. Juliette considers you such a great friend."

"Yeah, right," muttered Emma under her breath. Though the same age, Emma and Juliette had never been friends. When Emma had moved into the building, Juliette was just leaving for Bloomington, Indiana, where she had gotten a scholarship to study music.

"What was that? Did you say something, sweetie?" asked Belinda.

"I said, 'yeah, great,' Belinda. A recital is a fabulous idea."

Emma ran for the stairs before Belinda could delve into the subject of how Juliette, when she'd first come to live with the Bates as a traumatized 14-year-old, had barely spoken to anyone and made no friends.

EMMA WAS WEARING ONLY a towel and was rubbing her glorious hair dry with a second one when she opened the door.

"Help yourself to a beer or something while I finish getting dressed," Emma said by way of greeting. "I ran into Belinda on the way home, hence my semi-naked state."

Adam leaned in to give Emma a peck on the cheek and

breathed in a scent that reminded him of drinking cocktails on a Caribbean island. He tried to avoid looking at the gentle swells of her breasts above her towel or her trim legs below. Or to imagine what was hidden by the too-small towel. Adam moved toward the kitchen. A beer would definitely take the edge off.

"So you heard the news then?" he asked. The mental image of Emma sans towel behind her ajar bedroom door made him take a long pull of his beer. He'd definitely made the right decision regarding Brooke.

Emma emerged from her bedroom in a strappy dress thing that didn't cover much more skin than the towel. "About Juliette?" she said before disappearing into her bathroom. "Of course, given who the messenger is. But I don't buy it that Juliette just happened to have the summer off and wanted to spend it with her aunt and grandmother."

"Why not?" asked Adam, leaning against the open doorway to Emma's bathroom.

"Don't you find it highly suspicious," asked Emma as she applied makeup with a small flat sponge onto her face from a fancy-looking compact, "that a nanny would be given the summer off? With an A-list Hollywood couple like Blake Dixon and Genevieve Lane, it's not as though money's an issue. And even if they aren't filming, surely they must still have plenty to do: reading and memorizing scripts, discussing future projects, doing publicity for current projects."

"Maybe they'll be away for much of the summer," said Adam.

"From what I've read," Emma went on, her face tilted back, her mouth in an O, as she swept mascara onto her lashes, "they're going to be in the south of France for part of the summer. Wouldn't they want their French-speaking nanny around to help take care of the kids? I suspect there's more to the story than meets the eye."

"Maybe they thought she needed a break. Belinda was telling me that Juliette has been overtired and ill."

"That woman thinks anyone who coughs has pneumonia."

"Or maybe Juliette wants to spend some quality time with her grandmother because of the stroke?"

"If you ask me," said Emma, swiping lipstick onto her lips, "either they specifically didn't want Juliette with them or Juliette wanted the summer off. But which one and why?"

Adam couldn't have cared less. Sure Juliette was a nice girl. And for her aunt and grandmother's sake, he was glad she was going to be back. But he'd asked Emma to dinner tonight because he had something he wanted to tell her and was wondering just how much he should reveal and how she would react.

CHAPTER FIFTEEN

On the short walk over to their local Mexican, Emma told Adam about preparations for the following night's party to celebrate and promote her blog's relaunch.

As they settled into their booth and placed their orders, Emma looked forward to putting work out of her mind and having a relaxing evening with Adam. It'd been too long since they'd met for a casual dinner out, and she missed their usual bantering and teasing.

Emma was about to make a joke about Brooke letting Adam out of her clutches for the night when Adam said, "I have some news that might interest you."

"Really?" said Emma just as a waitress with extremely short black bangs and a mermaid tattoo brought them their drink orders.

When the waitress left, Emma said, "Don't keep me in suspense."

"Juliette is not the only new face we'll be welcoming to our building," said Adam. He squeezed lime juice into his bottle of Corona, pushed the lime wedge through the bottleneck, and took a swig.

"But how's that possible? We're already a full house." Emma paused from taking a sip of her margarita as an unpleasant idea began to take shape. It was too horrible for words. "No! No, you're not, Adam Knightley! Please tell me Brooke's not moving in with you? I'd never forgive you if she does. Especially if you didn't give me a chance to try to talk you out of it first."

Adam smiled, appearing more pleased than bothered by Emma's speculation, which only infuriated her more.

"I didn't know I needed your permission to ask my girlfriend to move in with me."

Emma's insides clenched. This was a disaster! If Brooke moved in, she could kiss her friendship with Adam adios. Emma gulped back something that felt like a hot, wet, sour lump. "So it's true then," she said, looking down at her hands, which were gripping her glass.

Adam placed a hand on hers. "No, Emma," he said.

She looked up. All the humor was gone from his eyes. In its place was that look again, the one that made her feel full and warm.

"Actually, I broke up with Brooke," he said, his eyes locked on hers.

Emma let out a slow sigh as she felt the knot in her stomach unravel and the pressure on her chest ease up. For a second she couldn't trust herself to say or do anything; the grip of fear and its subsequent release had shocked her system.

She freed her hand, raised her glass, and took a swallow from her drink. Ahh, the margaritas they did at this place were the best. Too bad Adam had had a bad tequila experience after the breakup of his marriage and wouldn't go near the stuff now.

By the time she set her glass down, her equilibrium had returned. "That's a relief!" said Emma, wiping the back of her hand across her forehead in an exaggerated fashion. "About time, too. What happened?"

"I just didn't feel it with her," said Adam with a shrug. "I didn't think it was fair to waste her time any longer."

"Poor girl," said Emma.

"What do you mean 'poor girl'? You didn't even like her."

"I can feel sorry for her now that she's out of your life," said Emma. "How did she take it?"

"As good as could be expected. I guess she probably saw it coming. She sensed that I was often withdrawn, which made her clingier, which made me pull back more. It became a vicious cycle. Another reason why I broke up with her is—"

"Yes?" asked Emma, feeling a small thrill of nervous expectancy. Then she followed his eyes toward the waitress, who was approaching their table with their food order.

"—she hates Mexican food."

Emma laughed, the tiniest bit disappointed. "Well, anyone who hates Mexican is definitely not a keeper."

They tucked into their food. After several bites of her chicken enchiladas, Emma paused. "Wait, if Brooke's not moving in, who is?" She took a sip of her margarita.

"Zak's new girlfriend."

Emma spluttered on her drink. "What? Zak has a girlfriend? And she's moving into our building? No effing way!"

"Apparently so. I saw him this morning as he was getting in from the airport. He was going on about this girl. Apparently, they'd met before and sparks had been flying but she'd had a boyfriend. This time there were no obstacles, they're supposedly madly in love, and she's moving in."

"Wow! You're not just shitting me, are you?" asked Emma, trying to wrap her head around this unexpected news.

Adam drew an X across his heart. "I guess you can halt whatever plans you had for him and Hailey," he added.

Emma cringed internally. Adam still didn't know about the disaster that was Hailey's broken heart. He probably assumed that all of her matchmaking had ground to a halt while Zak was away.

Let him think that. In fact, she could let him think that she had copped onto what a bad match Zak was for Hailey on her own.

"Don't worry," said Emma. "I've already discovered what an asshole he is; definitely not the guy for Hailey. You know what he did? A couple of nights before he left, he was all over me, telling me he *loved me*!"

"What do you mean?" Adam demanded.

"Just as you warned me," said Emma. "He wasn't interested in Hailey, he was interested in *me*. We shared a taxi home that night and he tried to grab me and kiss me."

"Why didn't you tell me? Did he hurt you?"

Emma liked that Adam seemed worked up over her. "No, he didn't hurt me. I was able to handle Zak."

"It still doesn't mean he can treat you or any woman like that!"

"You were right about him being a player and thinking he's God's gift to woman. Talk about fast: a new girlfriend! When's she arriving?"

"He said in a couple of weeks."

"At least I was right about him wanting someone serious. I'm really curious what Zak's girlfriend will be like."

EMMA COULDN'T SLEEP. She supposed part of it was nerves about tomorrow's party. This was a big deal for her, for her blog. Because if she didn't have that, what did she have?

Annalisa had an exciting new life with Tom and her dream career as a lawyer ahead of her. Isabel had her job and Garrett and two cute kids. Sasha had her successful event planning business. Lauren was quickly climbing up the masthead at *In the Know* and had the editor-in-chief role in sight. Even Juliette, though only a nanny, was an accomplished pianist. Had Emma had Juliette's talent, *she'd* certainly be doing something with it.

Just let the party go according to plan, she prayed. And please have everyone turn up who said they would turn up. You never really knew. In this city, socializing was not unlike dating: People felt no compunctions about ditching you if something better came along.

Of course, she was also running the events of her evening with Adam through her head. Brooke was out of the picture, thank God. But what did that mean? That now she would be able to hang out with Adam more than before? That their friendship would be able to go back to how it was before Brooke? Which was what she wanted, wasn't it? It wasn't as if she could ever imagine anything more with Adam than friendship, right? Then why had she felt that twinge of what—disappointment? relief?—when she'd thought he was going to say more just before their food had arrived?

Emma groaned, got out of bed, and snapped off the air conditioner. It was too loud and was making her bedroom too cold.

True, she'd had a bit of a college-girl crush on Adam, a good-looking, successful, older guy. But that was what college girls did. Plus that was ages ago.

But what if Adam did want something to happen with her now? Was that even a possibility?

He had kissed her the night she'd broken up with Jeremy, a guy she'd dated after college. But Adam had been drunk and feeling sorry for himself. And she'd pushed him away, of course, as soon as she'd come to her senses. He'd had no right to kiss her. Certainly not when all she'd wanted to do was think about Jeremy and how furious she was with him.

She touched her lips now. Jeremy was ancient history. What if Adam were to kiss her? Would she push him away again?

Emma's breathing deepened.

Adam had offered to escort her to her party. Was that just him being friendly and practical? Or was he suggesting that he come as her date?

And what about their friendship? Could she risk it for something more? Would she want to?

Emma kicked off her thin covers. With the air conditioner off, the heat really was unbearable. Seriously, what was wrong with her tonight?

CHAPTER SIXTEEN

From across the room, Adam heard Emma's tinkling laughter. Not that he needed to hear her voice over the din of the crowded lounge and music to know exactly where she was. He'd tracked her movements ever since they'd arrived together, never quite letting out of his sight a flash of red hair or the silky green fabric of her dress. Self-possessed and elegant, she was working the crowd like a pro.

He was proud of her. He knew she was talented, with business acumen, strong instincts and a good sense of what was on trend. It seemed with her blog, she'd found a niche worth exploiting that united her talents. And unlike many other bloggers, she had the money, connections and marketing know-how to throw a party *like this*.

Adam supposed it had gone well last night. Emma had clearly been upset when she'd thought Brooke was going to move in with him and relieved to hear they'd broken up. He was certain she'd felt the same charged awareness he'd felt the whole night. He'd wanted to say more about his feelings for her, but had held back, not wanting to get ahead of himself or to scare her off. Knowing Emma, he'd need to take it slow, gain her trust . . .

God, he sounded like some predator. What that woman did to him!

"Hi Adam."

Adam turned toward the quiet voice and saw Hailey, wearing a black dress that seemed more Emma's style than hers. He greeted the girl and they chatted about the party. Despite her efforts to be lively, she seemed dispirited.

"Is everything alright?" he asked. Perhaps she didn't know anyone else at the party and felt awkward and out of place?

"Is it that obvious?" said Hailey. "I always have such a hard time hiding what I'm feeling, unlike Emma, who seems so in control of herself all the time."

"If there's one thing I wish Emma was less good at, it's being in control of everything," said Adam, only half-jokingly. "Anything I can help with? Want me to introduce you to a couple of people? Though I admit I don't know most of the people here."

"No, that's okay. I don't really feel like meeting anyone new. Of course, it was important that I come to support Emma, and it is an amazing party. It's just that—I'm sorry, it's so cliché—I'm thinking about this guy, and it's making me sad. That's all."

"Sorry to hear that, Hailey. Want me to beat him up or something?" Adam said, trying for a light tone. She was probably missing her ex-boyfriend or something. He could understand that. How long had it taken him to get over Caroline? Much too long.

"Nah, it's not like he even did anything wrong, except for maybe not liking me as much as I like him. I guess I need to just accept that and move on. That's what Emma said. She said I need to forget about him and just have fun tonight, not waste time moping about him."

"You know, Emma's not always right. In fact, she's wrong far more often than she'd care to admit," Adam said.

"Oh, I wouldn't say that." Hailey was too loyal. "The thing is, I don't even know if he's back in New York. Emma doesn't know, either. Maybe he doesn't have my phone number with him, which is why I haven't heard from him? Or he lost it or he's too busy?"

Frowning, Adam asked, "Are you by chance talking about Zak?"

"Yes, I forgot you know him. Wait, you live in the same building . . . do you know if Zak's back in the city?"

A cold fist closed around Adam's heart. "When did you talk to Emma about him last?"

"I asked her about him today, when I was getting directions for the party."

"What did she tell you?"

"She said that she didn't think he was back yet."

"Did she tell you anything else?"

Hailey shook her head. "No, just that guys in bands can be flakey and maybe Zak wasn't worth it. I guess that's what I've been thinking about rather than trying to enjoy the party."

"Do you mind my asking what happened with you and Zak? Did you go on a couple of dates or something? If I'm being too nosy, just tell me to butt out, but it's kind of important."

"No, nothing like that. I, I . . . slept with him," Hailey said, her cheeks shiny red apples. "Please don't get the wrong idea about me, Adam. I'm not that kind of a girl. I can't believe I'm telling you this . . . I don't even know you that well. It's just . . . I was drunk and stoned and really into him. And he'd written me a song. And Emma kept telling me how much he was into me . . . so I went for it."

Adam felt like an old, lecherous tool, asking Hailey about her sex life. As for Emma, he was infuriated with her for lying to the poor girl and making her feel stupid, rejected and worthless. Emma, who was being lauded tonight for giving advice to young women like Hailey, and here was Hailey, obviously the worse for it. Much worse. Hadn't he warned her about meddling with Hailey's feelings?

"No, Hailey. Don't think that. Guys like Zak are players, and he probably saw you as someone he could easily . . . impress. It's not your fault, and you're definitely not stupid. Emma's the one in the wrong here for leading you on, letting you believe that Zak was into you, for not telling you—"

"Not telling me what, Adam?" asked Hailey, looking at him with round, doe-like eyes.

Adam ran a hand through his hair, not sure if he was helping matters by revealing the whole truth to Hailey. But she should know, shouldn't she? She was going to find out sooner or later.

"I hate to tell you this Hailey, but Zak's back in town and he has a girlfriend."

Hailey's face blanched and her mouth fell open.

He looked up and right into Emma's eyes. Frowning, Emma approached them, looking from Hailey to him.

EMMA HAD nothing to be nervous about. This was the party of all parties. Like Annalisa's wedding, and the launch party she'd helped throw for Luxe when the e-commerce site went live, everything was working out great. In fact, better than even she could have hoped.

Everyone seemed to love the redesign and the new direction she was taking the blog. Sasha had managed to get them booked into one of the trendiest lounges in the city, and it was packed. Lauren had brought a photographer and promised to put something in next week's issue of *In the Know*. A reporter was here from the *New York Post* and wanted to interview her for a story. There were plenty of people wanting her to recommend their bar/restaurant/salon/store/brand/products. (Of course, she would thoroughly vet any offerings before giving it a *Worth It* stamp; she couldn't be bought, and the blog had high standards. And, she wasn't making promises because, now with the advice articles, she had less capacity for reviews and would need to be more selective.)

She was in the middle of talking to a restaurant owner and a marketing executive when she spotted Hailey and Adam. Emma realized she hadn't even seen or said hi to Hailey yet.

Emma was already on her way over when she saw the look on Adam's face. Instead of teasing admiration, which was how he'd been with her on the taxi ride over, he looked furious.

Oh no! Adam must have found out about Zak and Hailey.

"What are you two chatting about?" asked Emma, plastering a smile on her face.

"Emma . . . " Adam said warningly.

"Emma, did you know that Zak has a girlfriend and is back in town?" Hailey asked, her voice shaky.

"Is that what Adam told you?" Emma asked.

Hailey nodded, her eyes pleading with Emma to say that Adam didn't know what the hell he was talking about. With Adam glaring at her like that, Emma was going to have to disappoint Hailey.

"Yes, now I remember. Adam told me that last night, too." Emma laughed. That nervous laugh of hers. "I'd had a couple of margaritas and totally forgot—"

"What the hell, Emma? What are you playing at?" Yes, Adam was definitely furious with her. "You lied to Hailey and you lied to me. I don't know what to believe anymore. Did Zak really throw himself at you, too? Or was that also a figment of your sick fantasy?"

The color drained from Emma's face. How could she, even for a moment, have imagined that she and Adam could get along as anything more than friends, when sometimes they couldn't even get along as friends? She itched to slap his face but didn't want to cause a scene at her own goddamned party.

"I definitely did *not* lie. About. Zak. Throwing. Himself. At.

Me!" she ground out through gritted teeth. "How dare you suggest otherwise, Adam Knightley!"

"What? . . . What, Emma?" Hailey looked like she was going to burst into tears. In her anger at Adam, she'd forgotten about Hailey.

"Oh, Hailey. I didn't want you to learn it like this."

Emma explained in straightforward terms what had happened with Zak in the taxi.

"I didn't tell you because I didn't want you to get hurt," she added.

"I should have known," whimpered Hailey. "I mean, look at you. Why would anyone want me when they could have you! And, I tried to blot this out, but he had this blown-up picture of you by his bed. When he was . . . on top . . . I could've sworn he was looking at it. Oh God, I think I'm going to puke!"

"I'm taking you home, Hailey," said Adam, without even a word or glance at Emma.

CHAPTER SEVENTEEN

Emma threw open the front door of her building, relieved to escape from another of Belinda's monologues, this one about the high cost of tuning a piano, not that she was complaining, of course, and it was all worth it because of Juliette being home, and for a whole summer, what a perfect niece she was, blahdy, blah, blah!

Hurtling herself out the door, not sure she could stand a whole summer hearing Belinda singing Juliette's praises, Emma could not stop her forward momentum when she realized there was someone on the other side of the door. She felt strong arms circle her. Then she was being lifted, swung and set down a few inches to the right while the arms' owner took a step to the left.

"Whoa!" the man said as he released his firm grip on Emma. Emma, who'd opened her mouth to berate this stranger for being in her way and manhandling her, shut it again. He'd done nothing wrong; had, in fact, made her feel like a dancer in a pas de deux while preventing what could have been a most inelegant and painful human collision.

"You alright there?" he asked, peering into her face with concern.

Emma registered a British accent at the same time her eyes met eyes startling in their blueness under insanely long lashes that were surprisingly dark for someone so blonde.

"Hi, sorry about that!" said Emma, all charm now. She laughed. "As you obviously noticed, I wasn't watching where I was going."

"No, it was my fault really, shouldn't 've been lurking in front of your door like some dodgy thug," he said with a winsome grin. "I'm looking for a friend, actually. I think this is her address, but there're no names on the buzzer, and I don't know which flat she's in. Hence the lurking about."

There was something familiar about him. Was this some guy she'd met at a party? An old acquaintance from NYU? A model she'd worked with at Luxe? Emma admired his lean, muscular build under a slim-fitted T-shirt. Unlike Adam's J. Crew T-shirts, this was definitely designer, and the fabric looked so soft she wanted to touch it. His face was breathtakingly handsome: defined cheekbones, well-groomed eyebrows, generous lips, and a long, straight nose. She was sure she would have remembered someone this attractive.

"Who are you looking for?" asked Emma.

"Her name is Juliette, Juliette Fairfax."

Emma's irritation returned. "Juliette? Yes, she's staying here with her aunt and grandmother, the Bates. They're in apartment number one. Juliette's not home now. I was just talking to her aunt and trust me, I wouldn't wish her on you," said Emma rolling her eyes and snapping her fingers and thumb together in simulation of Belinda's mouth.

He gave her a knowing look, and Emma's heart did a little skip, as though they'd just shared a secret. Feigning nonchalance, Emma asked, "How do you know Juliette? I didn't realize she was still well-acquainted with anyone in New York."

"Actually," said the man, rubbing his chiseled, slightly stubbled jawline with the heel of his hand, "we're not that well acquainted.

And I don't live here. I know the people she worked for in L.A.. I have a message for her."

The wheels started to turn in Emma's head. "L.A. . . . Oh! You're in that HBO show. The one about a TV show . . . ," she said, realizing why he looked familiar.

"*Episode*. Yes, that would be me. Ryan Churchill," said the man extending his hand and giving her a 'you've got me' smile.

She took his hand and smiled back. "Emma Worth," she said, glad she was dressed in her favorite yellow sundress, one that she knew flattered her especially well.

"I'm delighted to meet you, Emma Worth," said Ryan, lifting her hand to his lips, pressing a kiss on the back of her hand and then continuing to hold it for a few heartbeats before letting it go. "Now why does your name and face ring a bell?" he asked, looking her over in a way that made her pulse speed up. Emma could see why a number of women's magazines were claiming this British import was headed for stardom.

"Does it now?" she asked, an eyebrow arched.

He looked up to the sky as if for an answer and snapped his fingers repeatedly. "You're not going to help a bloke out, are you?"

"I guessed who you were."

"Hardly! What was it? 'You're in that show.' I'd hardly call that getting it correctly."

Emma pouted.

"I bet you're a model. Am I right?"

"Don't insult me like that!" Emma burst out with more playfulness than chagrin. "I can't imagine a more boring job than sitting around smiling, pouting or looking serious at will while draped in ridiculous clothing in ridiculous situations. Like running around an inner-city high school in 5-inch stilettos shooting a basketball."

Ryan threw his head back in amusement. "Or lounging about cuddling a baby leopard whilst wearing a leopard-skin bikini?"

"Exactly!" laughed Emma.

"Okay, so you're not a model. I give up."

Rummaging through her oversized Balenciaga, Emma pulled out a copy of that week's *In the Know* and flipped it open to an article about a new breed of It-girls. She, along with several other fashion and lifestyle bloggers, were mentioned in the article. A photo of Emma from her party was featured next to a blurb about *Worth It*.

"Maybe you saw this?" asked Emma.

"Yes, of course. I never miss an issue," Ryan said with a wink. She wasn't sure how serious he was. "Who'd have thought I'd meet THE Emma Worth in the flesh this very week? An It-girl! Blogger! Heiress! Well, there we go: No wonder you would look down at models and nameless actors, us working stiffs." Ryan said.

Emma, her hands in prayer position, channeling Oliver Twist, said, "Please, sir, don't hold it against me. I'm really just a normal, everyday kind of girl."

They both burst out laughing. Emma couldn't remember the last time she'd had this much fun.

"So you live here? In the same building as Juliette?" Ryan asked.

"That's right, apartment number three. Could I pass on the message for you? Her aunt said Juliette's not due back until later this afternoon."

"Oh, she isn't? No, no worries. I think I have her number; I'll reach her that way. I'll head back to my hotel then and settle in."

"Did you just arrive?" Emma asked, surprised.

"Yes, on the red eye," said Ryan. Emma found it strange that he would call on Juliette, who herself had only arrived yesterday, so soon after his arrival in New York. What was the nature of the message, she wondered, that he wanted to deliver it in person?

"What are you doing in New York, if you don't mind my asking?"

"I'm on hiatus from *Episode* and basing myself in New York this summer. My movie, *Between the Lines* co-starring Blake Dixon, is premiering here next month. So I'll be promoting it, doing loads of interviews and appearances and stuff."

Ryan's cell phone began to ring. He pulled it out of his jeans pocket, looked at the display, pressed a button and put it back in his pocket. "My publicist. I'll ring her back later."

"Sounds like you're busy; I won't keep you," said Emma. She would have liked very much to keep him.

"It was a pleasure to meet you," said Ryan, taking her hand again and looking into her eyes. Emma felt her knees go soft. "And I should apologize for taking up so much of your time. You were on your way out, after all."

"I'll let Juliette know you stopped by. Which hotel are you staying at?"

"The Gansevoort."

"Ah, that's nice and close by. Take care and maybe I'll see you again," said Emma.

"I'd like that, Emma Worth."

As Emma skipped down the steps, she made herself not turn around.

Walking down her leaf-shaded street, basking in the warmth of a perfect summer day, Emma thought of the encounter with Ryan and smiled to herself. She'd forgotten how much fun it could be to flirt with a charismatic, gorgeous guy. Famous, to boot. This was the kind of guy who should be blamed for keeping her up at night, not someone like *Adam*.

Emma started to feel annoyed again just thinking about him. That had been an entirely stupid idea to have even *considered* taking him out of the friend box and putting him in a different box, one which she didn't dare label. No, it was best to leave him in the friend box and keep the lid firmly shut.

After Adam had left the party with Hailey, Emma had had to work hard not to let the incident sour the rest of her night. Good thing she had practice controlling her emotions and could continue to put on a happy face. But there was no taming her subconscious thoughts, which had haunted more than a few of her nights in the last week.

Adam had had no right to tell Hailey about Zak. She had planned to do it in her own way and on her own time. And he certainly didn't have the right to nearly ruin her launch party. He'd offered to escort her, and for him to just leave like that was pretty shitty. She was still waiting for an apology.

At least Hailey had been understanding. She'd accepted Emma's apologies and reasons for not telling her everything about Zak right away.

No, when she couldn't sleep the night she'd had dinner with Adam, she told herself, it had had nothing to do with Adam. It had just been her subconsciousness telling her she needed to start dating again. It'd been far too long since she'd been with anyone, and having a guy in her life could be a good distraction. (Not to mention that dispensing dating advice while being in a relationship or actively dating would give her a lot more credibility than dispensing dating advice while single and not even bothering to look.)

And now she had the perfect candidate.

∾

"WHAT ABOUT THIS ONE, IZ?" Emma asked, holding up a cornflower blue dress that would work well with Isabel's dark-blond hair.

Isabel shook her head. "No, the bodice looks too tight. I'm still carrying all that excess midriff weight and with my boobs still huge like this, it would be indecent. God, I can't wait to have my body back! I swear, I'm never going to find a dress, and my lunch hour's almost over!"

When Isabel started acting like this, Emma knew something

was wrong. "You're stressed about going to Garrett's ex's wedding, aren't you?"

"Is it that obvious?" asked Isabel as she launched into another complaint about Bridezilla Beth, namely that no children were allowed at the reception.

"Why don't you leave them at home with your babysitter?" Emma asked.

"That's the thing, she's away this weekend. Plus we've never done an overnight with babysitters before. Adam and Brooke had offered to babysit. But now that they're not together, I wouldn't feel comfortable subjecting Adam to Mila and Felix on his own. Unless . . . "

Isabel let the word hang in the air. Emma understood now that Isabel didn't just want her shopping advice. Clearly, Isabel was desperate. And Emma was Mila's godmother and aunt, after all. If Adam was going to step up to the bat, and Brooke, who wasn't even family had offered, then she certainly could, too. "You want me to help babysit?"

"Oh, would you, Emma? Could you possibly babysit the kids with Adam on the weekend?"

Sometimes she wondered how it was that she, Emma, had the reputation for being the manipulative one of the two sisters. Of course, Emma couldn't say no.

This helped placate Isabel, who shortly afterward found a dress she liked.

While waiting in line to pay for the dress, Emma told Isabel about meeting Ryan Churchill.

Isabel was impressed. "I haven't watched his show, but I caught him in the BBC mini-series *The Soldier Poet*. He was divine. In fact, I think he's going to be on one of the morning shows this week; I saw a commercial for it."

"Really? I'll look it up."

"Are you going to see him again?"

"I sure hope so," said Emma, recalling the brightness of his smile and the blueness of his eyes. "The key, I suppose, is Juliette."

"She could probably use some friends. I've always felt so bad for her. Losing both her parents like that, and then going from her life in Paris to a new life with Belinda and her grandmother, who she barely knew."

Yes, Emma would befriend Juliette. And through her, she would become acquainted with Ryan, and then, well . . . Emma couldn't wait to see where that could lead.

CHAPTER EIGHTEEN

Emma rapped at Belinda's door. She hoped she would find Juliette rather than Belinda on the other side. What she wasn't expecting was to see Juliette dressed up and on her way out.

Juliette looked good in a simply cut dark pink sheath that flattered her shapely figure and olive skin tone. Juliette had always tended to pick clothes in more subdued tones and modest cuts. Maybe being out in La-La Land had finally rubbed off on her.

"Hi Juliette, welcome back," said Emma, touching her cheek to Juliette's. She recognized her perfume, an expensive, designer one. "How nice to see you again. You look well. That color really suits you, and what a gorgeous necklace."

"Thank you, Emma," said Juliette, fingering the diamond pendant at her neck.

The pendant looked familiar. Had Emma seen it in a magazine? Or maybe someone she knew had the same one?

"You're going out now?"

"Yes, I'm meeting . . . an old friend for a drink."

"How nice! It's great that you're in touch with some of your old friends," said Emma.

Yet, in the 15 months after college graduation, when Juliette had unsuccessfully looked for a job as a concert pianist in New York, Emma couldn't remember seeing Juliette with anyone their own age, anyone who could be mistaken for a friend or a date.

"Yes," was all Juliette said.

"We're all very excited to have you here this summer. Why don't we get together for dinner or drinks sometime soon to catch up?"

Emma thought she saw a flicker of surprise in Juliette's eyes before she smiled and said, "That's very kind of you to suggest it, Emma."

But you haven't actually agreed to it, thought Emma. Damn Juliette for being so noncommittal.

"By the way, Ryan Churchill was looking for you here earlier. He said he had a message for you from Blake Dixon and Genevieve Lane."

Juliette reddened. "Thank you for passing that on. We managed to, er, speak already."

"So what do you say? Shall we set a date to go out? How does this Friday sound?"

"Sorry. Adam stopped by half an hour ago and offered to take Aunt Belinda, Grandma and me out for dinner on Friday night."

He has, has he?

Juliette continued, "I haven't asked Aunt Belinda yet, as she's at work—"

"That Adam!" Emma laughed and hoped it didn't sound forced. "It seems he's gotten the plans mixed up. We'd both like to catch up with you, so when I mentioned dinner earlier, I forgot to tell you that Adam would come, too. We also discussed doing something with you and your aunt and grandma, but that was supposed to be next Friday or whenever we all had time."

"Oh," said Juliette. "Okay, in that case, I suppose Friday is fine."

"Great! I've been dying to check out this new Indochina

restaurant in the Meatpacking District. It'll be you, me, Adam. And you can bring a friend. Maybe whoever you're meeting tonight or Ryan Churchill. He told me he's staying at the Gansevoort; the restaurant is just across the street from him. I'll go ahead and make reservations for four people at 8 p.m.."

"I don't know Ryan well, but I suppose I could mention it to him," said Juliette. She took a look at her watch. "Sorry, Emma, I've got to run now."

Now that that was settled, Emma just had to inform Adam about the change in his Friday evening plans. And break the news to him that she was going to be babysitting with him on the weekend.

Of course, she hadn't fully forgiven him yet, but she could let him think she had.

Just at that moment, Emma's phone beeped.

Meet me for a drink? I want to apologize for how I acted at your party.

～

For DAYS ADAM had been infuriated with Emma and disgusted with himself.

Yesterday, he'd stopped in at Café Bisou, primarily to check up on Hailey, who hadn't thrown up after they'd left Emma's party, but had hiccupped and sniffled her way through the taxi ride to her apartment in Boerum Hill. The frost around his heart had thawed a little to hear that Emma had taken the initiative and apologized to Hailey, explaining everything.

"I felt so bad for Emma," Hailey had said. "I know now she was just trying to protect my feelings. I couldn't believe that I was causing her such anguish."

Really, Hailey was much too loyal and forgiving.

What about him?

He could believe, as Hailey did, that Emma had lied to protect Hailey from being hurt.

Nevertheless, what Emma had done was wrong. She'd ignored his warnings (not that that was anything new) and convinced Hailey to go after Zak.

And what about Zak throwing himself at Emma? Adam winced. What he'd said to Emma had been a low blow.

He'd let his romantic hopes about Emma cloud his judgement; he'd taken it personally when she hadn't actually done anything to *him*. She'd only wronged Hailey, and she'd already righted that wrong.

For that reason, he decided he should apologize.

So he was surprised when she didn't let him apologize. Instead she flashed her smile and green eyes, told him it was okay, and asked if they could go back to how they had been.

All the ice around his heart melted. Perhaps there was hope for them yet.

She wanted to have dinner with him and Juliette on Friday. He didn't mind if the older Bates women didn't join them. From what Emma said, it sounded almost like a double date. And then she said she'd offered to babysit Mila and Felix with him.

A whole weekend with Emma. He smiled, the flicker of hope growing.

CHAPTER NINETEEN

Clad in a flirty little black number, and dry-oil sprayed, shimmer powdered and bronzed, Emma felt every bit the It-girl *In the Know* had dubbed her. Thanks to the publicity from that and the *New York Post* article that had also come out this week, her blog had gotten tons of traffic and now had thousands of new subscribers.

She and Hailey were good again, now that Hailey knew about Zak's betrayal and new girlfriend.

She and Adam were friends again, just as it should be. And tonight there was a good chance she would see Ryan Churchill again. She didn't dwell on the disappointment she'd feel if Ryan wasn't there, convinced that he was as eager to see her again as she was him. Juliette was cagey, only saying she'd mentioned it to Ryan and had no idea if he was coming or not.

At Maison Dalat, an Amazonian blonde hostess with smoky eyes and chandelier earrings led Emma, Adam and Juliette to their table. As they passed the busy bar, Emma spotted Ryan talking with two girls. Emma gulped. He was even better looking than she'd remembered. Spotting them, Ryan extricated himself from his companions. His eyes skimmed over Juliette, then alighted on Emma with what she felt was true delight.

"Emma Worth, it is lovely to see you again," he said giving Emma a peck on each cheek before doing the same with Juliette.

Turning back to Emma, he said, "Juliette mentioned you would be having supper here, and I basically invited myself. I hope you don't mind. I don't know many people in New York, so it's brilliant to be able to escape my hotel room and have some company. Anyway, we can't let this bloke," he said, acknowledging Adam with an outstretched hand, "have you two beautiful women all to himself, now can we? That wouldn't be fair to the rest of us poor S.O.B.'s."

Considering the number of mascaraed eyes that had slinked over Adam and Ryan's tall forms as they shook hands, Emma knew Ryan did self-deprecating to an art form.

"Shall we continue to your table?" The hostess sounded impatient.

Ryan waved his goodbyes to the girls at the bar, who pouted in disappointment.

At their seats, Emma declared the dark, exotic interior of the trendy two-story restaurant to be "decadent and sumptuous" and demanded the others' opinions. While they looked around and made their assessments—"over the top" from Adam, "like a colonial gentleman's club" offered Ryan, and "I can see the French influences" contributed Juliette—Emma performed her own study of the dynamic between Ryan and Juliette. Seated in low wicker chairs across from one another, Juliette and Ryan seemed to avoid eye or physical contact, exchanging only the usual pleasantries and the occasional smile.

Poor things, how awkward for them, thought Emma. They feel uncomfortable in a social setting together because Ryan is in a whole other league from Juliette, who's basically his colleague and friend's hired help. Emma determined to take over the conversation, putting them all at ease while spotlighting her own inclusiveness, big-heartedness and social adeptness.

As the four perused their oversized, red, leather-bound menus, Emma commented on different dishes she'd read about in a review.

Orders placed, Emma praised Ryan on his *Live! with Regis and Kelly* appearance and said, "So you really used to take ballet lessons? I should have guessed after the way you did that lift-and-spin thing on my stoop the other day. I felt like a ballerina."

"Ha, yes, six years, in fact. Ballet is fabulous for body control, which is great for an actor, particularly stage actors. My mum was keen for my little sister to do ballet, but she didn't fancy it in the least, saying it was for stupid prissy girls and not for girls who were going to grow up to be doctors. So I went to the studio instead—I'd always admired dancers like Astaire and Baryshnikov, and I was hoping to get the lead role in a school production of *Joseph and the Amazing Technicolor Dreamcoat.* More importantly, we couldn't get the money back otherwise."

At Emma's prompting, Ryan revealed more about his acting history and what it was like growing up in England. Then a would-be debate began over the merits of Los Angeles vs. New York. A fair or long debate it wasn't since Ryan and Juliette, the only ones to have actually lived in L.A., weren't partial to the sprawling city. "It's a strange place. I don't get it. I much prefer New York or London or Paris," said Ryan with a smile at Juliette, who nodded her agreement.

The evening continued with Ryan and Emma taking over and regaling the others with funny stories—Ryan about Hollywood and acting and Emma about New York and the life of an It-girl. Adam, Emma noticed, was grumpy and did not warm to Ryan. She also noticed that Juliette was mostly quiet, which wasn't surprising. After a while, Adam turned to Juliette and engaged her in conversation. Emma continued to talk and flirt with Ryan, while straining to hear what Adam and Juliette were saying.

Several sumptuous courses, a round of cocktails and two bottles of wine later, the check arrived. Ryan reached for it. "It's on me."

"Thanks, but I was planning to get this," said Adam.

"Mate, it's good, I got it," said Ryan.

"No, I'd like to pay," answered Adam, producing his wallet. "It was my idea."

Watching this display of masculine pride, Emma rolled her eyes at Juliette to suggest a shared understanding of how this happens every time you go out with men for dinner. Juliette didn't seem to understand. Poor thing, she probably doesn't find herself in this kind of situation very often, thought Emma.

"Ryan, thanks for the offer, but you're the guest. Why don't you let Adam get it this time. You can buy us a round at the next place and pick up the tab next time. Shall we go up to the top of the Gansevoort? Or would you like to go somewhere a bit further afield?"

With her arm linked through Ryan's, Emma navigated them over the cobblestone streets to their next destination, a dive bar which was known for sexy barmaids dancing on the saloon-style bar.

Juliette ordered a club soda. Emma knew she should probably have something non-alcoholic but ordered a Ketel One tonic anyway. Someone, she herself probably, suggested a game of pool: Emma and Ryan against Juliette and Adam. Adam sank ball after ball, more than making up for Juliette's poor performance. Upon losing, Ryan said good-naturedly, "Good game, mate. Where'd you learn to play like that?"

"Used to play a lot with my brother and friends when I was younger," said Adam.

Emma wondered at his ungracious tone.

Later, when Ryan and Juliette weren't paying attention, Emma hissed at Adam, "What the hell is wrong with you? You've been acting pissy all night."

"I thought the point of tonight was to catch up with Juliette. Not to hear about you and Ryan's celebrity histories."

Really, what was up with Adam tonight?

"So what were you and Juliette talking about all this time? Surely you two did a bit of catching up or did you just eavesdrop on Ryan and me the whole night?"

"I thought *you* were the one who wanted to see Juliette, which is why you hijacked tonight. Now it's clear to me exactly why you arranged this cozy foursome," Adam said, scowling over to where Ryan and Juliette, standing a good foot or so away from each other, were talking.

"Feeling a bit jealous, Adam? Now that you don't have Brookey-Wookey to fawn all over you?"

Adam glared at her. "What about *you*, Emma? You've long since left charming Emma behind and are getting into drunk-Emma territory. Not your best side. Anyway, *I* for one, am meant to be babysitting my goddaughter and Felix tomorrow, so I'm going to bed. I'd suggest you do the same. Not that you ever listen to me."

Emma opened her mouth to retaliate, certain that Adam was exaggerating her drunkenness. She felt fine. Better than fine. But having already secured what she was after—Ryan had asked to see her again, and numbers had been exchanged—Emma decided there was no point arguing with Adam tonight.

Anyway, Adam was right. Her niece and nephew were a handful at the best of times; dealing with them while hungover and tired would not be fun, even without Adam being annoyed and angry with her.

CHAPTER TWENTY

It took two rings before the door opened. Garrett was holding on to a bawling Felix, who was naked and not exactly fresh from the waist down. In the hallway, a half-dressed Isabel pleaded with Mila: "Mila, where did you hide Mommy's shoe?"

"I didn't *hide it*, Mommy!" said Mila, exasperated, as if she'd had to explain this countless times already to someone who was too slow-witted to understand. "I was using it as a bed for Mousey to sleep in. Mousey has reflux like Felix does. So the slantiness of those shoes lets her sleep better."

Emma and Adam looked at each other in amusement. On the journey over, they had hardly spoken, Emma fighting a headache and Adam apparently still annoyed with her.

"Okay, I don't mean 'hide' it, but where were you playing with it?" Isabel demanded with as much calmness and reason as she could muster, which didn't seem to be much at this point.

"I don't remember."

Isabel flung up her arms as a growl escaped her lips.

Turning from this scene, Garrett said, "Hi Emma, hi Adam, am I relieved to see you two! Izzy, as you can see, is going mental trying to pack and get everything ready here—and that was before she started looking for her shoe! I'm afraid she might strangle Mila. And Felix, my boy, has just done the most disgusting poo—right after we'd just changed and dressed him."

Adam and Emma turned to one another and waved their fists: once, twice and on the third count Emma splayed her hand and wrapped it around Adam's fist. "Paper, I win," said Emma.

"Alright, give him to me," said Adam, reaching for the baby.

"Thanks, bro," said Garrett, unburdening the crying, squirming bundle from his arms.

"And I'll go see if I can wrangle more information out of Mila," said Emma. "Maybe then you can help Isabel finish packing so she can at least finish getting dressed."

"Thanks, Emma, though I'd rather stay as far away from that woman"—Garrett nudged his thumb in the general direction of Isabel—"as I possibly can right now. I might get my head bitten off if I so much as looked at the suitcase."

Finally, after detailed instructions repeated several times, a last-minute feed, a story and lots of hugs and kisses, a frazzled but fully dressed Isabel was able to leave.

When the door closed behind her parents, Mila gave a sigh of relief with an eye roll. "Thank goodness they're gone. They were driving me crazy!"

Emma and Adam burst out laughing.

Later that evening, spaghetti Bolognese plates cleared and bowls of organic ice cream in front of them, Mila asked, "Uncle Adam, where's Aunt Brooke tonight?"

"I don't actually know, Mila. We are no longer friends like that. So you probably won't see her anymore."

"Oh," said Mila, looking subdued for a moment before brightening up. "Does that mean now you and Auntie Em can get married?"

"To each other?" Adam croaked as Emma coughed into her water.

"Yes, silly," said Mila. "What else?"

"Why do you think your Auntie Em and I should get married?" Adam seemed genuinely curious.

"Well, you live together and you are my godparents together. 'Parents' are supposed to be married, like Mommy and Daddy. And Ellie's Mommy and Daddy are also married and her godparents are married. And Felix's godparents are also married."

"A child's godparents don't *have* to be married, and they certainly don't have to be to each other," said Emma. "They could even be married to other people."

"Oh," said Mila, quiet for a moment as she considered the information. "But don't you love each other?"

"Of course, we do, Mila, but not in the way that your mommy and daddy love each other," said Emma, raising laughter-filled eyes to Adam's but finding his thoughtful and hooded. "We love each other as friends just like we love you as our goddaughter."

"But maybe you should get married, since you are friends and you are my godparents together and you live together. And then maybe you will love each other like Mommy and Daddy love each other," said Mila decisively and triumphantly. "Can I also be the flower girl at your wedding?"

"Uh-oh! Looks like you've inherited your Aunt Emma's matchmaking skills," said Adam, giving Mila an affectionate tap on the nose.

At around half past nine, Adam and Emma tiptoed out of the children's room. Mila had kept asking for another book and wanted Uncle Adam and Auntie Emma to do all the animal sounds over and over. Even Felix had been gurgling with laughter.

"Phew, that was exhausting!" said Adam. "I'm too old for this."

"I don't think age has anything to do with it. I'm exhausted too, and I'm way, way younger than you."

"Not that much younger," Adam said with a mock-cautioning tone.

"You'd make a fantastic dad. You're so patient and know

exactly how to talk to them. And I didn't know you were so good at accents and animal sounds."

"I'm full of surprises," said Adam, raising and wiggling his eyebrows until Emma laughed.

"What do you want to do now?" asked Emma, stifling a yawn.

"Pass out on the couch with a beer and a movie," said Adam, plopping himself down on the protruding part of the L-shaped couch.

"That sounds perfect," said Emma, going to the fridge for the bottles then sitting down next to Adam. "How does one little girl have so much energy? I thought she would never fall asleep."

"Tell me about it. And boy can she talk. You'd hardly guess she was only five," laughed Adam.

"Yeah, five going on fifteen."

In the middle of the night, Emma's sleep was interrupted by a baby's cry. She couldn't imagine where the sound was coming from and tried to shut it out. She felt something heavy on her and realized it was Adam's arm. The cry came again. Felix! Emma scrambled off the couch, where Adam lay sleeping, undisturbed by the baby's cry. Just like a man, she thought, as she ran to Mila and Felix's room, her hand massaging the crick at the back of her neck.

"Hello, little man," she said, seeing Felix's red face. She cooed at him as she lifted him out of the crib. "Are you missing your mommy a bit? How about, a snuggle with your Auntie Em and a lullaby?"

Felix settled down while she rocked him and sang, but when she tried to put him into his crib, he protested again. "Perhaps you're hungry, little man? Or don't want to go to bed all alone? Ha, you're practicing to be a real little New York dude already, eh? Alrighty, let's warm up a bottle for you."

Easier said than done, thought Emma, as she tried to warm up a bottle of expressed milk according to Isabel's instructions while juggling Felix. She struggled to get the damn milk warmer to open, which wasn't helped by Felix's wiggling and whimpering. When it opened, she couldn't remember whether she was supposed to remove the cap, replace it with a teat, or leave it closed. "You don't know, do you, Felix?" Emma asked. He replied with a wail. "I guess that's a . . . leave off the cap?" She couldn't believe Adam was still asleep despite the noise they were making.

Finally, the milk was ready, and she managed to get the bottle to Felix while only spilling a quarter of the bottle. Felix drank his milk greedily, his eyelids already falling before he'd finished. Emma removed the bottle, rocked him again, and settled him back into his crib, thankful that he didn't protest this time, just sighed and went to sleep.

She tucked the kicked-off covers back around Mila's sleeping form and took the alpaca blanket that was draped on a chair in the children's room into the living room. Adam was curled up on the sofa, trying to fit his long length onto the space. She debated whether to wake him and send him to a real bed but decided against it; he was sleeping so soundly. She smiled, thinking that he looked very young asleep. She covered him with the blanket. Then she changed into her nightgown before crawling into Isabel and Garrett's bed.

THE EARLY MORNING light poured through the living room windows. Adam stretched out his achy limbs. He could hear traffic, activity and voices outside, never distant sounds in New York, even on a Sunday morning in this section of Brooklyn. Inside, it was quiet. Upon investigation, he found Felix deep asleep, but Mila was missing from her bed. He found her and Emma in Isabel and Garrett's bed.

Adam looked at the two sleeping females. They were sharing a single pillow and facing each another. Something tightened in his chest. He pulled the covers a bit higher over Mila and tenderly swept her sweaty hair off her face. He glided his fingertips over Emma's bare shoulder, causing her to murmur something in her sleep, and pulled the cover higher over her as well. He then leaned over and kissed Mila's slightly chubby cheek and Emma's brow. After another few moments looking at this sight—they were like a sleeping Madonna and child—he headed for the bathroom to take a shower.

EMMA WOKE to the delightful smell of coffee and bacon. Entering the kitchen, she saw Mila in her pajamas, sitting in her designer wooden high chair, explaining to Adam how to make eggs. Emma laughed to witness the little girl lecturing the man who was so good at lecturing *her*.

Adam turned from the stove, freshly showered and wearing Isabel's frilly apron over his T-shirt and jeans. Emma went to him, as though for a couple-y peck on the lips, lulled by the domesticity of the scene. Just in time, she turned her face and accepted the kiss he pressed onto her cheek.

"Look who slept in late," he teased.

"Look who slept through the baby crying," returned Emma.

LATE THAT AFTERNOON, Emma and Adam reversed the steps they had taken the previous morning, on considerably better terms than on the way over. Their chatting was broken by companionable silence. As they drew near their building, Adam turned to Emma, glum at having to say goodbye to her and the prospect of a quiet Sunday evening alone before him. "Emma, how do you feel about getting some take—"

He was interrupted by the ringing of Emma's cell phone.

"Hello?" said Emma, who'd dug her RAZR out of her purse

and answered it as they walked. "Hello, Ryan. . . . Yes, me too."
Here a laugh. "Tonight? No, I don't have other plans. . . . Sure, I'd
love that. . . . Yes, I know it. . . . Okay, see you there at eight. Bye."

With a smile she turned to Adam, who by this time had let
them into the building and had already retrieved two bills and a
manila envelope from his mailbox. "Sorry, that was Ryan. What
were you going to say earlier?"

"Don't worry about it; it was nothing important," said Adam,
crushing Emma to him so she wouldn't see his disappointment.
He rested his chin on her head for a moment and then said into
her hair, "Just that the babysitting was really fun. Have a good
time with Ryan tonight."

He then took the stairs two at a time and had already shut the
door to his apartment before Emma had even closed her mailbox.

CHAPTER TWENTY-ONE

Emma stepped into the upscale sushi restaurant in Chelsea excited to see Ryan again.

She swept her eyes around the waiting area and bar. He wasn't there, even though she was a fashionable 20 minutes late. Fashionable because she had changed her outfit about 15 times trying to find the right balance of interested-but-not-overeager, stylish-but-not-trying-too-hard.

Normally she was good at this; but tonight she may have overthought it. She hadn't trusted her instinct, which had told her a cool minimalist top, jeans and heels might have been more appropriate than the figure-hugging femme fatale dress she had finally settled on.

After giving the hostess Ryan's name, Emma was led to a table. Ryan was engaged in conversation with two other people. Half-drunken glasses of beer, empty plates, chopsticks, a skinny white porcelain jug, and three sake cups littered the tabletop.

"Emma!" said Ryan upon seeing her. Trapped between the two others in the semicircular booth, he made helpless gestures with his hands and indicated that she should slide into the booth next to the man on his left.

This wasn't exactly the reception Emma had hoped for.

Ryan apologized that a work meeting had gone over and made the introductions—the man was his manager, Gavin, and the woman, his publicist, Amalia.

"Don't worry, we won't be staying long. Got to catch a flight back to L.A. early tomorrow morning," said Gavin.

A lychee martini was ordered and soon appeared for Emma. Still somewhat miffed, Emma sipped her drink as she listened to Gavin, Amalia and Ryan discuss plans for the premiere of *Between the Lines* in just over two weeks' time. Or rather, Gavin and Amalia discussed the premiere while Ryan rolled his eyes at Emma to show he wished they would hurry up and finish.

Mollified, Emma offered input about the theater and after-party location.

When the topic turned to who Ryan would be taking to the premiere, Amalia and Gavin suddenly appeared to take an interest in her. Emma answered their questions about her blog and background and life in New York.

Amalia interrupted her to say, "I hope you don't mind if I order some sushi. The appetizers did nothing to tide me over."

After a round of miso soups, a selection of nigiri, a crispy lobster roll, a house roll and a sashimi dish all washed down with Asahi and sake, Amalia and Gavin finally agreed that business had been conducted and they could go.

"Emma, it was a pleasure to meet you. I hope to see you soon, perhaps at the premiere," Gavin said, reaching out a hand to shake Emma's.

"Yes, Emma, delightful to meet you," said Amalia to Emma, then wagging her finger at Ryan, she said, "I would not mind seeing this beautiful woman on your arm at the premiere."

"Sorry about that!" said Ryan when they were finally alone. "I feel like they're my parents, trying to embarrass me in front of a girl I like."

Emma's heartbeat quickened. "Yes, it was like being in high

school and my date's parents are trying to see if I'm good in enough for their son."

"Well, if that were the case, Emma, you passed with flying colors. They adored you. Thanks for being such a good sport. So, since I can't really do anything but, will you be my date to the premiere of *Between the Lines*?"

"Are you just asking me because your parents gave you their approval?" teased Emma.

"Yeah that, and it's too late to find another date," said Ryan.

"I doubt that," said Emma, ecstatic that Ryan had chosen to take her to the red-carpet premiere of a Hollywood blockbuster.

EMMA WAS STILL THINKING about the dresses she'd tried on during her preliminary shopping trip—with only two weeks to go, she needed to make the most of her time—when she noticed the truck in front of her building.

Two men emerged from the back of the truck, maneuvering a large covered item between them. A piano! Emma hurried through her building's double doors, which were propped wide open. The door to the Bates' apartment also stood open. Emma stuck her head in and saw Juliette holding a broom and dustpan next to a slightly darker rectangular patch of hardwood floor where the previous piano had been.

"Hi, Juliette. Are you getting a new piano?"

"It would seem so," said Juliette, heading to the kitchen to empty the dustpan and put it and the broom away.

Shortly afterward, the two movers appeared at the doorway. "Same place as the other one?"

"Yes," said Juliette.

The men moved the piano into the empty space then removed the cushioned covering. A small gasp escaped from Juliette as the shiny black upright was revealed. Juliette gazed for a long time at the new piano before opening the lid and fingering the keys reverently.

"It looks like a nice piano," Emma said.

"It sure is a beauty," agreed the man gathering up the packing material. "Top-of-the-line Yamaha."

"Miss, would you mind signing for this?" asked the other man. "It's just saying you've received the piano in good condition."

"No, of course not," said Juliette, taking the proffered pen and clipboard. She read through the form clipped onto it and then signed it.

The man took back the clipboard, separated the carbon forms, and gave Juliette the pink customer copy along with a business card. "Here is the number for the tuner. Just give him a call to schedule an appointment. As I said before, the first two years of tuning is paid for, up to four times a year. Anywhere in the country."

"Thank you," said Juliette, taking the card.

"You enjoy playing it, you hear. This is one fine gift. Your boyfriend must really love you."

After Juliette had shown the men out, Emma asked, "You have a boyfriend, Juliette?"

"No," Juliette snapped. "The mover was just joking."

"But it was a gift?"

She nodded and, before Emma could ask who it was from, added, "It must be from Blake and Genevieve, a kind of thank you gift or bonus."

"But you don't know for sure?"

"It couldn't possibly be from anyone else," said Juliette with finality.

The way Juliette ran her fingers over the polished white and black keys and the longing looks she gave it made it clear she couldn't wait to try the piano, even in its untuned state.

On her way upstairs, Emma wondered if Juliette could have been lying about who'd sent her the piano. Emma recalled the fortune cookie from last night's takeout. The little piece of paper had read: "A romantic mystery will soon add interest to your life." Maybe this was exactly what the fortune was referring to, thought Emma, rubbing her palms together.

She certainly wouldn't mind a bit of romantic intrigue in her life. In fact, she was as good a sleuth as she was a matchmaker.

CHAPTER TWENTY-TWO

"I'm sorry about the other night. Amalia insisted that I meet with this stylist," said Ryan, as he greeted Emma a couple of days later. "You don't believe me, do you? I just saw the way you rolled your eyes."

True, Emma had been upset by Ryan's last-minute cancellation of their planned Tuesday night date. But now, in his presence, with that dimpled smile and those baby blues, all was forgiven.

"Apparently, Jace is extremely in demand and, on Amalia's begging, agreed to see me Tuesday evening to help get me suited up for the premiere," continued Ryan. "Speaking of the premiere, you are still going to be my date, aren't you? I hope I didn't just shoot myself in the foot."

"Hmm . . . " Emma pretended to think it over. "You're not going to stand me up again, are you? I'm not some starry-eyed ingénue that you can walk all over."

"I promise I will not stand you up to my own premiere," said Ryan, the twitching of his lips betraying his attempt to look earnest.

God, he really did have the most amazing lashes.

"In that case, I suppose I could be persuaded to go with you," Emma said, laughing at their silliness. Then on a serious note she asked, "Would your stylist or Amalia have to approve what I wear as your date?"

"You're an It-girl. People idolize your style. You set the trends, Emma," said Ryan, looking appreciatively at Emma's asymmetrical turquoise skirt and white top, accessorized with a feather necklace and Roman sandals—she was going for boho chic— perfect for an afternoon stroll through the Village.

Emma could get used to this. "Well, I'll definitely need to give it some thought."

"I trust you completely . . . as long as you make *me* look good." He grinned.

Emma raked her eyes from the tips of his golden-blond quiff down to the toes of his tan leather brogues (Italian, no doubt) before saying, "As if you need anyone's help to make you look good."

Did Ryan actually blush?

"Shall we?" Ryan offered Emma the crook of his elbow.

She linked her arm through his and felt a flutter of excitement to finally have Ryan to herself. Wandering through her neighborhood, they admired brownstones that were particularly manicured or interesting, and Emma pointed out locations where various films and TV shows had been shot.

At the Coffee Bean, waiting for their Ice Blendeds, Ryan said, "So, I have four extra premiere tickets. Would you like to invite some of your friends? I was thinking Juliette, of course, and perhaps her aunt? Adam. You'd mentioned Hailey."

"Yes, that might cheer Hailey up a bit. It's Adam's kind of movie, so he'll certainly enjoy it. I guess it would be nice for Juliette to attend her boss' premiere. But Belinda wouldn't know what to do with herself, and what would she wear?"

"It won't matter what they wear. They won't be walking the

red carpet, at least not on my arm." He looked meaningfully at Emma as he held the coffee shop's door open for her.

Don't swoon, Emma.

"If Belinda goes, then we will hear about nothing else for weeks—months—afterward."

"Then I will have done my job. It is my goal, after all, to fuel every woman's fantasies and conversations," said Ryan with a wink.

Emma snuggled close to him, charmed as hell. We look just like one of those celebrity couples you always see strolling hand-in-hand on the pages of magazines like *People* and *In the Know*, she thought, wishing a paparazzo would snap a picture of her and Ryan right now.

"By the way," said Emma, remembering her news, "Juliette has got a new piano!"

"Really? She must be very excited. I understand the piano at her aunt and gran's was very old and not very good."

"Yes, they've had that one for ages, and it was secondhand to start with."

"I'm glad to hear it. With her talent, Juliette deserves a good piano to play on."

"The person who gave it to her obviously feels the same way." Emma took a sip of her drink, feigning nonchalance.

"What? Are you saying it was a gift?"

"Yes," said Emma, then explained that she had been there when the piano was delivered. "Juliette said it was likely from Blake and Genevieve, but she didn't know for sure."

"Was there no card?"

"Not that I'm aware of. If there had been, she'd have said definitively that it was from them, wouldn't she? So I suspect," said Emma, leaning in, "that Juliette has a secret admirer."

"You do?" said Ryan. "Why do you think that?"

"The mover said Juliette's boyfriend must really love her to give her such a nice gift. Juliette denies having a boyfriend, but it planted the idea in my head that it was a kind of lover's gift."

"Hmm . . . " said Ryan, rubbing his chin. "I'd place my cap on it coming from Blake and Genevieve."

Emma took a long draw through her straw. "Let's assume it's *not* from Blake and Genevieve. Who else could it be from? Do you have any ideas? Was Juliette seeing someone in L.A.?"

"I certainly wouldn't know anything about her private life."

"So that means there *could* be someone. Maybe an ex trying to win her back? I swear I won't be able to rest until I figure it out!"

"Well . . . " Ryan drawled

"Well what?" asked Emma as they wandered into Washington Square Park.

"It's just an idea," said Ryan, looking thoughtful, "a half-formed one at that, but . . . what if it *is* from the Dixons—but not from both of them?"

Emma looked hard at Ryan, who was preoccupied by a gray squirrel trying to steal discarded food out of the trash can.

Was Ryan implying there was something going on between Juliette and Blake Dixon, an A-list Hollywood actor? That was preposterous! Yet it would explain why Juliette was in New York and not with the family in France right now. If she, Emma, were Genevieve Lane and suspected her husband of being attracted to the nanny, she'd also have sent her packing; the last thing she'd want would be a shapely, bikini-clad nanny ruining their summer beach vacation.

"Oh. My. God. I see," said Emma, breathless. "Yes, now it all makes sense! It's from Blake, isn't it? He's Juliette's secret admirer. That's why Juliette's been banished here for the summer; Genevieve wants her as far away from him as possible."

"Emma, you do have a devious mind," said Ryan, with a conspiratorial smile.

"So you think my theory is correct? You know Blake; do you

think Juliette was having an affair with him right under Genevieve's nose?"

"Blake has always been very professional," said Ryan, seeming to choose his words with care. "He's good-looking, suave, famous, so naturally a lot of women fancy him and try to get close to him. He and Genevieve seemed like a typical married couple the few times I saw them together. I must admit, however, it did strike me as odd that Genevieve would hire someone as young and pretty as Juliette to live with them and watch the children."

"Do you think Juliette is Blake's type?"

"Possibly. She is very attractive—dark hair, olive complexion —same as Genevieve, just—"

"—a younger model!" finished Emma.

"And Blake loves classical music and plays the piano himself, so he no doubt appreciates Juliette's talent."

"And Juliette's also very discreet," Emma pointed out, "which would be handy if you were trying to fool around behind your wife's back."

"Good point. So yes, I could see how a man like Blake might fall for Juliette's charms," said Ryan. "This is pure speculation, of course. Just between you and me."

"Of course," nodded Emma, thrilled to be sharing secrets with Ryan Churchill.

Then Ryan added, "Of course, maybe by now, Juliette has received a postcard from Corsica saying: 'Surprise! Hope you like the piano. Wish you were here. Love, Genevieve, Blake, Camden, Olivier and Sansa.'"

"Oh, I should hope not," said Emma, much preferring her own theory.

CHAPTER TWENTY-THREE

The next day, Emma was at home working when she heard scraping sounds above her and then muted music. The roof terrace—her *private* roof terrace—was above her, with access from her apartment and the hall landing.

Emma climbed up the stairway from her apartment to investigate.

Beyoncé was "uh-oh"-ing out of a portable bar speaker on which an iPod was docked. A woman with long, wavy, high-lighted hair in tiny flamingo-pink bikini bottoms lay face down on one of Emma's cushioned wooden sun loungers. It had been dragged from where Emma had carefully arranged it to a part of the deck that was in full sunshine. Next to her was a small table, also moved from its previous location. On the table, in addition to the iPod speaker, were issues of *Star*, *In the Know* and *Life & Style* and a bottle of Hawaiian Tropics Dark Tanning Lotion SPF 4.

"Excuse me," said Emma over the music, "this is private property."

Leisurely, the woman raised her head and turned it toward Emma's voice, lowering her oversized, gold sunglasses as she did so. "It's okay, I live here now. You must be Emma. I'm Chloe. I'm sure you've heard all about me from Zak."

Emma's jaw dropped. She clamped it shut again and clenched her teeth. So this woman, who thinks she owns the place, is Zak's girlfriend and her new neighbor. Being preoccupied with, among other things, Juliette's arrival and Ryan, Emma had forgotten about Zak and the mysterious girlfriend. She had, indeed, not really believed an actual girlfriend would materialize.

"I'm so glad you're here," the woman said. "Would you do me the biggest favor in the world and put some sun lotion on my back? I may have missed a few spots and I'd hate to have an uneven tan."

The nerve of this woman, seethed Emma, eyeing the deep, dark, even tan the woman was sporting. "I'd rather not," said Emma, "my hands are, er, dirty; I was chopping some stuff in the kitchen."

Emma cursed herself, wondering why she'd felt it necessary to make an excuse as to why she didn't want to rub lotion on the bare back of a woman she had never met before. The same woman whose boyfriend had thrown himself at *her* and slept with one of her friends just a few weeks ago.

"Jesus, it really is hot! Such a gross, humid heat, not like the dry heat we get in L.A., where even when it's like 100 degrees, it doesn't feel so sticky and disgusting like this. I sure could use an ice-cold drink right now. But my apartment's sooo far away ... "

Emma ignored the pouty tone and blatant hint. She was not about to go fetch a cold drink for this woman like some servant.

Chloe sat up suddenly, exposing two large, nipple-tipped spheres, the taut, glistening skin several shades whiter than the rest of her body.

"Oops," said Chloe, reaching for her discarded tank top and holding it in front of her boobs. She gave a little laugh that to Emma's ears sounded as fake as her breasts. "They're nice, aren't they? Everyone tells me they look very natural. I have an amazing plastic surgeon, one of the best in L.A.." She then looked pointedly at Emma's chest. "If you feel like a bit of a boost, I can give you his number. Put in a good word to get you to the top of the waiting list, y'know."

Emma gasped. A perfect B-cup, she had never felt inadequate with her shape before. Now she felt positively livid that this hideous Barbie doll of a woman had just insulted the size of her chest.

"Would you like to feel them?" continued the woman, her modesty obviously forgotten as she lowered her shirt. "It's funny because it's always the women who are curious about them. Probably because they're secretly thinking about getting some themselves. Guys, on the other hand, just love boobs. Doesn't matter if they're real or fake as long as they're big. Zak just adores them!"

Emma was no prude, but she was not someone who let it all hang out. And she was certainly not interested in seeing, let alone feeling, this bimbo's fake tits.

"If you want to stay up here this afternoon, fine. But please move the furniture back when you leave. And in the future, I have to ask that you not use the roof-deck; it is only for the private use of the top-floor apartment. You are welcome to the back garden just outside your apartment; it'd certainly be more *convenient* when you want a cold drink."

Spinning on her heels, Emma made for the stairwell, disregarding Chloe whining about how there wasn't enough sunlight or a sun lounger in the garden.

Emma returned to her desk and couldn't believe that Zak had chosen this ridiculous bimbo over someone sweet and kind like Hailey. She reached for her cell and dashed off a text to Adam:

Zak's gf just asked if I want to touch her fake tits!!!

His reply was nearly instant: *Did you? ;)*

No! Suggested that I needed a boob job!!! Can u believe the nerve? Yours are fine as they are! :P

CHAPTER TWENTY-FOUR

It was going to be another sweltering New York summer day. Coming down the stairs to check her mail the next day, Emma heard voices. Or rather, Belinda Bates' voice.

" . . . of course, we have fans, but have you heard? It's dangerous to have a fan blowing on you while you sleep. People in Korea have died of it! That's what Gina Kim from work told me. She's Korean so she would know. Since hearing that, I've been afraid to keep the fan on while Mother sleeps. And, as I was telling you before, it's much too loud for me with the windows open. I will just have to wait until next month's paycheck to buy a new air conditioner. Of course, Juliette has offered to buy one, but I told her, 'Absolutely not. You are a guest here.'"

Adam, in a sweat-soaked T-shirt and running shorts, was doing stretches in the foyer. Emma could imagine just how hot and sweaty he was from his morning run, which obviously wasn't early enough to beat the heat; he was probably dying for a shower. Rather than turning tail and escaping back to her apartment, Emma decided she'd help extricate Adam from the grip of Belinda's jaws.

"There you are, Adam. Remember you were going to help me with that thing on my blog? Sorry, Belinda, Adam and I were planning to do some work this morning."

"Of course, of course, Emma, don't let me keep you. I was just finishing up here with Adam, wasn't I? But since I have you both here at the same time, two birds and one stone and all, there's something I wanted to ask you. You've both heard about Juliette's new piano, I'm sure? Fifteen-thousand dollars! That's what Mrs. Goddard says it's worth. Can you just imagine? Genevieve and Mr. Dixon must just cherish Juliette, but then again, how can they not?"

Emma tapped her foot. What was so great about Juliette, anyway, besides that she could play a stupid piano?

Adam seemed to be sweating more than he was a minute ago, and Emma could smell the maleness of him, a thought that was strangely intimate. She went to her mailbox.

"So I've been thinking what a shame it is to keep such a treasure hidden away here in our little apartment with no one to hear its sweet sounds except for me and Mother, and she's so hard of hearing, it's just wasted on her, though she does so like to watch Juliette play. Juliette has such a wonderfully calm demeanor when she plays. She just shines like an angel—her inner beauty really comes through."

Adam smiled and nodded. Emma wanted to kick him. "So what was it you wanted to ask us?" prompted Emma.

"Oh yes, so I thought—you know how I've been wanting to hold a welcome-back thing for Juliette anyway—that it would be a lovely idea to hold a recital here. That way we can all appreciate Juliette's new piano and her playing. Chloe thought it was a wonderful idea. Have you met Zak's girlfriend, our new neighbor? What a lovely girl!"

Emma rolled her eyes. Adam cupped his hands in front of his chest and winked at Emma. Emma suppressed a giggle and swatted at his hands with the envelopes in her hand.

"I haven't had the pleasure," said Adam, "but I've heard she's very big hearted and easy to get a feel for. Emma thinks they are going to be real bosom buddies."

Emma stuck her tongue out at Adam's grinning face.

"Yes, I thought the very same thing myself! Both of you so lovely and young and into fashion. I must say, Adam, that between Emma, Juliette and Chloe, we have three of the most beautiful women in the whole of New York all under one roof!"

"Oh, I have no doubt of that whatsoever, Belinda. So you would like to hold a recital here?"

"Yes, Adam. I was thinking Sunday, a week from tomorrow. In the afternoon. Chloe's offered to help; she says she loves throwing parties. And then you can meet Chloe for yourself, Adam."

"Are you free next Sunday, Emma?"

Even Adam's usual patience with Belinda was wearing thin, she noticed.

"Yes, I am," said Emma. It would be most expedient to simply accept; she could always back out later.

"Perfect. Belinda, Emma and I will be there next Sunday. We look forward to it. But I really need to grab a shower now and, uh, talk with Emma about her blog as I'd promised. Thanks for the invitation."

"Thanks," called Emma behind her, as she and Adam jogged up the stairs. Adam unlocked his door. She followed him in.

"Did I forget something? Or were we really supposed to meet this morning?" asked Adam, reaching one arm behind his neck and pulling his T-shirt over his head.

Watching Adam stride to the fridge and pour himself a glass of water, Emma's mind wandered to Ryan as she wondered what he looked like without a shirt on. Were his shoulders as broad as Adam's? Probably not, though he was leaner than Adam, who, although clearly in good shape, was probably not as chiseled as Ryan was. Adam had a sprinkling of dark hair covering his chest and a happy trail that disappeared past the waistline of his shorts. Would Ryan also be as hairy? Not to say that Adam was hairy, Emma decided. He was just the right amount of hairy. No, somehow she imagined Ryan with a hairless chest. Probably waxed. She supposed she could Google for a picture of a bare-chested Ryan. But she'd be able to see for herself soon enough, surely?

When they were saying goodbye at the end of their date, she'd looked expectantly at Ryan, feeling like a 16-year-old on her first date, wondering if she was going to get kissed or not. Ryan had leaned in. She'd closed her eyes and lifted her face, and she'd felt his arms go around her . . .

"I see that the sight of my bare chest has caused you to drool and rendered you speechless."

Emma blinked, then smiled. "Sorry what, Knightley? I was thinking about Ryan."

With a snap, Adam unfurled a maroon yoga mat. He lay down on it, put his arms at the sides of his head, and started to do crunches.

Emma's mind went back to the end of her date with Ryan. He'd wrapped his arms around her, pulled her close, and planted a big kiss on her cheek. Her cheek! It was definitely *not* how she'd hoped the date would end.

After his set of crunches, Adam propped himself up on an elbow and panted, "So you really like him or are you just starstruck?"

"You know I don't do starstruck," huffed Emma. "But yes, I think about him all the time. I feel completely swept off my feet. He asked me to be his date for the premiere of his movie with Blake Dixon and Jacqueline Boucher."

Adam lay back down and resumed his crunches, this time alternating from side to side. When he'd finished his obliques, Adam said, "It's been a while, hasn't it, since you've really fallen for someone? Not since Jeremy, was it?"

ADAM REGRETTED SAYING it the moment it came out of his mouth. He remembered with a pang of guilt, desire and humiliation the night Emma had come home from a night out with her boyfriend Jeremy.

He himself had been out with old college friends. On baby-moon in New York, David and Maureen had tried to downplay their joy at the impending arrival of their first child in deference to the fact that he and Caroline's relationship hadn't worked out. The imbalance caused by the missing fourth wheel made the whole evening awkward; Adam had drank far too much.

Against his better judgement, Adam was having a nightcap when a tear-streaked Emma materialized in his apartment. Had he let her in? Did she just walk in? He couldn't remember, but she was the one person he most wanted to see right then and there. It was as if he'd conjured her up.

"Can you please pour me one of those?" she'd said.

"You don't like scotch," he'd answered.

"Doesn't matter, I want one," Emma had answered in that defiant Emma way of hers. He'd shrugged, taken down another rocks glass and sloshed in some amber liquid from his uncapped bottle of Macallan.

"Bad night?" he'd asked, clinking glasses with her. He took a large swallow and saw her grimace after she'd done the same. "I thought you were with Jeremy?"

"That dickhead? Yeah, I was, but I'm so over him! So over him! You know what he did? He was flirting with the waitress the whole time. When I called him out on it, he just shrugged nonchalantly, told me he felt 'compelled'—that was his word, compelled!—to flirt with other women, and that it obviously means he's not as into me as he thought he was! He would continue seeing me, if I wanted to, but he wanted to make sure I knew where things stood between us. What. An. Asshole!"

Adam had wrapped his arms around Emma. They'd hugged plenty of times like that. But her proximity, the tantalizing scent of her and, he had to admit, her availability and vulnerability, was messing with his head. "There are much better guys out there for you, Emma," he'd said to her, stroking her luxuriant hair. "Other guys who'd love you and treat you much better than he does. Who'd want to be with only you. He doesn't deserve you."

He heard her sniff. When she'd looked up at him, her eyes green and luminous, eyelashes spiked, eye makeup smeared, delicate freckles peeking through, he didn't know what had possessed him. He could only blame it on drink and his own miserable state. "Someone like me," he'd whispered and brought his lips down on hers.

He could have sworn she'd relaxed into his kiss, even returned it. Though that could have just been wishful thinking. Because next thing he knew, she'd laughed and pushed him away.

Adam grimaced, remembering. He quickly flipped onto his stomach to do push-ups.

He'd taken advantage of her while she'd been pining for someone else. Forced himself on her even. He had hoped Emma had forgotten the incident. Hoped she'd been too drunk to have emblazoned the memory into her mind, as he'd done. Certainly it had never been repeated and never come up in conversation, for which he was grateful. But a part of him was disappointed Emma hadn't remembered the incident, that a kiss from him had meant so little.

It was after that night that he'd started to seriously date again. During his first years in New York, too broken by what had happened with Caroline to entertain any thought of a serious relationship, he'd focused on his work and had casually hooked up with women he'd found attractive when they'd thrown themselves his way. After Emma's rejection, he'd actively moved on and looked for someone with long-term potential. Hence Tricia and briefly Sara and more recently Brooke.

"I'm so excited about the premiere," Emma was saying. She didn't seem to notice his discomfiture.

Of course she wouldn't. She could think of nothing but Ryan effing Churchill.

"Guess what? Ryan says he has extra tickets and wants to invite you and Hailey, Juliette and Belinda, too. Thursday after next."

"He's certainly charming his way into everyone's hearts, isn't he?" said Adam after his first set of 20 push-ups.

Emma missed the sarcasm, unsurprisingly. "Yes, he is so easy-going and charming. Not at all an egotistical Hollywood type. I go soft in the knees just thinking about his accent. And he's so drop-dead good-looking, you can't help but want to stare at him all day," chattered Emma as Adam grunted through a second set of push-ups.

Adam got up, sweat running down his face and chest. The heat was really getting to him.

"Was there something you wanted to talk to me about, Emma?" he snapped. "If you just want to swoon over Ryan, you can do that much better with Annalisa or Hailey. I really need a shower now."

The last thing Adam wanted was to hear just how close Emma and Ryan were getting.

She hopped down from the barstool. "My, who's a grumpy one today! So, was that a yes? I figured, being as it's a spy movie, you'd be interested. Shall I tell Ryan you'll be coming?"

Ryan, indeed! There was definitely something he didn't like or trust about the guy. Ryan seemed too smooth, somehow, too sleek. Like a fox. No one was that perfect; Ryan must be hiding something. Adam did not want Emma to get hurt. He should probably go along to the premiere and watch out for her.

"I suppose I could skip the running group that week," he said. He knew he sounded ungrateful.

He put his hands to his waistband and started to peel off his shorts. He was almost pleased to see the back of Emma as she shut his door behind her.

CHAPTER TWENTY-FIVE

Emma was applying a final coat of mascara when someone knocked on her door.

"Come in," she called. As the front door opened and shut, Emma stepped out from the small hallway to see who had entered.

"Oh, it's you," said Emma to Chloe. "Just give me a sec to finish my makeup," she added as she disappeared into the bathroom again.

"Don't mind me," said Chloe, striding into Emma's living room as through she'd been invited and had every right to wander about. She took in the setting sun. "Nice place! So much brighter than ours. I feel absolutely claustrophobic down there in the basement."

Chloe poked her nose into Emma's bedroom and her office like a potential buyer at an open house. "Our place is sooo dark, I don't want to know what it'll be like in the winter. Though by then, I'm sure, we'll be somewhere nicer. I picture a big airy loft-type place, with floor-to-ceiling windows and views of the whole New York City skyline."

Emma clenched her teeth, annoyed that, once again, Chloe had invaded her property and was acting like she owned it. If she wasn't running as late as she was, she'd never have let Chloe just come in like this.

Chloe continued talking. "Our place is so different to what I'm used to in L.A.. We have a big house in the hills there, Benedict Canyon, y'know? It's stunning. Six bedrooms, a separate guest house, an infinity pool, and the best view of the whole Valley. Daddy's an entertainment lawyer, y'know. He has big-name celebrities for clients but, of course, I can't reveal who they are, confidentiality agreement and all that."

Emma finished her makeup and emerged from her bathroom. She wore an oatmeal-colored jersey dress that was blousy on top and ended in a clingy miniskirt on the bottom.

"You look good, Emma. The dress plays up your figure well, much better than the thing you were wearing when we met. But that color washes you out. I have a fake-tan spray for legs. Want me to get it for you?"

Emma decided she would stay sane only by ignoring everything Chloe said about her appearance. Anyway, she had no interest whatsoever in the fake-and-bake look that Chloe preferred. New York was a totally different creature from L.A., and Chloe was going to learn that for herself sooner or later.

"Where are you going tonight? Hot date?" asked Chloe, as though they were indeed friends. Emma was glad she had a legitimate excuse and would be able to get rid of this woman soon enough.

"I'm meeting a friend for afterwork drinks. She's a senior editor at *In the Know,*" said Emma, knowing that mentioning the popular gossip magazine, which young women associated with crack cocaine—bad for you but addictive as hell—would impress Chloe.

"Really? I wonder who her sources are? I, obviously, always

hear the best celebrity stories first because of Daddy's job, y'know? Some of them are so incredible, you would never look at a particular celebrity in the same way again if you knew about the lawsuits and settlements that come up. Of course, my lips are sealed," said Chloe, drawing an invisible zipper across her lips. "Oh the stories I could tell. I should write a tell-all one day. Anyhoo, I'm free tonight and I'd be happy to come along with you. I'm sure there's some stuff your friend might find useful, though, of course, I can't name names. But I think my descriptions could be enough so that you know who I mean without getting anyone into trouble, if you catch my drift."

"What's Zak up to tonight?" asked Emma. She couldn't help adding in a voice laden with false sympathy, "Leaving you home alone on a Friday night right after you've just arrived, shame on him!"

"You haven't heard? About their record deal with BMG? Recording starts in three weeks. So they've got to rehearse all the time and finish a few more songs. So obviously, he's very busy right now. I don't mind; I make friends easily. And I don't mind making a few sacrifices now 'cause soon he's going to be a huge star. Huge! He's so talented. And once the money rolls in, we'll be able to leave this dump. I can't believe the amount of rent he pays to live in a basement. If it were this apartment with the roof-deck, that would be a different story."

Emma wanted to snort, thinking of Chloe and Zak living in her apartment. "If I'm not mistaken, Zak's parents are paying for this place." Emma knew that an aspiring musician/waiter, who only worked weekday lunch shifts, wouldn't be able to afford a one-bedroom apartment, even a basement one, in this neighborhood. "And, I might add, the rent on your place is less than what some of the other basement dwellers on this street are paying, and for far more of a 'dump' than this place. Now if you'll excuse me, I really need to go."

Emma grabbed her clutch and stood outside her apartment, waiting for Chloe to exit. As Chloe huffed down the stairs muttering something about how much ruder New Yorkers were than Angelenos, Emma slammed the door shut and deadbolted it behind her.

CHAPTER TWENTY-SIX

"What's new in the world of celebrity gossip?" asked Emma as she walked into the wine bar and joined Lauren at the small corner table.

Whenever she got together with Lauren, Emma was never quite sure what to expect, though entertainment was generally on the cards. Often at the expense of other people.

"The usual," said Lauren, launching into commentary about certain members of Hollywood royalty, hangers-on, wannabes, models, boy band members and a laundry list of B-celebrities. Lauren's brush was wide. And usually scathing. "The biggest news this week is, get this, that according to a source close to her"—Lauren named a bubbly actress who had recently gotten married—"is pregnant. We had to pull one of the evergreens, a cellulite story, to make room for this one. Seriously, right?"

Lauren took a greedy gulp from her glass. There was a kind of irreverent fun in being with Lauren.

"So, how's your blog doing? The It-girl article we ran was good wasn't it?"

Emma had been expecting this. Lauren didn't do favors for free. That was what made an encounter with her sometimes unpredictable. At Luxe, Lauren had been editor-in-chief of the online magazine. Emma had wanted to lead the marketing campaign for the magazine's launch, and thanks to Lauren, had gotten to head up the project. Emma was grateful to Lauren for the favor, but for weeks after, Lauren was relentless in bringing it up any chance she got. When Lauren developed a mad crush on a videographer Emma had worked with, Lauren had gotten Emma to fix them up; Emma had been more than happy to comply. Emma was curious what Lauren was going to ask for this time.

Emma told Lauren about the steady increase in traffic to her blog and the number of new partnerships and advertisers she'd acquired. There had always been a bit of one-upmanship with them, so Emma fibbed the numbers a bit. To satisfy Lauren's ego, Emma made sure to give the *In the Know* article credit for getting *Worth It* some welcome attention. But she downplayed the extent the article had helped by saying how much the *Post* article, blog interviews, and Emma's own marketing efforts had also contributed.

After they'd caught up on work and gossiped about mutual acquaintances, Emma asked, "Are you still dating the investment banker?" Lauren had brought him to the *Worth It* party as her date.

"Oh God, him, no! He wanted us to make animal sounds every time we fucked, I swear! The first couple of times it was kind of funny, maybe even a turn-on, but then I just could not deal with his weird fetish anymore," said Lauren with a shudder. Then without missing a beat she asked, "Any chance you can set me up with that hot neighbor of yours?"

"Who? *Zak?*" asked Emma frowning. When would Lauren have met Zak?

"No, that wasn't his name. He was at your party. We chatted a bit and then he disappeared with that anemic-looking wallflower. God, I hope he's not fucking dating *her!*"

Lauren could really be such a bitch sometimes. Emma would

have defended Hailey had she not been reeling from the mental image of Adam grinding Lauren to a soundtrack of the bleating and neighing he'd done while reading to Mila.

"Adam?" she croaked, reaching for her Marlborough Sauvignon Blanc. She took a long swallow.

"Yes, *him*! You two aren't together, are you? I did wonder at your party. There seemed to be some . . . tension . . . there."

Emma's cheeks went hot. She laughed. That nervous laugh of hers. "We're just friends."

"Not even fuck buddies, then?"

Emma shook her head.

Lauren continued, "I personally don't see how you can live in the same building and not occasionally want to let him fuck your brains out."

"I guess I've never thought of him in . . . *that* way," said Emma, picturing a sweaty, bare-chested Adam doing push-ups over her. She shook her head to dislodge the discomfiting image and took another swallow to rehydrate her suddenly dry mouth.

"So he's available then?" Lauren demanded.

Emma looked at Lauren, who was pleasant-looking enough in a wholesome, slightly horsey kind of way. A bit like Brooke, she supposed. "No, he's dating some woman called Brooke right now," lied Emma.

"Well, when they break up, I've got first dibs," said Lauren with a bark of laughter that Emma found obnoxious. "Remember, you owe me one."

Surprise, surprise.

"So, are you seeing anyone?" asked Lauren.

Having anticipated this question, Emma was prepared for it. She looked away and let her eyes soften and a smile play at her lips, which wasn't hard to do as she conjured up Ryan. "Well, sort of," said Emma. "It's way too early to tell if it'll lead anywhere, but . . ."

"But what?"

"He's kind of famous, so I'm not sure if I should say anything yet, especially to someone like you, you working for *In the Know* and all that," said Emma with a flick of her hand.

"Emma Worth! Who are you dating? Now I'm really intrigued! And this can strictly be between you and me, girl talk between friends."

"He's not that famous—yet—maybe you haven't even heard of him . . . " said Emma, stalling, enjoying keeping Lauren in suspense.

"Remember, you're talking to *me*! It's my job to know anyone who's remotely famous. Fucking spill the beans already!"

"I'm seeing . . . Ryan Churchill. I'm going to be his date for the premiere of *Between the Lines* next week at the Ziegfeld Theatre."

Lauren didn't say anything for a second, then, "Well, if you have fucking Ryan Churchill asking you to red-carpet premieres, I can see why you might not be so bothered that you have an HFH living right under you."

HFH—Lauren's shorthand for highly fuckable hottie. She swears too much; Adam wouldn't like that, thought Emma, pleased she'd thought of at least one reason why Adam and Lauren would most definitely not be a good match.

To Lauren she said with a little grin, "So you have heard of him?"

"Not heard of Ryan Churchill? He is only the hottest, and I mean that in both senses of the word, up-and-coming actor. *Between the Lines* got a lot of attention at Cannes this year. There's talk of Blake Dixon being up for a Best Actor nominee and the movie getting a Best Picture nod as well."

Emma hadn't been aware of this and was suitably impressed. Ryan was good at being self-deprecating which, she decided, was infinitely better than someone who blew his own horn, like Zak.

She went on to tell Lauren about the idea she'd had while dress shopping with Hailey the other day. Unable to decide which dress to wear to the premiere, Emma had narrowed the choices down to three; she was leaving it up to her blog readers to select the winning dress.

"That's a fucking fantastic idea, Emma. You're a marketing genius, but then I knew that already otherwise I wouldn't have suggested you to lead the Luxe launch."

Emma smiled, as much for Lauren's predictability as for the praise of her idea.

"We can definitely run something on it in the magazine. Readers love looking at red-carpet dresses. And we're always being asked to introduce web or interactive elements. My editor will love this."

Thoroughly enjoying herself now, Emma felt the rush of running the show. Lulled by the familiarity of a good girly gossip session over a few glasses of wine, something that had been a regular occurrence with Lauren when they'd worked together, Emma opened her mouth and the words spilled out:

"Apropos Blake Dixon, I have reason to believe that he might be cheating on Genevieve Lane."

This could be payment to Lauren for helping her get her blog, once again, into *In the Know*. And maybe if Lauren had this nugget, she'd back off about Adam. Anyway, she wouldn't actually name names.

"Really? You are full of interesting tidbits this evening, Emma! There's certainly been speculation about their marriage being on the rocks, but who knows what's fact and what's fiction?" said Lauren lifting and dropping her bony shoulders. She then raised her wine glass up to the light, swirled the red liquid then downed the dregs. "I don't suppose you know who he might be cheating on Genevieve with?"

Emma took another sip, savoring the power of possessing a piece of information that someone else wanted. Leaning in, she whispered, "The nanny."

"Another nanny scandal! Now that *is* interesting. Do tell."

Emma felt warm and fuzzy, the wine hitting the spot and

loosening her tongue. "Well, she's an accomplished pianist. Blake sent her a $15,000 Yamaha last week."

"I'm assuming you know all this from Ryan Churchill, he and Blake being well-acquainted with one another?"

"In a manner of speaking. This is pure speculation, of course."

"Of course," said Lauren, motioning to the waitress for another round of wine. "And is the nanny with the Dixons at the moment?"

"No, she's in New York," said Emma.

Lauren whistled her admiration. "Emma, this just gets more and more intriguing! You're a gold mine! What else do you know? What does she look like?"

"Just between us?" asked Emma. Surely it couldn't hurt to divulge what she knew about Juliette. It wasn't as though any of this was a secret.

"Yes, of course," said Lauren.

"Well, she's exactly Blake's type, if his type is Genevieve. She also has long, dark brown hair, nice curves, a regal elegance."

"Blake used to date that brunette Victoria's Secret model, remember?" added Lauren.

"I hadn't even thought of that. Yes, I guess one could say that Ju—, the nanny, has the same kind of look."

"What else do you know about her?"

Emma leaned in again. "She was raised in Montreal and Paris. Her dad's Canadian, her mom's from here. Her parents were killed in a car crash when she was 14."

"How tragic!"

"Yes," said Emma, relating that that was how Juliette came to live with her aunt and grandmother, who lived in her building.

"How did she end up nannying for Blake and Genevieve?"

Emma explained that when Juliette hadn't been able to find a job as a concert pianist, she was recommended to a family with two girls who needed a nanny slash piano teacher.

"So let me guess . . . after that position, someone recommended her to Blake and Genevieve, who wanted a French-speaking American nanny for when they were filming *Between the Lines* in France a couple of years ago?"

"Exactly!"

"And now she's here and you're dating Ryan Churchill, Blake's co-star. So how does that work? Are you guys like double dating or something?" Again that obnoxious laughter. How had Emma never noticed that before about Lauren?

"Ryan was literally just outside my building one day as I was leaving. He had a message for *her* from Blake."

"Wow, this girl is popular!"

"Oh," said Emma, putting a hand to her mouth. "I just realized something that points more to *her* and Blake being together. Ever since she's been back, she's been wearing this necklace with a gorgeous solitaire diamond. It was only later that I remembered seeing it at Tiffany when I was wedding-band shopping with Annalisa. What nanny would be wearing that unless it came from a rich boyfriend or admirer?"

Emma paused to drain her glass. Perhaps it hadn't been such a good idea to have three glasses of wine on an empty stomach.

"Do you know who Blake will be bringing to the premiere?" asked Lauren.

"No. But Ryan had extra tickets and invited my neighbor's niece to come. It'll be interesting to see how Blake and his children's nanny behave with one another."

"Yes, interesting indeed," said Lauren, nodding into her wineglass.

CHAPTER TWENTY-SEVEN

"What are you up to today?" asked Annalisa.

Emma groaned into the phone. "Ugh, I'm heading downstairs later to Belinda's place for, get this, a recital and English tea party in honor of Juliette. It's just an excuse to show off Juliette's new piano and her playing."

"Did you find out if it's definitely from Blake and Genevieve?"

"Actually, Ryan and I think the piano is just from Blake," said Emma as she updated Annalisa on her theory.

"Really? Blake and Juliette? Based on the few times I've met Juliette, I just don't see it. Actually, I have a better theory."

"Yeah?"

"I think that Adam and Juliette might be a thing."

"What? Adam and Juliette a couple? That's ridiculous! I can't think of a worse match!" Emma laughed at the absurdness of Annalisa's suggestion.

"Wait, listen. It makes so much sense: Adam dumps Brooke. Juliette shows up in New York shortly after. You said yourself that it seemed suspicious. We both know how patient and attentive Adam is with the Bates. He's probably more than happy to hear Belinda gabbing on about Juliette. And didn't he spend a couple of weeks on business in L.A. last fall? Remember how Belinda asked him to bring that care package to Juliette? Maybe that was when this whole 'affair' kicked off. And now the piano."

Emma listened to Annalisa's words with conviction that her friend didn't know what she was talking about. The thought of Adam and Juliette together felt almost physically wrong to her.

"I don't buy it for a second. I can't imagine him with someone like Juliette. She's just so boring. Too meek and quiet. They'd have nothing in common."

"I don't know about that. I've seen many far more unlikely people hit it off. They're both smart, educated, attractive people. He's successful and, I suspect, ready to settle down. Juliette's into kids; I mean I assume she is since she nannies. And she's musical and talented, but not overly success-oriented, which would be good if you want to start a family. I can totally see them together. You can't?"

"No!" said Emma with vehemence. "Save your arguments for the courtroom."

Emma felt almost queasy as she pictured Juliette and Adam pushing a stroller, cooing over the baby in there with a little Mila-like person at their side. "Anyway why would he keep the piano a secret? Why would they bother keeping the relationship a secret?"

"They obviously want to keep it hush-hush because they don't want it to be on Belinda's radar until they know if it'll work out. If it doesn't work out, Juliette can go back to her job in L.A. and they wouldn't need to cross paths again, except for the rare occasions when Juliette visits New York; so no one need be the wiser."

"There's a hole in your argument, prosecutor. Why would he send her a piano if he's trying to keep it all hush-hush, especially from Belinda?"

"Adam loves Juliette so much, he can't bear to have her wasting her bountiful talents on a crummy old piano. So he sends her the new piano and lets everyone think it's from the Dixon-

Lanes. He's not after the glory, he just wants Juliette to have her precious piano."

"You think you've got it all figured out, do you? I thought I was the only matchmaker here."

"I only learn from the best," laughed Annalisa. "Plus, it's not like just anyone could afford a piano like that, but Adam could. And he'll be at the recital, won't he?"

"Yes."

"Of course he will. Check it out. See how they act with each other. I'll bet you a drink I'm right."

"You're on, and you're wrong, I'm sure of it," said Emma with more conviction than she felt.

CHAPTER TWENTY-EIGHT

Annalisa's suspicions about Juliette and Adam would not leave Emma alone. Emma tried to work, but couldn't focus, the idea of Adam and Juliette together turning round and round in her head.

The necklace and piano could just as well be from Adam as they were from Blake. And Adam had been annoyed with her when she'd wondered what Juliette was doing back for the summer. On the night they'd all gone to dinner at Maison Dalat, he and Juliette had certainly seemed cozy together. Even more damming, Adam had called her out at the end of the night for disrespecting Juliette. For him, it was meant to be Juliette's night, and he'd resented that she and Ryan had hogged the spotlight.

Emma gave up trying to work.

She was even glad when it was 3 p.m. and she could head downstairs and apply her powers of observation to prove that she was right and Annalisa was wrong. Though the longer she thought about it, the less she was certain.

Emma barely had time to greet Juliette, who'd opened the door for her, before she was summoned into the kitchen by Belinda.

"Emma, dear, you are so punctual today. Not to say that you're usually not but, never mind, we're very grateful to have you grace our small salon here today. Do you know Ryan?" Emma and Ryan's eyes met over the small kitchen table. They nodded and smiled at each other. "Oh yes, of course you do! You were recently all out together with Juliette. Juliette told me it was a lovely night. I'm so happy Juliette has found such terrific friends, you know she had such a hard time—"

Emma shut out the rest of Belinda's words as she feasted her eyes on Ryan. As much as she was able to, anyway, considering her mind was in the living room with Adam and Juliette.

Belinda had jumped from Juliette's past to gushing about Ryan: "Emma, he brought these flowers for Mother and I. Aren't they just beautiful? I was putting them into a vase right here in this kitchen not two minutes ago when the temple of my glasses just broke off. Ryan said he saw the little screw bounce off the floor and then he was crawling on my kitchen floor trying to find it. Good thing I mopped it earlier today. Can you imagine when I tell the girls at work that Frank from *Episode* was crawling around on my kitchen floor! They'd probably ask me something indecent, like how his—"

"You could ask me if you need help with anything like that, Belinda," said Adam, who'd come into the kitchen while Belinda was talking. His somewhat peevish tone made Emma smile to herself. Was Adam, normally so cool and unruffled, jealous of Belinda's praise of Ryan?

"Of course, Adam, you are the best neighbor two old ladies could have, and so handy. Ryan, normally Adam helps us with these kind of repairs, and he does an excellent job, I might add—" and Belinda's mouth was off and running again.

Due to the minimal space in the kitchen, Adam was close enough to Emma that if she leaned back slightly their bodies would touch.

"Emma, did I tell you what an amazing gift Adam has given

us? Yesterday, or was it two days ago? It was the day that I had to work, so yes, it must have been Friday because it was just Juliette and Mother at home. Adam bought us an air conditioner—and not a cheap, no-name one either! You know, Ryan, ours had broken just before Juliette had arrived. And Adam installed it himself. When I came home, it was already on. I could immediately tell the difference the minute I walked in here . . . "

As Belinda continued talking, Emma could only dwell on Adam's generosity and the fact that he had been here alone—Mrs. Bates didn't really count—with Juliette. Annalisa's words sprang tauntingly to mind.

" . . . such an amazing, thoughtful gift! Between the air conditioner and the piano, you'd think we were royalty, getting all these fine, fine presents."

Belinda was paused by the doorbell ringing. But only momentarily. "Oh that must be Chloe and Zak. Have you met them yet, Ryan? Chloe's from L.A. too, and also has connections in Hollywood, so you'll have lots in common. Such a fine addition to our building. So interested in befriending Juliette."

While Belinda went to greet the new arrivals, Emma half turned to face Adam. "What a nice gift you've given the Bates."

"It's no piano," quipped Ryan.

"Such a tremendously generous gift as the piano is," Adam said, addressing Ryan, "practical it is not. It's so large and domineering, it crowds the rest of the living room even more so than before. The Dixon-Lanes, in their mansion in the Hollywood Hills or wherever it is people like that in L.A. live, clearly have no conception of how small an old apartment in Manhattan can be; or they simply don't care. What's to become of it when Juliette leaves? Either she'll have to pay dearly to transport it and tune it herself, or let it sit here, unused, taking up precious space."

Ha, thought Emma, that proves the piano couldn't possibly be from Adam.

"I believe," said Ryan, "that tuning the piano for the first two years is paid for, as well as the next relocation of the piano. That's what Juliette told me at least. Most uncommonly thoughtful of Blake, don't you think, Emma?"

Emma and Ryan exchanged knowing glances.

"Oh yes, most thoughtful," said Emma. "See Adam, more thought was put into it than you give the giver credit for. And you must agree that it is the finest, most valuable thing anyone, any admirer of Juliette's, certainly, could give to her. I quite agree with Adam, though, that the piano is far too large for this apartment, which is already overcrowded as it is. But Blake, I mean the *Dixon-Lanes*, couldn't have known this. However, I think your gift is a far more practical one, Adam, or we'd all be sweating and suffering through the heat this afternoon."

"Ah, finished," said Ryan, holding up the glasses to inspect them. "Let me return these to Belinda and let us go meet the new guests."

"Do we have to?" said Emma under her breath to Adam. Coming around the table, Ryan hooked an arm around Emma's waist to escort her out of the kitchen, leaving Adam to follow.

Introductions were made. Zak, Emma noted with glee, avoided her eyes. And she was relieved to see Chloe take more of an interest in Adam and Ryan than in her. She sat down next to Juliette on the sofa and watched the proceedings from a distance.

Chloe was looking around at the drab furnishings in the Bates' cramped apartment with barely hidden disdain, while her mouth dripped untruth after untruth. "Oh Belinda, what a lovely collection of china teacups you have!" "Mrs. Bates, did you crochet these doilies yourself?"

Approaching the piano, Chloe opened the lid and let her fingers trail on the keys. "Juliette, you are a lucky girl. Do tell who your secret admirer is! I will say one thing, you sure do know how to pick them, he's clearly a rich one. Why something like this must cost, what $5,000!"

"Oh no, dear," said Mrs. Goddard, Belinda's friend and Juliette's former music teacher, "this one's worth at least three times as much."

Belinda, having heard the train of the conversation, approached the ladies. "Yes, indeed, $15,000! You can buy a new car with that much money! Can you just imagine it? It's like we have a car in our little apartment."

It certainly feels that way, thought Emma.

Belinda looked alarmed. "Maybe I shouldn't be telling as many people as I have about it. You know, me with my big mouth. Now everyone knows we have a $15,000 piano in our home. We could be robbed! Perhaps we need to put bars on our windows or get a security alarm!"

"Auntie, it's not as though anyone could steal a piano out from under our noses and out the window," said Juliette with a soft smile.

"Oh yes, how silly of me. Of course not. Anyway, welcome, please sit down everyone. Oh, I haven't offered anyone anything to drink yet. What a bad hostess I am."

Belinda brought tea and other refreshments to her guests. One could see how much effort she had gone to to make her cucumber sandwiches, scones, and a layered Victorian sponge cake.

"Belinda, you are a fantastic baker," said Ryan after a bite of his scone. "These scones take me right back to England, to my gran's kitchen. And where did you ever find clotted cream? I've tried looking for it in L.A., but no luck!"

Seeing Chloe peel the bread off the top of a cucumber sandwich, shake her head, and whisper something to Zak, Emma felt offended on Belinda's behalf. Perhaps the sandwiches were on the soggy side, but Chloe had no right to laugh with Zak about it.

Adam had taken the free seat on the sofa on the other side of Juliette. His head was next to Juliette's, and he was saying something to her in a way that made her smile. Observing this,

Emma's heart lurched. Could Annalisa be right about them, even if the piano wasn't from Adam?

After the tea things were cleared, Juliette played a long classical piece with such serene joy that even Emma was moved by it. She looked over at Adam and saw that his eyes were fixed on Juliette. After that, Juliette said she'd be happy to take any requests.

"However wonderfully Juliette can play, she can also sing beautifully," said Ryan, "and I would love to hear her voice again. Juliette, could I request the song that you sang at Blake's birthday party?"

Juliette blushed. Ryan had mentioned Blake's name, after all. But could Juliette have something going on with both Blake *and* Adam? Was Juliette stringing Adam along, waiting to see if Blake would leave Genevieve for her while keeping her options open? Emma felt indignant for Adam's sake, and her dislike for Juliette increased. This was not helped when, during the next song, Ryan's rich baritone joined Juliette's silky soprano while she accompanied them on the piano.

Near the end of the song, Emma discerned that Juliette's voice was taking on an edge of hoarseness. When the song finished and Ryan suggested another duet, Adam spoke up: "I think that's enough singing from Juliette. Don't you hear how hoarse her voice has become? Emma, would you mind bringing Juliette a glass of water, I think she could really use one."

That was really too much, thought Emma, incensed. Granted, she was closest to the kitchen; Belinda was sitting on a chair squeezed between the loveseat and the piano. Resigned, Emma rose to do Adam's bidding.

After Juliette had taken a few gulps of water, Mrs. Goddard said, "I, for one, would love to hear you play Chopin's Scherzo No. 2, Op. 31 on this piano."

As Juliette played, Emma's mind wandered back to Adam and Juliette. Could Adam have, earlier in the kitchen, so vocally opposed the piano because he knew it came from Blake, his rival for Juliette's affections?

Emma had worked herself into such a state that she barely realized the recital was over; Juliette had shut the piano and couldn't be persuaded to play more, despite Belinda's protests.

Later as the guests, plied with more refreshments, stood about and chatted, Emma found herself standing with Juliette, Adam, Chloe and Zak.

Chloe was saying, "Juliette, you are a great piano player. I used to play when I was a girl, but then I switched to dancing. I would so love to take up the piano again. I was quite good, y'know. I wonder what would have become of me if I hadn't quit? I might be a classical pianist myself! Zak will definitely talk to his agent about you, won't you, Amore Mio? You stick with us and we'll make sure you become famous."

"That's very kind of you, Chloe and Zak. I have no desire to be famous; I just want to play for myself and for an audience who can enjoy the music as much as I enjoy playing it. Maybe even write some of my own songs."

"All you need to do then is, like, marry a rich man and you'll be golden," said Chloe, as though she had made the wisest pronouncement ever. "I can be lots of help. I've got tons of connections in L.A. through my dad, who's an entertainment lawyer, y'know, so he knows everyone worth suing, ha ha. Isn't that funny?"

"Ha ha, yes, I get it," laughed Zak, looking adoringly at Chloe. "You are so clever!"

Emma rolled her eyes at Adam and mouthed, "Kill me now!"

"And Emma, you've yet to take me up on the offer of a shopping trip. I think we both have a similar respect for fashion, though obviously very different tastes. We could learn a thing or two from each other."

At this, Emma's eyes skimmed over the overly tight, short and entirely trashy outfit Chloe was wearing and didn't deign to answer. Instead she appeared not to have heard and turned to Adam as though to discuss a very important matter that she had just remembered.

Thus she missed the question that Belinda, who had joined them had asked, but couldn't help hearing Chloe's response. "Oh, I did everything. Modeling and acting, commercials and music videos. You know that commercial for Heineken, when there are three girls at a pool party? The middle one was me! But what I'd really like to do is star in a reality show. I've pitched a producer in Hollywood, a friend of my dad's, to follow Zak and me around. It'd be about his journey to becoming a rock star and how I'm there to support my man and how I adjust to living in New York and our amazing relationship. It'd be like that show with Jessica Simpson and . . . "

Shortly after, to Emma's relief, Chloe and Zak had to leave for another engagement. After their departure, Ryan took the opportunity to invite Belinda to his film premiere.

Belinda could not imagine going to a film premiere, no she didn't deserve to, not silly old her, and who would be there to watch Mother? "Oh no, you young people go." The more Belinda demurred and declined and said how it was impossible for her to go, the clearer it was to everyone present that she wanted to go.

The problem of what she would wear was solved by Adam, who told her that she could wear what she had worn to Annalisa's wedding, which "was very elegant and suited you well, Belinda." Mrs. Goddard offered to watch Mrs. Bates if Belinda was truly concerned about her mother being left alone for the night. Finally, it was decided that Juliette and Belinda would go, escorted by Adam. Emma suggested that Hailey might join them, and Adam readily agreed to the arrangement.

CHAPTER TWENTY-NINE

Emma stepped into her gown.

She'd posted her final three choices and received a flurry of responses—with a spike in votes since *In the Know* had hit newsstands on Monday. It was gratifying to know she had so many readers who were interested in what she had to say and wanted a say in what she had to wear. She was also delighted with the result of the poll: Her readers had chosen the cerulean gown: a vintage couture creation out of chiffon and scalloped lace, accented with feathers and sequins. It was truly a stunner.

As the final touch, she pinned to her bodice the dragonfly brooch Adam had given her for her 25th birthday; it complimented the dress perfectly.

Yet, as she surveyed herself in the full-length mirror, two small lines formed between Emma's brow. Her accessories were too understated. For a night like tonight, to stand out on the red carpet, she needed something more.

Emma cocked her head to the side as she tapped her forefinger to her lip. She remembered the way the creative director at Luxe would fly into a rage when he'd look at photographs from a fashion shoot and find that nothing "popped." That's what's she needed now, something to make her outfit pop. Otherwise there was no sense of surprise, especially since the dress had been on her blog and in *In the Know*.

And then inspiration hit Emma upside the head.

Teetering precariously on her office chair, Emma pulled down the large round striped box at the back of the top shelf of her closet. She didn't know why she still had it; it took up too much precious storage space. She'd never worn it before and had no intention of ever wearing it. She supposed she couldn't bring herself to get rid of it, being as it was one of the few presents she'd ever received from her mother. Emma removed the lid of the bandbox, spread the crinkling tissue paper, and lifted out a glittered turquoise bird with peacock feathers perched on a tiny chapeau that clipped onto the head.

Emma had been surprised when the box had arrived, even more so when she'd seen who the sender was, and flummoxed when she'd seen the extraordinary headpiece inside. She had no contact with her mother other than the infrequent birthday cards and random postcards from hotels or exotic locations she'd received through the years. The scrawled messages always held a familiar tone, as if they knew each other, or would be seeing each other soon, when they'd never known each other and would never be seeing each other again. The messages were full of back-handed compliments: how beautiful Emma had become when once she'd been such an "ugly duckling" or how Little Orphan Annie had blossomed. Those messages had always wrenched Emma's chest open, hate warring with the little voice in her head that said, *Remember those soft arms that had hugged you and held you so close? She must have loved you once.* Emma would retaliate, *Then how could she have left me?*

The note that had arrived with the bird had only said that her mother had purchased it for Ascot but then found something that worked better with her outfit. Since Emma's birthday had so recently passed, she'd thought Emma would like it. Emma had not dwelled on the fact that it had been a good couple of months after her birthday or that it was one of her mother's rejects. She'd just shoved it in the back of the closet, where she'd mostly forgotten about it.

Yes, it just might work, thought Emma, as she set the bird atop the nest of her hair that Marcello had arranged in a loose updo.

The contrast of the blue bird to the red of her hair was startling.

Dare she wear it? It was so over the top, the naysayers were bound to hate it.

But it added an outrageous twist; it made the outfit pop. If she wanted to stand out tonight, gain attention, not just for Ryan and his movie, but for her blog, too, this was perfect.

Except for one thing.

Emma unpinned the dragonfly from her dress. Let's not go overboard with the winged creatures here, she thought, as she rested it on the tray on her dresser table.

Yes, she would do Ryan proud.

And tonight, Ryan was going to kiss her. It was seriously time to progress their relationship from flirting and casual daytime dates to the big time.

CHAPTER THIRTY

Hailey, upon seeing Emma gave a small yelp of appreciation. "Wow, Emma! You look like a goddess! I so need to get a photo with you." She took out her mini Pentax camera and attempted to take a photo of herself with Emma, with unflattering results. Emma suggested asking Adam to do the honors as they were all meeting at his place anyway.

After greeting and complimenting Hailey, Adam turned to Emma. "You're breathtaking, Emma."

Emma felt warmth suffusing her cheeks, pleased by the simplicity of his statement. "Thank you. And you don't look too shabby yourself," she said, observing that his normally finger-combed wavy hair was slicked down, his strong jaw was close shaven, and he wore a well-fitted black suit and shirt. "You'll hold your own against the likes of Blake and Ryan," pronounced Emma, adjusting the knot on his tie, then patting his chest when she was satisfied.

The smile he gave her, like the one he'd given her on the night they'd met, made her actually believe her statement.

Before long, Juliette and Belinda came up to Adam's apartment. In the midst of introductions, gasps of admiration and compliments, Ryan's limo arrived and Emma was whisked off in it, leaving Adam and the three women to follow in a taxi.

Emma and Ryan barely had time to exchange a peck on the cheek and compliments on each other's appearance before Amalia, who was also in the limo, took command. She inspected Emma with a precision that would have made anyone less confident than Emma uncomfortable. But Emma did not twinge.

Amalia nodded. "I read your blog series about choosing the dress; that was inspired. Nice work getting some press coverage on it in *In the Know*. I wasn't convinced that this dress was the best choice. But I think you manage it well. Love the bird. Nice touch."

She then instructed Emma and Ryan on how to act on the red carpet: "I know you two have not been dating long and don't necessarily want the press to draw conclusions before you yourselves have. But the goal tonight is to draw people in, make them root for you, because people love to see two beautiful people falling in love. They want to believe in fairy-tale romances. Let them believe. Emma, be an actress tonight, shine, make them love you and Ryan. But give the ladies hope that perhaps Ryan may be their prince, too. And Ryan, you aren't as big a star as Blake and Jacqueline—yet—but after tonight, after the film hits the theaters, all bets are off. So don't forget to make love to the camera."

Emma knew exactly what Ryan's publicist was getting at, she being no stranger to the business of selling images. Ryan found her hand and gave it a squeeze and raised it to his lips for a kiss as the limo pulled up to the historic single-screen Midtown theater and Amalia turned her attention to what was happening outside the limo.

"Ready?" Ryan asked.

Emma nodded, admiring her swoon-inducingly handsome date in his slim-fitting charcoal gray suit, his short hair styled and spiked just so.

Emma was as starstruck as the rest of them. She had been to

her fair share of parties and big events, but to be surrounded by A-listers like Blake Dixon and Jacqueline Boucher, to be part of the main event, with photographers' bulbs flashing and blinding her, was a novel experience. She was surprised that there were even a few fans there for *her* when she saw the sign, "Emma, you're Worth It!" being waved. Then there were microphones being thrust into their faces. Ryan was asked about the movie or her. Emma was always asked who she was wearing. And everyone commented on the bird.

Emma smiled for the cameras and the fans. She waved, flirted with Ryan, and felt a charge, a high, a rush from the experience that she had never felt before. It was a little like when she had been named Homecoming queen her senior year in high school, and she had smiled and waved from the back of the convertible as it made its way around the football track, but magnified a hundred fold.

They were led before the step and repeat for more photos including one in which Ryan pulled her close and kissed her on the lips. Spotting Blake, who was escorting Jacqueline Boucher, Ryan took Emma over and made the introductions.

Later, while she and Ryan were chatting with Blake and the producer in the lobby of the theater, Emma saw Juliette entering. Blake appeared to see Juliette at the same time. Excusing himself, he made his way over to greet Juliette. Emma watched intently as Blake enveloped Juliette in a brief hug. Then hands at their sides, they exchanged a few words before Blake patted her on the arm and went to shake hands with a crew member he'd just spotted. Even in Emma's wildest imagination, she could not see anything untoward about the exchange between Blake and Juliette. They had seemed to be exactly what they were: a man with a woman who was the nanny of his children. There was a familiarity, but also a formality, and not a flicker of lust or any emotion beyond basic respect and politeness.

Emma's smile faltered as she saw Adam lead Juliette toward

where Belinda was talking to Hailey. She pulled the corners of her lips back up, aware of all the flashbulbs. How had she never noticed what a striking pair Adam and Juliette made? It must be the clothing, Emma thought, admiring Juliette's form-fitted royal blue column dress. Ryan, she noticed, was looking at them, too.

~

THE EXPERIENCE of watching the film sitting among the cast and crew, the director speaking on the stage before and after the curtains, the applause and whistles, the whole energy surrounding the screening had been electric. Emma, in the midst of it, couldn't help but be swept up.

At the premiere party afterward, a happy and pumped Ryan worked the room, accepting congratulations, exchanging high fives, and catching up with co-stars and crew members. He was attentive toward Emma, introducing her around, but the various sets of faces and names and roles blurred together in Emma's mind; she couldn't follow the anecdotes and jokes being traded among those who'd been on set.

After a while, she left Ryan and went in search of her friends.

She found Adam sitting on his own and joined him, happy to be off her feet for a while.

"Having a good time?" he asked, leaning against her slightly so their shoulders brushed.

"Yeah, it's been pretty magical," she sighed.

They sat in companionable silence for a few moments, lost in their own thoughts. While she had enjoyed being in the spotlight with Ryan and meeting the other stars, it was nice to hide out in the corner for a bit and just hang with Adam.

She looked over to see Adam staring at her.

"What?" she asked, feeling suddenly overheated and self-conscious.

"Sorry, nothing," he said, shaking his head as if to clear it.

"Getting tired I guess. I'm going to head soon. Got a lot on my plate at work tomorrow. I'm pretty sure the others are ready too. Want to come with us or will you be going with Ryan?"

Emma got up reluctantly. It would be so easy to head home with Adam and the others.

But she was determined to take her relationship with Ryan to a new level tonight despite the fact they'd barely had time to chat all night. The moment in the limo right before they'd arrived had probably been the most intimate of the whole night, and even then, it had been in front of Amalia's watchful eyes.

"You guys go ahead," said Emma.

After Emma had said goodbye to the others, she half-heartedly chatted with a few different people she'd been introduced to earlier. She found it hard to concentrate; her mind kept on going to how the evening would end for her and Ryan cut through by images of what Juliette and Adam were doing. Had work just been an excuse so Adam and Juliette, all dressed up, could continue their night alone? Picturing Adam kissing Juliette's neck and unzipping her blue gown so it pooled onto his bedroom floor, Emma felt disgusted, voyeuristic and ashamed of herself. *What the hell was wrong with her?*

She caught Ryan waving and smiling to her from across the room. Putting on a sultry smile, she made her way over to him.

What was wrong with her was that she couldn't wait to be alone with Ryan, to find out just how hairy or broad his chest was, and to get kissed senseless so all other thoughts would disappear.

And if he wanted more than some serious making out, she wasn't going to stop him.

CHAPTER THIRTY-ONE

Still fuzzy with sleep, Emma yawned and stretched languidly. She recalled a smooth shirt and being encircled by strong arms. She'd felt safe and at home. The way those warm brown eyes had looked at her had made her insides melt. Wait, thought Emma, Ryan's got blue eyes. She shook herself awake and her dreamy feeling was instantly replaced with embarrassed chagrin.

Ryan's blue eyes, indeed! She was done with them.

Emma pulled herself out of bed and went to wash away the stubborn remnants of her makeup and hairspray.

How could she have been so blind, she thought, as the warm water hit her.

On the way home last night, she'd cozied up to Ryan in the backseat of the town car. She'd drawn circles on his palm with her thumb. She'd leaned toward him while squeezing her arms together to give the push-up bra an added boost. She'd even fluttered her lashes.

Emma snorted in disgust as she worked her hair into a lather.

All her efforts had been for nothing; Ryan hadn't even noticed.

Of course he wouldn't have!

Still high on the night, Ryan had chatted the whole ride about the red carpet, the film, the people he'd worked with on the film. When the car drew up to Emma's building, she'd invited him in for a nightcap. He'd been undecided. She'd suggested they could check out the view from her roof-deck and he'd agreed.

They'd barely sat down on her outdoor sofa when Ryan had jumped back up and gone to the edge of the terrace.

"Nice view," he'd said, looking at the lit-up skyscrapers in the distance. When she'd approached him and ran her hands up his chest—she could confirm it was rock hard—he'd grasped her hands.

"Emma," he'd said, lacing his fingers through hers. "I want to thank you again for being my beautiful, brilliant date tonight. I couldn't have been prouder to stand there next to you. You stole the spotlight from Jacqueline, you know. And half the men were drooling over you."

She'd quivered with happiness and expectation, already anticipating those perfect lips on hers.

"But I—I haven't been fully honest with you." His gaze had been earnest. "I asked you to be my date for the premiere under false pretenses. I was pressured into it by Amalia and Gavin."

A heavy blackness had swooped down upon Emma, and the taunting voice in her head had told her he didn't want her. Either. She'd known what was coming, the dreaded "It's not you" speech. The one people told you when they wanted you to feel better. To feel less rejected. The one everyone must have told that heartbroken little redheaded girl after her mother had left. Not that it had helped.

Goose pimples had surfaced on her bare arms; the weather had cooled down significantly.

"I'm sorry, Emma," Ryan had said, "I never meant to lead you on. I know you'd like something to happen, but I can't be with you now, *in that way*, because—"

And then it had hit her. The blackness had lifted away. Of course! She hadn't known whether to laugh or cry.

Why would someone like Ryan need to have a beautiful, attractive woman by his side at the big-deal red-carpet premiere of the movie that was going to make him a star? Why would his publicist and manager push him into taking someone like Emma as his date? Why had they vetted her on her dinner "date" with Ryan? It had all been a set-up.

Now it all made sense—the ballet dancing, the musicals in school productions, his almost feminine beauty, his obsession with his looks. It explained how he could be immune to her charms. Emma was Ryan's beard!

She no longer felt rejected. Stupid, yes. Used, yes. But at least not rejected. Anything was preferable to that.

"You don't have to tell me, Ryan, I know," Emma had said. If she had to choose, then it would have been laughter. A relieved laughter.

"You do?" Ryan had looked surprised. "Did Juliette tell you?"

"Does she know, too?" Emma had asked.

"Of cour—" Ryan had started to say, then stopped himself.

Emma had continued to think out loud, placing the last pieces of the puzzle in place. "Yes, of course, she would, wouldn't she? She knew you in L.A.. Maybe there, among industry folk, it's kind of an open secret."

"No, actually, not that many people know," interjected Ryan. "Amalia and Gavin, my family, a few close friends, but that's about it."

As much as she'd wanted to lash out at him for using her, Ryan's frowning, distraught face had given her pause. He wasn't out of the closet. He wasn't okay with his sexuality. The last thing she wanted to do was to make him feel worse for it.

"Don't worry, I won't tell anyone you're gay."

Ryan had opened his mouth then closed it. Clearly he thought he was better at keeping secrets than Emma was at figuring them out.

"Yes, please, Emma," Ryan had finally said. "I would really, really appreciate it if you could keep this conversation between you and me. Because of my career, I can't have people thinking that I'm . . . *you know*. That's why Amalia insisted I walk the red carpet with a gorgeous woman like you. I'm sorry. Could you ever forgive me?"

He'd pled with those baby blues; Emma had nodded.

"Thank you, Emma. I hope you're not too disappointed. Believe me, if the situation were . . . different . . . I'd be all over you now. Friends?"

Emma had felt a little mollified and let Ryan hug her.

So much for getting some action, thought Emma with a rueful smile as she snapped off the shower.

CHAPTER THIRTY-TWO

A mug of coffee in hand, Emma turned on her computer. Emma clicked over to *Worth It*.

Below her latest post, the one in which she had announced the winning dress, dozens of new comments filled her screen. Most of them remarked on how amazing Emma had looked at the premiere. Others asked what it was like to walk the red carpet with Ryan Churchill. A smaller contingent of readers complained that they would have preferred one of the other dresses. And then there were people who were less than impressed with Ryan Churchill's choice, with her and her blog.

Why is he with a nobody like her and not Evangeline Ross?

Obviously a fan of *Episode* who wanted Ryan to date his on-screen on-again-off-again love interest.

You're just a spoiled little rich girl with your "look how wonderful my life is, look at all the great places I can go eat and shop and get my hair done and do Pilates at." Give me a break! Obviously, you have no clue what it means to be a struggling New Yorker. This blog is so Worth-less!

Ouch.

Why do the skinny, shallow, stupid women always get the hot guys?

Okay then.

Nearly everyone mentioned the bird, though not everyone was a fan.

What the f*** is in your hair? It's like something died up there. What were you thinking, Emma????

You can't please everyone.

Next Emma began clicking on the links that some readers had left, which sent her to pictures of her and Ryan on the red carpet as picked up by various celebrity and entertainment websites and blogs.

The phone rang. It was Hailey.

"Oh my God, Emma! Have you seen all the pictures of you on all the websites?"

"Yeah, I'm just looking at them now. I had no idea!"

"Looks like you got all the attention. You're like Liz Hurley in THAT Dress!

Emma disconnected with Hailey, and her phone immediately rang again. Ryan.

"Thank you again for last night. For being my date and for . . . understanding."

"You're welcome," said Emma, slightly embarrassed for herself and for Ryan.

"Amalia was really pleased with how it all went," added Ryan.

"As she should be! Have you seen all the pictures of us all over the Internet?"

"Yes, Amalia already told me. It's mad! The people loved you, Emma. Your hair, your dress, *that bird*."

"No, not everyone. But it was clearly you they loved, Ryan. You're the star."

"Judging from some of the headlines I've seen, I'd say it was the other way around, or rather, the bird stole the show." They both laughed. "Either way, it's great publicity for the movie, which was the whole point. Thank you again."

Ryan continued talking. "Listen, I need to head back to L.A.

for a week or two to do some more interviews, meet with my agent, all that fun stuff. I head out tomorrow. So I guess I'll see you when I get back?"

"I'd like that," said Emma. Looking at the pictures of herself on her computer screen, and still reeling from the huge spike in traffic her blog had received, Emma decided it definitely wouldn't hurt to have Ryan as a friend. In fact, it could have its uses. "You'll probably be asked about me when you get interviewed, right? If it would help you to continue to . . . pretend that we're an item, I'm okay with it."

"I hadn't even thought of that. Yes, I think it would be helpful to me . . . to make it sound like we're getting to know each other . . . better. You don't mind? I wouldn't want to infringe on your single life."

"Don't worry about that. Dating's overrated anyway," said Emma, renewed in her belief that getting close to someone romantically would only lead to problems. Thank God her little romance with Ryan had been nipped in the bud when it had. No, it was best to focus on herself, her career, especially now that it seemed things were taking off.

For the rest of the day, Emma fielded calls, e-mails and blog comments. Marketing managers called wanting to speak to her about modeling or representing their products. She got e-mails from numerous companies offering her money to promote their products on *Worth It*. Some journalists and bloggers wanted to interview her. The comments on her blog kept coming. She tried to reply to as many as she could and managed to write a short entry to post with a few behind-the-scenes photos from the premiere.

At the end of the day, Emma shut her laptop; she could not look at the screen another minute. Plus she'd hardly moved all day, had barely eaten anything and was starving.

Dinner? She texted Adam.

Warming up leftover beef stew. Plenty left. Come on down.

When he opened the door two minutes later, she collapsed in his arms for a hug.

He held her for a moment. "What was that for?" he asked, stroking her hair, running his hand up and down her back.

She sighed against him, not wanting to move, not wanting his hand to stop moving. Finally she pulled away and said, "Just happy to see a friend. I'm exhausted, haven't left the apartment all day. The phone's been ringing non-stop."

"I've been buried with work. What's happened?"

"Have you not seen the news?"

"Just the headline stuff this morning, what's happened?" repeated Adam, alert.

"The premiere . . . All the articles, photos . . . Have you not seen?"

Adam appeared to relax. "No, I don't make a habit of checking the entertainment headlines on a daily basis," he said, going to the stove to stir the pot.

"Apparently, the world seems to love me and my dress and the bird," said Emma, plopping herself down on a bar stool and putting her elbows on the bar. "It's like I've become an overnight celebrity or something. There's pictures of me in most of the entertainment outlets. I've been getting calls with offers to be the face of this or that, even to star in a reality show."

"Whoa, Emma. I'm not sure whether to congratulate you or feel sorry for you. How do you feel about it?" Adam poured red wine into a wineglass and handed it to her before filling a glass for himself. He sliced up half of a baguette and set it on the bar along with a dish of butter. Then he ladled the steaming stew into two large bowls and set them on the bar.

"Overwhelmed, but kind of elated, I guess," said Emma, breathing in the comforting smell of Adam's beef stew. She picked up her spoon as Adam came around the bar and took the barstool next to her. "You should see my blog, I've gotten thousands of hits on it today. It's kind of like a dream come true."

"I'm happy you got so much attention, if that's what you want. Think about what you really want before accepting any offers. Don't let it all go to your head. Things move fast in the media, yesterday's news is old news, and all that. I'm not saying that's how it will be in your case, but don't rush headlong into anything before fully considering it."

She supposed that was sound advice. It was good to have someone like Adam in her life, a steadying influence.

They ate for a while in silence, Emma too hungry and too exhausted to talk. Her mind was still playing catch-up. She hadn't had the time to fully process her revelation about Ryan and her feelings about that. Or the conviction that Juliette couldn't be with Blake, which meant there was a good chance that Adam was Juliette's secret admirer—which still didn't explain the piano—and her feelings about that. All that on top of today's media attention and too little sleep, and Emma felt like her head would explode.

Now that she was at least fed, she just needed to shut down her mind and relax, to listen to Adam. He was talking about the movie and grudgingly acknowledging that Ryan was a very good actor. "But I can't shake the feeling somehow that he's always acting. The way he's so charming to everyone, it just seems forced somehow."

Normally Emma would have disagreed with him. Was it just to be contrary because that was how their relationship worked? Yet knowing the truth about Ryan, and why he would need to "act" all the time, it was clear that Adam had been more perceptive about Ryan than she had.

"Yes, he's a good actor," Emma said. Adam seemed surprised that she didn't say more.

"So," Adam said, carrying their empty bowls into the kitchen, "things are going well with you and Ryan?"

She would have liked to tell Adam the truth, to have a friend to confide her disappointment about Ryan in. But remembering her promise to keep Ryan's secret, their plan to keep on pretending they were seeing each other, Emma nodded. "Yes, yes, everything's great."

Adam refilled their wine glasses and brought them to the sitting area. "Okay. Just make sure he treats you well. Don't let him put his needs before yours. I, for one, didn't care one bit for how he took over the show from Juliette on Sunday, and then kept on wanting her to sing, even if her voice had gone hoarse. Just wanted to hear his own voice, if you ask me."

Again Adam seemed to expect her to retaliate. Instead, Emma found it as good an opening as any to ask about Juliette.

"Juliette looked very good last night, I thought," said Emma, curling her feet under her and getting comfortable on the leather sofa.

"All of you looked beautiful. You, Hailey, Belinda, Juliette."

Emma couldn't help getting in a little jab: "It's like the pot calling the kettle black. You put Ryan down for being charming to everyone and what are you doing now? You're the picture of charm."

"Ah, but I say it in complete honesty." Adam smiled. "But you were asking about Juliette . . . I always think she's lovely."

"Her playing is exquisite and she has a beautiful voice, doesn't she?" continued Emma.

"Yes, without a doubt. Emma, what are you fishing for?"

Emma sighed. "Okay, Annalisa and I have a little bet going. She thinks that there's something between you and Juliette."

Adam smiled slowly. "I see. You've been speculating about my love life again."

Emma was in no mood to be kept in suspense. "Well? Is there?"

"Would it bother you if there was?" asked Adam, peering at her.

Emma lowered her eyes and took a sip from her glass. "No, of course not, except . . . "

"Except what?"

"Except that it would mean I'm wrong, and you know how I hate being wrong. And I'd owe Annalisa a drink next time we see each other."

"Is that all this information is worth? A measly drink? You should have double downed, at least. Gotten two drinks out of it. No, there isn't anything between Juliette and I."

Emma let out her breath. Had she been holding it? "Ha, I knew it," she said, relief, lightness, glee flooding her. "Annalisa is so wrong. I told her it was ridiculous. Juliette's so not your type."

"And you know what my type is?"

"Obviously," said Emma. "Not Tricia, certainly not Sara, not Brooke—"

"So you've told me, many a time."

"See, you should listen to me more often. You forget, I am a very talented matchmaker," Emma said, feeling like her old self again. She supposed the stew and a bit of wine and bantering with a friend was doing the trick.

"What about Zak and Hailey?"

"Okay, so that was one bad call. And it wasn't my fault. It was Zak's. For being so not who I thought he was."

"Anyway, so what's my type? I'm very curious."

"You need someone who is kind, has integrity. She's got to be intelligent, charming, feisty and funny—someone playful you can joke around with. She should be successful, career-oriented. She also shouldn't be totally selfish or superficial, but she would be attractive."

"Not bad, not bad at all," he said. "Sounds like some pretty big shoes to fill, though. Guess I'll be destined to be single forever."

"Don't give up hope just yet. Not with me around."

"Good, that gives me hope, Emma," said Adam.

After a beat, she said, "I can't wait to tell Annalisa that she's wrong about you and Juliette."

CHAPTER THIRTY-THREE

"How long have I been asleep?" Isabel yawned and sat up on the red-and-white-checked picnic blanket.

"Mommy, finally!" said Mila, running over to the blanket. "Auntie Em has been playing with me but now I'm starving, and she doesn't know how to make the egg salad sandwich the way you do."

Emma had attempted a sandwich, but it had been rejected by Mila. She had tried to offer Mila other snacks, but all her efforts had been refused. What five-year-old refused snacks and wants an egg-salad sandwich? Giving up on feeding Mila, Emma had worked on entertaining and keeping an increasingly hungry and cranky Mila from waking up her mother and baby brother.

Rubbing her eyes, Isabel asked, "Is Felix still asleep?"

"Yes," answered Emma. "Did you have a good rest, Iz?"

"I totally passed out, didn't I? I just meant to close my eyes for a bit."

"Don't worry about it. You needed the rest," said Emma, who'd noticed Isabel's lack of makeup, hair hastily pulled back in a ponytail, and crumpled outfit. "I guess with Garrett away, you've got your hands full?"

"Do I ever! It was the worst timing, too. Last week we had to complete a pitch for a new account we're trying to get. It was a couple of late nights, and with Felix not sleeping at night, I'm—"

"Mommy! My sandwich! I'm starving!" Mila started to beat at her mother with her little fists.

"Ow, Mila! Please." Isabel grabbed at Mila's fists, gave her a glare, then flashed Emma an apologetic glance. "Fine, I'm going to make your sandwich. But please don't hit me or wake your brother. And while you eat it quietly, I would like to talk to your Auntie Em before Felix wakes up."

After the sandwich was made and Mila was happily munching away, Isabel turned to Emma.

"Probably not how you wanted to spend your Saturday? When you could be having a cozy brunch with Ryan right now," Isabel said.

A young couple strolled by arm in arm. Emma looked away from them and back to Isabel. "No, he's currently in L.A."

"Oh, okay," Isabel replied. They made short work of talking about Ryan; Emma didn't want to say too much, and Isabel seemed surprisingly disinterested. "I really want to discuss something with you, Emma, which is why I asked you to meet me today. Besides wanting adult company to help me keep my sanity, of course."

"Sure," said Emma, who'd been waiting for an opportunity to ask what Isabel thought she should do about the various offers she'd received. But it seemed she'd have to wait until Isabel was done with whatever subject was on her mind.

"So, you know, Mila's starting kindergarten in September," said Isabel. Apparently, Isabel and Garrett weren't excited about the local school and Mila was on the waiting list for the private school they'd liked best. With September approaching fast, it seemed there was no chance Mila was going to get a spot.

Emma tried to give Isabel her whole attention but wasn't quite sure where her sister was going with this. She probably wanted Emma's opinion on whether to go with a second-choice private school or to just suck it up with the public school.

Of greater concern to Emma was how she could leverage the attention she'd received from the premiere into something more. Her readers were begging for more party pictures of Emma, wanted to know her style secrets, and asked about her romance with Ryan. They were interested in her not so much as a blogger but as a personality.

Of the offers that had come in, the most promising were a print ad campaign for a national jewelry chain and a multi-channel campaign that would feature Emma as the face of a new perfume. Could this lead to an acting career? Modeling assignments? Would she want that?

"Emma, what do you think?"

Emma shook her head. "Sorry, Isabel, my mind wandered off. What was the question again?"

"You haven't been listening to anything I've been saying, have you?" Isabel fumed.

"Of course I have. You were talking about Mila's kindergarten options for next year."

"I started with that, but you completely missed what I said about my job and Hartfield."

"Did I? I mean, yeah, sorry, Isabel, I did." Emma shrugged, trying to look apologetic. Isabel's face remained pinched. Emma admitted, "I was thinking about all this media attention and how I could leverage it to advance my career. But in what direction? How can I—"

"Shit, Emma, sometimes you're so self-involved!"

Ouch, that stung. Especially coming from Isabel, who normally wouldn't lash out like that. Something must really be bothering her.

"Mommy, watch your mouth!" chided Mila. "You said that the s-word is a no-no word." At the same time, crying exploded from the stroller.

With a groan of frustration, Isabel shoved herself off the blanket and stomped over to the stroller.

Emma pulled a face and saw the same expression reflected in Mila's face. Leaning in close to Mila, Emma asked, "What was your mom telling me about earlier?"

Mila stage whispered back, "That she's gonna quit her job, and we're moving to Hartfield. Isn't that great? I managed not to say anything at all about it to you while Mommy slept. I'm very good at keeping secrets."

~

IT DID MAKE SENSE, Isabel and Garrett moving to Highbury-on-Hudson. In some ways, it was even inevitable, the trajectory of many a Manhattanite being to move to Brooklyn, ideally Park Slope, once the children came along before moving north when the children started school, if not to make a direct exodus to Westchester County.

To Emma, it felt like a betrayal.

While Highbury-on-Hudson was still commuting distance, without her job, how likely was Isabel going to be in the city? Their lunches and occasional weeknight Pilates class or drinks would be no more. The onus would then be on Emma to make the trip up to Highbury if she wanted to see her sister or niece or nephew.

Even worse, it was as if Isabel was choosing Morley over her. Their father was getting old, Isabel had said, and she and Garrett wanted the children to grow up near at least one grandparent.

"What does Dad think of the idea?" Emma had asked, remembering how unavailable he'd been during most of her childhood and how he'd shot down her idea to work at Worth Papers & Stationery.

"He loves it. In fact, it was his idea," Isabel had said, detailing how, ever since Annalisa's wedding, Morley had been trying to sell them on Hartfield's plentiful indoor and outdoor space and Highbury's highly regarded school district and charming, lively center. "The more Garrett and I talked it over, the more it seemed to make sense, especially as there's a good train connection to his job, and I was getting so frustrated at mine." Emma knew Isabel's ad agency was not friendly to working moms and was never going to promote her to creative director.

Of course, Emma was happy their father was welcoming Isabel and her family with open arms. But it hurt.

Isabel was always the lucky one. And now Isabel had everything: two mothers and a father (not to mention Adam and Garrett's wonderful, down-to-earth parents), a husband, two children. Yes, they were planning to get a dog, too.

And who did Emma have? Neither mother, nor father, at least not one that she had a good relationship with. Everyone thought she was having a steamy love affair with a dreamy movie star, but she hadn't actually been intimate with anyone in far too long to remember. Her best friend had just moved across the country and now her sister, niece and nephew would be moving away.

Emma had tried to argue that once Isabel left her job, it would be hard for her to get back into the rat race. She would turn into a soccer mom, just shuttling the children around the suburbs. Isabel had explained that as a graphic designer she could easily freelance and wanted to focus on illustrating and other applications for her art, anyway.

Yes, art was another one of the things that Isabel and Morley had in common. Though Morley never made art anymore, she'd known that in his younger years, he'd been something of an artist.

Sometimes life wasn't fair.

Well, at least Emma could make the most of what she had. And right now, that seemed to be a star that was rising. If she was strategic about this, for example, by getting lots of photo ops with Ryan, getting on Sasha's guest list every night, and planning amazing outfits to wear to each of the parties, then maybe everyone would envy *her*, would be proud of *her*.

CHAPTER THIRTY-FOUR

On Monday morning, Emma was awakened by a call.

"Hailey. Why are you calling me at 7 a.m.? What? You want me to go and get a copy of *In the Know*? Now? What's so explosive? Something about Ryan and me? No, Juliette? Juliette and Blake? Oh no!"

Emma threw on a T-shirt dress and dashed to the newsstand on Hudson Street. She begged that it was not what she thought. Staring back at her from the cover was Genevieve Lane, looking disheveled and devastated. In the corner was a picture of Blake giving Juliette a hug at the premiere. Emma had witnessed that hug herself, and it had looked perfectly innocent. But the camera had captured it in a way that looked suggestive. Splattered in large type across the top was: "Blake caught with nanny. Genevieve says 'Don't come back!'"

Emma turned to the inside spread and saw another picture of Blake and Juliette together from the premiere, and one grainy one of Juliette with the Dixon-Lane children. Emma read the article—some of the words seemed to have come word-for-word from her own mouth—and knew that it had to have been Lauren who'd written the story.

The information, according to the article, came from "a source close to Juliette." All of it was there: the anonymous gift of a $15,000 Yamaha, the Tiffany necklace around Juliette's neck. There was even a sentence that "Blake's handsome British co-star is said to have had suspicions." At the bottom was a box featuring pictures of three women: Juliette Fairfax, Genevieve Lane, and Blake's ex-girlfriend, the Victoria's Secret model. The implication was that Blake liked a certain type of woman. There was also a sidebar titled, "Who is Juliette Fairfax?", with facts about Juliette, including her childhood in Paris and Montreal, the death of her parents, her lonely years in New York. Emma was mortified and couldn't begin to imagine how Juliette would react.

That bitch, Lauren!

Emma chewed on her lower lip. What the hell was she going to do? Did Juliette already know? Could she get away with pretending she knew nothing about it? Should she break the news to Juliette? She raced downstairs and knocked on Adam's door; he'd know what to do.

"Emma, what are you doing here at this time of day? Is everything okay?" asked Adam, his hair messier than usual, stubble back in force. Emma walked in and showed Adam the cover.

"What kind of bullshit is this!" he said. "The junk these magazines print. What would give them this idea?"

Emma bit her lip.

He snatched the magazine from Emma and flipped through the pages until he'd found the article.

"Juliette having an affair with Blake? Her boss? It's the most idiotic thing I've ever heard!"

Adam sank down on the sofa and ran his hands through his hair. "Who could have put the magazine up to this? Who knows the Dixon-Lanes and Juliette?"

Emma remained silent.

Adam suddenly lifted his head. "Was it Ryan?"

"No, no, it wasn't Ryan!" said Emma. "Why would he say that stuff, anyway?"

"I don't know; publicity for the movie? Maybe he and Blake had a falling out? I don't care about them, it's poor Juliette that's going to suffer the repercussions here. She doesn't deserve this. She's the last person to deserve this kind of treatment."

"Maybe it was Chloe?" Emma squeaked. She'd screwed up royally and Adam was not going to be happy when he found out she was behind it.

"I don't think she knows enough about Juliette's past and . . . " he looked up again at Emma, his eyes slits. " . . . as far as I know, she doesn't have a friend who works for one of these rags. Like that woman who wouldn't leave me alone at your party. Did you tell her this stuff about Juliette?"

Emma couldn't answer. She cast her eyes down, not wanting to see disappointment in Adam's eyes.

"You did, didn't you?"

Emma sighed; the game was up. "I didn't think Lauren would actually print any of that stuff. Honestly I didn't. I was just gossiping with her as I would with Annalisa or any other friend, just repeating Ryan's suspicions. And I never once said Juliette's name."

Adam blew out his breath in a huff. "Emma, you know what you've done, haven't you? You've spread lies that could ruin lives! Juliette's for one." Yes, he was angry indeed. "You have got to stop meddling in other people's lives."

"I get it, okay?" snapped Emma, sick of Adam being on her case. She immediately regretted her tone with him. He was right; it was her fault. "I'll make it up to Juliette. I'll publish something on my blog retracting it."

"It's too late; the damage is done. We need to go downstairs and warn Juliette. There could be paparazzi waiting outside."

"Oh God, I hadn't even thought of that. This is worse than I thought!" said Emma.

It was clear from Juliette's red-rimmed eyes that she was aware of the news.

"I just don't understand," she said. "I don't know why they would print these lies. Why would they think there was anything, anything at all between Blake and I? I would never . . . ! Poor Genevieve . . . the kids!"

Emma's sense of shame deepened.

"These magazines are despicable!" Adam said. "They make up lies to sell copies. I can only hope, for your sake, Juliette, that it blows over quickly." Adam cleared his throat and Emma felt his elbow in her ribs. "Emma would like to say something, too."

Damn Adam for making her feel like a chastised five-year-old who'd pilfered something from kindergarten and now had to return it to the teacher. But admit the truth she must.

"Juliette, I'm so sorry. It was my fault. Ryan and I were joking that you and Blake were having an affair—"

"It was *you*, Emma?" asked Juliette, incredulous, turning to Emma.

Emma couldn't look Juliette in the eyes. "Then I told a friend who's an editor on the magazine. We were just gossiping."

"Why do you hate me so much? What have I ever done to you?"

When had she ever been hateful toward Juliette? No, Juliette wasn't being fair. She'd never done anything cruel to Juliette before, had she? Certainly never tried to cause Juliette pain intentionally?

"Juliette I don't know what you're talking about," Emma started, her cheeks aflame. No, she'd get through with her apology before addressing anything else. "I didn't think she would print it. Not without evidence. And even if it were true, it wasn't my right to gossip about it. I'm so sorry, Juliette."

"I've lost my credibility and almost certainly my job because of you and your idle gossip." The chill behind Juliette's words cut Emma. "Sorry is not enough, Emma. Get out of my apartment."

"I understand that you must hate me now, but—"

"Just. Go. Now."

Emma was surprised at Juliette for possessing more control and backbone than she had supposed.

Back in her apartment, Emma stared at the cover of the magazine, which she still held in her hand. She'd really messed up. She had presumed a relationship between a person she didn't know well and an A-lister she didn't know at all, and she had speculated it as fact to someone who worked on a national gossip magazine and was obviously not to be trusted. The result of her meddling was staring her in the face.

She dialed Lauren's number. She got ready to lay into her, to vent her anger at being put in such an awful and awkward position.

Lauren got in first. "Emma, I am so fucking sorry! I only found out about it myself on Saturday, when the issue had already shipped. I accidentally let it slip to one of my colleagues and she commissioned the photographs and did the research and wrote the article. I swear!"

"Save it, Lauren," said Emma.

"Fuck, Emma. I'm serious. I suppose I should have given you pre-warning, but I was worried you wouldn't believe me. I'm really sorry."

"Yeah right, Lauren, you don't have a sorry bone in your body. You forget I used to work with you. I heard you lie all the time to cover your ass." It was true, and remembering this, Emma realized that she had been a bigger idiot than she'd thought telling Lauren what she had that night. "I'm going to post a public apology on my blog. I'm going to take the blame for opening my mouth, but don't think you're going to get away with it, either."

"Is that supposed to be some sort of threat, Emma?" Lauren cackled. "It's not like anyone reads your stupid blog, anyway."

"No, Lauren, it wasn't a threat. I was just informing you of what I was planning to do. It was common courtesy, something you obviously know nothing about."

Lauren's voice went cold. "How soon we forget those who've helped us out. You owe me, you know, for all the good press you and your fucking blog have been getting. If it wasn't for me, you wouldn't have any readers at all."

"I didn't ask for your help," said Emma, "but I'd say we're even now. More than even."

"Oh, I wouldn't say that, Emma," said Lauren. "By my count, you still owe me one."

GOOD TO HER WORD, Emma wrote and posted the apology, knowing, as Adam had pointed out, that it was too little too late. Her tiny blog readership was nothing compared to the reach of *In the Know*, whose cover was going to be seen by every person in the country when they paid for their groceries or walked by a newsstand. For the rest of the morning and into the afternoon, Emma tried to concentrate on work. There was so much to do: so many e-mails and comments to reply to, a blog post to draft, another to edit. She had a few calls to make, an interview to do. The last thing she needed was guilt about the Juliette situation eating away at her. Finally, after she'd gotten a few of the more urgent things out of the way, Emma couldn't sit still at her desk any longer.

She went downstairs to find Juliette.

"Who's there?" came Belinda's voice when Emma knocked. It sounded like Belinda was expecting the Big Bad Wolf. She was either afraid it was reporters or . . . *Emma?*

"Belinda, it's me, Emma."

The door opened, but the chain hadn't been unlatched. Emma frowned; she didn't think that had ever happened in the 10 years she'd been living in the building.

"Is Juliette here? I wanted to apologize to her. I didn't really get to this morning as I'd wanted to."

"No, no, Juliette's not here," said Belinda, even though Emma could hear whispering inside, voices that sounded suspiciously like Juliette and Chloe's. "Mother's sleeping, so I'd better go in, keep it quiet for her."

That had never stopped Belinda before, Emma thought.

"Oh, okay," Emma said, retreating, as the door shut in her face.

Emma had never gotten such a frosty welcome from Belinda before, and she felt a strange ache. She wouldn't even have minded one of Belinda's monologues right about now.

What a day! sighed Emma. Neither Juliette or Belinda was speaking with her. Adam never came back to talk to her this morning, so he was probably still upset with her. Her friendship with Lauren was beyond over. Was Ryan going to hate her too for dragging him in the mud with her?

CHAPTER THIRTY-FIVE

"Omigod, omigod, Emma, there he is," said Hailey a few evenings later at Emma's local Mexican.

"Who?" asked Emma, looking discreetly around and seeing no one she recognized.

"Rob. You know, the guy who works for Adam, who asked me out?" said Hailey through clenched teeth.

Emma had to keep from laughing at the way Hailey was raising her eyebrows and shifting her eyeballs toward a guy standing at the bar. Subtle she was not. "Oh him. Has he been stalking you at the café?"

"No, I haven't seen him since he gave me that note. Oh no, I think he's seen me," said Hailey, raising the menu and hissing to Emma around its side. "What if he comes over? What if he asks me why I didn't call him? It looks like he's trying to pretend he didn't see me. This is so embarrassing!"

Emma rolled her eyes, wondering why Hailey was getting so worked up about some loser.

"Anyway, as I was saying," said Emma, "Ryan was surprisingly okay about it. He called to apologize, saying it was his fault for leading me to believe that Juliette and Blake were a thing. Amalia, his publicist, thinks, if anything, it'll bring more publicity for the mov—"

Emma sighed. Hailey wasn't paying attention to what she was saying; instead she was peering over the top of the menu and Emma's shoulder, trying to look at Rob without being seen.

"He's paying for his order. Oh no, he's going to have to walk by us to leave . . . "

Emma turned around, wondering what was so much more interesting about Rob than what she was saying.

No, he hadn't improved with time, thought Emma, seeing the deer-caught-in-the-headlights look he gave her when their eyes met. He changed his path from the beeline to the front door he was on to come toward their table.

"Hi Hailey, uh, I thought that was you, but I wasn't uh, sure. And it's Emma, isn't it?"

"Yes, hi Rob," Emma said for both herself and Hailey.

"Dinner in with the roommates tonight," he said, lifting the white plastic bag with a stack of Styrofoam containers inside. Then looking full at Hailey, he said, "Hailey, are you, uh, still working at Café Bisou?"

"Yeah, you should come in again sometime."

"Really? Okay, I will. It was good to see you again."

"Yeah, me too, bye."

After Rob left, Hailey let out a groan. "'Yeah, me too!' Ugh, that totally didn't come out right!"

"I think it was fine, Hailey."

"And what about what I said about him coming to the café? Was it too much? Will he think I'm leading him on?"

"Honestly. Don't worry about it. Don't worry about him."

"Oh, okay," Hailey said, looking down and taking a sip from her margarita.

Now that she had most of Hailey's attention again, Emma continued telling her about the fallout from Monday's scandal.

She'd found out from Adam that Juliette had exiled herself with Chloe in Amagansett, where Chloe had an aunt.

At first Emma was surprised that Juliette would take Chloe up on her offer. But putting herself in Juliette's precarious shoes, as Adam had suggested she do, she decided it was probably as good an offer as Juliette was going to get to escape the paparazzi. Juliette probably also relished being trapped in a hot, cramped two-bedroom apartment with her nosy, overprotective aunt and grandmother less than she relished being trapped with Chloe and her unknown aunt in what Chloe suggested was a huge house near the beach, private and a world away from the teeming city.

From Ryan she had learned that Juliette had been let go from her position as nanny to the Dixon-Lane children. Genevieve, having been in the business long enough, was used to how the gossip magazines and paparazzi could twist the truth; she had no compunctions that there was anything untoward between her husband and the quiet, musical nanny. But under the circumstances, she could not keep Juliette employed as it would draw too much unwanted press attention, which was unfair to the children. There was no hard feelings and they would be happy to give Juliette a good reference and provide her with a not unreasonable severance package.

Emma had been relieved; she supposed it could have been worse, much worse. At least Hollywood seemed to be taking it in stride.

The biggest fallout was that Juliette had no job, and therefore, no home to return to after the summer. Perhaps Emma could help her find something? That would help make up for what she'd done, and perhaps Adam would see that she could be helpful in a good way.

Thinking about jobs reminded Emma of something.

"Hailey, I nearly forgot, with all the other stuff going on: I might be able to get you a job interview."

"Really?" squealed Hailey.

"Yes, at Estée Lauder in Midtown." Emma told Hailey about running into an old NYU classmate, who now had a very senior role in the company. Her friend had complained about how busy it was and how their marketing assistant in the consumer marketing group had just left. "I said I knew someone who'd be perfect for the role. They want someone with a couple of years of experience; you'll help coordinate marketing campaigns, do market research, benchmarking and competitive analyses."

"I couldn't do that! I don't even know what those terms mean. And I have no experience."

"Lesson number three, Hailey: You need to think more confidently, spin things positively. What do you do all day at Café Bisou? You interact with consumers, you market, upsell, cross-sell different products to them, you get their feedback, you juggle many tasks in a fast-paced, high-pressure environment. See, it's just about tweaking things here and there to make your résumé look good. Don't worry, I'll help you with that and then I'll coach you so you'll do great. Of course, appearance will be important. I'll help you choose an outfit and do your makeup and everything. I can turn it all into a blog post about getting a job."

"But I don't even know if I want to be in marketing. Or work in a corporate job. Or even work in an office."

"Nonsense, Hailey. You're just scared. You need to get out of your comfort zone, start somewhere. This friend, Liz, she started as an assistant, too. And now she's practically a VP. It's a huge opportunity. I can totally see you in marketing."

"Really? I've never thought about going into marketing."

"Well, now you can! Can you e-mail me an updated résumé ASAP. In Word, please, so I can make edits to make it sound really good."

"But I wouldn't want to feel guilty lying about my experience or anything."

"Don't worry, I won't be lying, just stretching the truth," said Emma. Was this what Adam meant by meddling? But she was just trying to help Hailey. That couldn't be bad, could it? "Lots of people do it on their résumés. Otherwise, it's so competitive in New York, you would never even get an interview."

"If you're sure. I totally trust you."

"As you should," said Emma. No, she wouldn't screw this up. Adam would see, when she got Hailey a great job, that she was a helper, not a meddler.

CHAPTER THIRTY-SIX

The next week flew by for Emma as she dealt with the offers that had rolled in following the premiere and began to put into place her plan to get as much media attention as possible.

In addition to Sasha's parties, she herself was receiving enough invitations to parties, openings and events, that she could head out every night of the week, sometimes to two events. During the day, she attended meetings, gave interviews, went shopping, planned her outfits, working on the blog in between. The following week, she was scheduled to do the photo shoot for the diamond chain, and Ryan was due back. She was also hashing out her contract with the perfume, Enchanted. At least she'd fixed up Hailey's résumé and had sent it out already.

Just over a week after the Juliette and Blake story broke, Juliette and Chloe returned to the city.

As soon as she was able to get Juliette alone, Emma approached her to apologize.

Juliette looked more subdued than ever.

"How was it in the Hamptons?" asked Emma.

"It was good, thanks."

"How was Chloe's aunt and her house?"

"Marianne was very hospitable, and her house was comfortable."

Aargh, thought Emma, it was like pulling teeth. How different Juliette was from her aunt, who at least was speaking with Emma again, though not quite as profusely as before. Emma should have been happy about this, but somehow it still hurt.

"Did being around Chloe for so long get annoying?" Emma asked, trying to take a light-hearted approach that would invite sharing. Juliette didn't or wouldn't bite.

"I am very grateful to her as well as to her aunt. Look, Emma, was there something you wanted to say?"

"Yes, Juliette. I want to very humbly apologize to you for the part I played in the scandal between you and Blake. I was wrong, and I want you to know how sorry I am for whatever pain I might have caused you or Blake and Genevieve and their children. I'm also sorry that you lost your job over it. Please, if there's any way I can help you to make it right or help get you a job or something, I hope you will let me know."

"It's okay, Emma. Despite what I said the other day, I know it wasn't meant personally. But you've done enough as it is; I don't need your help."

Emma left then, not sure whether her apology had been accepted or she'd been dismissed again.

Ryan returned to New York the day after. Emma was meant to be having dinner with him after he'd dropped off a letter of reference for Juliette from Blake and Genevieve.

She was surprised to see that the cozy dinner for two had turned into dinner for four. Apparently, Chloe had seen Ryan arriving, had invited herself along—both to drop off the reference letter and to dinner—dragging Juliette with her.

The night was dominated by Chloe complaining about how much friendlier the service in L.A. was, detailing how evil carbohydrates were, and crowing about how she'd rescued Juliette.

When Chloe began to talk about "sending out feelers to her

extensive network" in order to find Juliette a new nanny job, Ryan had asked, "Is that true, Juliette?"

"Since I have no job, I need to think about what I'm going to do next. And Chloe has been kind enough to ask around to see if anyone needed a nanny."

"We need to watch out for our friends." This from Chloe with a pointed look at Emma.

Ryan turned to Juliette again. "Is that what you want? I thought you wanted to pursue teaching privately. With the new piano you could."

"But I couldn't teach from here," said Juliette, looking down. "I mean Aunt Belinda's place. I'd need a home of my own. It couldn't be in the city; I'd never be able to afford the rent. I don't think I have any choice but to get another nanny position," said Juliette.

"Of course, you do, Juliette," said Ryan. "What about L.A.?"

"I'm over L.A.," said Juliette. "No offense, Chloe, but it's just not the place for me."

The same charming Ryan that Emma had been expecting didn't make an appearance that night. Instead he was petulant. He probably feels guilty, thought Emma; it was, after all, indirectly his fault that Juliette was out of a job.

"It was kind of a weird night," Emma related to Hailey later that night, as Hailey was closing up at Café Bisou. "Maybe because of the dynamic with me and Juliette there in the same room after what had happened. And then throw Chloe and Ryan in the mix. It was an odd group."

"At least you got to see Ryan again, even if it wasn't quite the intimate date you were expecting. I'm so jealous you're going out with someone dreamy like *him*."

Emma felt bad for pretending to Hailey that she and Ryan were actually together, especially as she could see that Hailey's mood was maudlin.

"Sometimes I wonder if this has all been a mistake," Hailey

said. "Maybe I should go back to Rochester. I mean, what am I even doing here? I miss my family and my old friends. Here I've only got you, a few people from work. I never talk to my roommates. You know, Chris, my ex, has been trying to contact me."

"No, Hailey, you can't! You can't go back to Chris, not after what he did to you. It takes time to make friends. Anyway, you're just in a summer sublet, you can move out and get new roommates."

"Yeah, that's what I mean, my sublet is ending soon, so should I even bother to stay?"

Panic gripped Emma. Hailey couldn't leave. First Annalisa, now Isabel. Not Hailey, too!

"Hailey, you've only just got here. It's way too early to leave. You haven't given the city a chance yet," said Emma. "Anyway, I've got some great news that might convince you not to leave. Liz, my friend that works at Estée Lauder, came back to me and said she was impressed with your résumé and was going to pass it on to HR to schedule an interview with you."

"Really?" said Hailey, seeming to be more bemused than excited. "That's great. Thanks, Emma."

"It will be great. I promise."

CHAPTER THIRTY-SEVEN

Three weeks later

"We need to plan a farewell party for Adam."

Emma's hand was already on the banister, her foot on the first step, eager to get away from Belinda's chatter—How had she ever missed it when Belinda was giving her the silent treatment?—when Belinda's words stilled her.

Emma spun around as Belinda continued to speak. "I still can't get over the news. Mother and I are simply devastated. And to think, it's thanks to him and that wonderful air conditioner that we can sleep at night. Not to say we don't appreciate you, Emma, letting us live here. And Chloe and Zak; what a service Chloe did for Juliette. We can never repay her for that. By the way, are you going to Chloe's birthday party on Saturday?"

Emma's mind had stopped registering anything after Belinda's initial words. "What did you say about a farewell party for Adam?"

"Oh yes, yes. My mind is like a pool table and each thought is like a ball, always spinning in tangents. Did that make any sense?

No, not really; I suppose that was a bad analogy. Forget about that, maybe a better analogy would be a pinball table—"

"Please Belinda, what about a farewell party for Adam?" repeated Emma, enunciating each word slowly and with emphasis, as though she were talking to a foreigner.

"Yes, a farewell party for Adam. He deserves no less, after being here for nearly a decade. This building just won't be the same without him! What a loss! Who will help us fix things? Who will bring Mother her favorite flowers? He is simply irreplaceable." Celia shook her head and sighed, looking truly mournful. If Emma wasn't experiencing a small death herself, she would have even felt sorry for Belinda. "Chloe has already agreed to organize it, you know how she loves parties. She suggested doing it on your roof-deck. She thinks the theme should be—"

"When should we have the party?" Emma cut in.

"Not too late at night so Mother could attend, too."

"No, I meant when as in which date?" squeaked Emma. Her throat scratched. Her heart raced. This couldn't be! Adam moving out? Where? And the worst of it was her not knowing anything about it. The fact that Chloe not only knew but was planning to host the party . . . that was just fucking unbelievable! And here Emma was, having to pretend she already knew when she wanted to shake Belinda and get her to tell her everything.

"Chloe's thinking a week from Saturday."

Emma gasped. "That soon?"

"Is that too soon? He'll be out before the end of the month he told me. I could just cry thinking about it!"

"Let's talk about the party later," said Emma, having heard enough. "I'll check the date with Adam." Emma raced to her apartment. She slammed the door shut and sank against the back of the door, the staccato hammering of her heart painful. She didn't give her heart rate a chance to return to normal. She needed to know everything. Now. She threw open the door, ran down the stairs, and rapped on Adam's door. Her knuckles stung.

"To what do I owe *this* honor?" said Adam when he opened the door. He didn't even bother to hide his sarcasm.

"When were you fucking going to tell me?" she spat at him.

"That I'm moving?"

"What else? Or is there more you're hiding from me?"

"Wait a minute here. I wanted to tell you right away. I would have told you . . . had you given me the chance to. Had you had the decent courtesy to return my text messages. Had you ever been around. I just assumed you were too busy to care."

"What's that supposed to mean?" demanded Emma, unable to believe Adam was turning this on *her*.

"As if you don't know. But I'll spell it out for you: You've gone completely AWOL on us. We haven't seen you for weeks. You're hanging out with your fancy friends all the time now. Hailey says she hasn't seen or talked to you, either."

"Oh, have you seen, Hailey? I wonder how her job interview went."

"Exactly, Emma! How did you expect it to go when you'd completely lied about everything on Hailey's résumé? And then broken your promise about helping her prepare for the interview? Can you imagine how embarrassed she was when they asked her about experiences she's never had? She felt like a total fraud having to fudge her way in front of people who made her feel like she was just wasting their time, which she was. She was in tears afterward."

"Poor Hailey," said Emma, chewing on her bottom lip. She'd totally forgotten about the interview until after the fact. She knew she should have called Hailey when she'd remembered, returned all those missed calls. But she'd been in a photo shoot all day. Those things were exhausting. Then she'd had to rush home to change for some party thing with Ryan. And since then she'd simply had no time. "She could have been better prepared."

"Yes, *she could have.*" Emma flinched at Adam's tone. "When you started hanging out with Hailey, I'd thought she'd be a bad influence on you. That the way she looked up to you in adoration would only increase your sense of superiority. But you want to know what, Emma? I was wrong. She's the one who drew the short end of the straw; being friends with you has been the worst possible thing for her. She's too good—literally—for you!"

Emma's face tingled hotly as if she'd been slapped. Why were they even discussing Hailey right now? When the only thing she could think about was Adam moving out.

"Where are you moving?"

Please, please, please, don't say California or anywhere far away, Emma prayed to herself.

"I got an offer I couldn't refuse. A place in Tribeca. A realtor friend showed it to me before it went on the market. I had one weekend to decide. I tried to get a hold of you; thought your opinion was worth something, maybe for you to see it. You didn't seem interested in getting back to me."

The relief that it wasn't across the country or even across the city was short-lived. It was exactly as Belinda had said—the building just wouldn't be the same anymore without Adam in it.

"Why? Why now?"

ADAM HAD WONDERED the same thing. He told Emma what he'd told himself: "Why not? I was looking for an investment, had been planning to buy something for a while. But I got comfortable. Now with the housing market as it is, it would've been stupid not to. The offer was too good to pass up."

But the reason he couldn't admit to Emma and didn't want to admit to himself was that he needed to move on. He needed to get out from under Emma, literally and figuratively. It was torture to be in such close proximity to her and not be able to have her the way he wanted her. Seeing her all loved up with Ryan was nearly his undoing. He couldn't bear to lose her to

Ryan and his ilk, to this world of celebrity that she'd begun courting. But he already had, he told himself.

It was well past time he left.

"Belinda says you move out at the end of the month?" Emma blinked back her tears.

"Yeah. Escrow should close on the 20th if everything goes as planned. I could move in anytime after that. I'm getting quotes from some movers now."

Emma squeezed her eyes shut and pressed her lips together so hard they practically disappeared. Adam had expected her to be upset about the news, but not look this heartbreakingly wretched. How easy it would be to draw her into his arms and let her cry on his shoulder. To tell her he would stay if she wanted him to. The train of his thoughts only made him more annoyed with himself. It wasn't as if she cared; certainly not in *that* way. He was more stupid than he thought if he could be taken in by her tears.

"And in case you weren't aware, Mila was really upset that you didn't come to her farewell party. Annalisa's also been trying to get a hold of you."

"I already explained to Mila I was going to be in the Hamptons that weekend. And it's not like I'm not going to see her again. Do you know what Annalisa wants? It's just been so busy lately, the perfume campaign and interviews and everything. But it should calm down a little after tomorrow's shoot, and I'll be able to get back to everyone."

"Are you sure, Emma? Because it doesn't seem like all work to me. You've been going out a lot recently. Every night, from what I can tell."

"Oh, have you been spying on me or something?" Emma's eyes were flashing and narrowed. She was in battle mode.

If that's what she wanted, he could give as good as he got.

"I often hear you clattering down the stairs at night. And I did stop by a few times. To try to tell you about the offer and to tell you I was moving out. You weren't ever home. So if that constitutes spying, then sure, I've been spying on you! And if so, don't come barging in here demanding why I didn't tell you I'm moving out!" He was shocked at his own outburst.

"Why are you yelling at me?" demanded Emma.

"Sorry," he said, the anger releasing with a long sigh. "I'm disappointed. We miss you and feel abandoned, Emma. For Ryan and your glamorous new lifestyle and friends."

Emma swallowed. "I've just been really busy with work, okay? It's not like you don't know how that is, Adam Knightley. You sometimes disappear for a couple of weeks at a time or have these big deadlines where we don't see or hear from you for days."

"That's different, and you know it, Emma," said Adam shoving his fingers through his hair.

"Is it? This is work, too. The parties and stuff, it's all about networking and building awareness."

"What? So you can be some C-list celebrity who's only known for who she dates and what she wears?"

"What's it to you?"

Adam sighed. He didn't enjoy lecturing Emma, but sometimes she needed it, and he was the only one to do it. "Emma, I'm glad you're enjoying your 15 minutes. But making a career out of it? Have you learned nothing from the whole Juliette scandal? That's what your life will be like. Your every move will be scrutinized and judged by millions of people who don't know you. Your love life—who you're sleeping with—will be fair game. You're going to have to watch everything you eat—and I know how much you enjoy a good meal—and constantly be at the gym. And then there's the whole nightlife scene. Lots of booze and drugs." He thought about Caroline. "I'd hate to think of you getting into that. And what for, Emma? What would you get out of it except for becoming more shallow, self-centered—"

"Are you done now?" asked Emma, "Because I need to get ready to go out."

"Fuck, Emma. Have you not listened to anything I've been saying? Hailey was freaking out before her interview. Annalisa's been having problems with Tom, but I guess you don't care. Isabel's also trying to get a hold of you. They all call me looking for you as though I'm your fucking boyfriend." He snickered and tasted the bitterness in his mouth. "You have better things to do. Go, Emma, good night."

"Just back the fuck out of my life, okay!"

The door to his apartment slammed shut.

With pleasure, thought Adam in the echoing silence. He didn't need this in his life. He didn't need *her* in his life. Moving out was the best decision he'd ever made.

CHAPTER THIRTY-EIGHT

Emma's tears were flowing unchecked now.

She didn't care. Adam was just trying to hold her back. All he ever did was lecture and find fault with her. She didn't need people like that in her life. She needed people who believed in her and her potential.

She was achieving a kind of recognition she'd never known, and it made her feel like someone special; it was her due. She was associating with people who were worth something, not stuck with her crummy neighbors, the Belinda Bates of the world and wannabes like Chloe.

She'd call Annalisa back. Definitely. Tomorrow evening or maybe on her way home tonight; it wouldn't be too late on the West Coast yet. And she'd try to stop into the café sometime soon and see Hailey.

But now she had a party to get ready for and she needed time to look her best. She'd already wasted precious time arguing with Adam. Maybe his moving out wasn't such a bad thing after all; she didn't need him looking over her shoulder, watching her every move. Emma swiped on her lipstick, wishing she actually believed it.

The party was for a hot new menswear brand at a swanky Soho hotel. Still seething from her encounter with Adam, Emma reached for the first glass of white wine and quaffed it down upon entering the party.

She took a second one from a passing tray to sip while she made the rounds. Standing there, looking for Sasha or someone she recognized, Emma heard a familiar, slightly nasally female voice behind her describing an "Italian stallion" who was "hung like a horse" and could "go on all fucking night" followed by cackling laughter.

Shit, Lauren was here, thought Emma. Should she confront her, let her know she was here? Or try to avoid her all night?

"Isn't that Emma?" she heard a woman say to Lauren. It took Emma a bit longer to place the new voice. Well, there was no hiding now, thought Emma, spinning around to face Lauren and her former boss, Anja Theussen.

"Why you're right, Anja, it is Emma!" said Lauren, her tone sugar coated over something more unsavory.

Emma was still reeling from the surprise of seeing the two women, together no less.

"I didn't know you were friends," blurted out Emma. When they had all worked together at Luxe, Lauren had constantly bad-mouthed Anja, calling her a cold, calculating bitch. Emma had heartily agreed.

"What a nice surprise, Emma," said Anja in a tone that didn't quite match the words. "How are you doing?"

"Fine, excellent," said Emma, raising her glass in a small toast and taking a large swallow. She needed something stronger. "How are things at Luxe?"

"Oh, you know, the usual," said Anja with an airy wave of her bejeweled hand.

"How are things with you and Ryan Churchill?" asked Lauren.

So, is that how you want to play it? thought Emma. Pasting on a wide smile, she answered, "Wonderful! I couldn't be happier. It was a shame he couldn't be here tonight, but he had other commitments. *Between the Lines* is still topping the box office chart, as I'm sure you know, so he's very busy."

Emma had no idea what Ryan was up to tonight. He could have been on a secret date with some guy, for all she knew. But Lauren didn't need to know that. Because for all Lauren's sexual predator talk, the one thing that Lauren desperately craved, Emma knew, was a man. A boyfriend. A potential husband. She only settled for sex for lack of anything more meaningful. So having a boyfriend, even a pretend one, gave Emma one up on Lauren. "Are you still single and looking?" asked Emma, feigning friendly curiosity.

Lauren narrowed her eyes slightly, but her tone was friendly, conspiratorial. "I've got plenty of company. But let's just say, I'm leaving my options open. There are a few HFHs at this party," said Lauren, doing a quick scan of the room, "Plus, I'm still waiting for dibs on your hot neighbor, Adam."

At the mention of Adam, Emma's face flamed, her mind returning to their fight from earlier. This time, however, the passionate words lobbed between them were swallowed by rough, burning kisses, the anger between them building and fanning the flames of lust until the inevitable explosion. If Adam were her fuck buddy, is that how the night could have ended? She deleted the mental image and her mind replaced it with images of Adam being Lauren's stallion. She shuddered. That was far, far worse.

Damn Lauren and her insinuations about Adam!

Two downed glasses of wine started to do their work. The fight with Adam, and now these unsettling visuals, compounded with her unresolved anger at Lauren's betrayal meant Emma had plenty of fuel to work with. "For your information, Lauren, Adam would not go for you even if you were the last woman on earth. You exemplify everything he dislikes in a woman: obnoxiousness, deceitfulness, maliciousness. He thinks *In the Know* is despicable and hates you for the lies you printed about Juliette."

Lauren's face had taken on an almost cartoon-like look of apoplectic shock. Emma wanted to laugh, but Lauren had already recovered herself. Anja meanwhile was looking from one to the other as though she were at a Wimbledon match.

"Watch out, Emma, or you just might topple from that high horse you love prancing around on. In fact, I look forward to helping you fall. Take that as a threat if you wish. And by the way, it was me who told Anja that she shouldn't promote you to the marketing director position." With that, Lauren whipped around and stalked away. Anja shrugged at Emma, a look of apology? pity? indifference? in her eyes and followed Lauren.

Emma tossed back her wineglass. Damn, it was already empty; not a single drop left. She had the sudden desire to fling the glass across the room and watch it shatter. Instead she headed for the bar. Something harder was definitely in order. Whiskey came to mind.

It had been Lauren, all along, who had sabotaged her career at Luxe? Emma had complained to Lauren about how unfair Anja's decision to give the job, which Emma had coveted and clearly deserved, to one of Anja's minions had been. Lauren had agreed and assured Emma that she had wholeheartedly recommended Emma for the role. What a total liar! Was Emma such a bad judge of character that she'd chosen to be friends with Lauren all these years without realizing what kind of a person she was?

Forget Adam, forget Lauren. She was not going to let them bring her down. She was here and she intended to have a good time.

It wasn't like the night could get any worse, anyway.

At that moment, a deep, accented voice near her asked, "What are you having?"

Emma turned and nearly lost her breath at the sight of the large, swarthy and sexy stranger. Without doubt, he was someone

Lauren would dub an HFH, a highly fuckable hottie. Or was it highly fuckable hunk? Either way, this guy fit the bill.

"What are *you* having?" she tossed back, a raised eyebrow. Was she issuing a challenge?

He looked her up and down, unabashedly. "I know what I'd like to have. I just don't know if it's available."

A punch of desire hit Emma right at her core. Okay, it had been awhile since she'd felt *that*. With Ryan, there'd been attraction, but this was pure animal lust. Perhaps this was a wake-up call, her long-dormant body trying to tell her something. *Forget about Adam. So what if he's moving away. Forget about Lauren and her betrayals. Forget about the fact that you have a sham relationship with a guy who will never find you attractive because he's into guys. Here is a guy who desires you, and you want to feel desired, deserve to feel desired. So why not?*

CHAPTER THIRTY-NINE

Emma didn't want to wake up. "Fuck!" Filming the perfume commercial was taking place today. What the hell time was it? In her bathroom, she considered her bloated, mascara-streaked face and the red marks on her neck. She didn't recognize the person in the mirror and didn't care to know her. Is this who Adam saw when he looked at her?

Shit, Emma thought, remembering a call of some sort to Annalisa. She flipped open her phone. Yup, at 4:38 a.m.. On the West Coast it would have been 1:38 a.m., not as bad, but . . . shit. Emma had no time for contemplation. She disrobed and let the shower work its magic. Her head pounded, her body ached, her skin chafed, but at least she felt somewhat revived afterward. She pulled on a dress, popped a couple of Advils and was out the door.

Now at the shoot, she had to endure two hours of sitting in a chair having her hair and makeup done. The headache had not gone away, and she had the dreaded feeling that she was still drunk, that she reeked of alcohol and sex.

The HFH's name was Diogo, and he was a pro soccer player from Portugal, Emma had learned. His team had made it to the semi-finals of the World Cup in Germany in July. Emma had no idea who he was or what that meant, but it sounded impressive.

They had started with dirty martinis, flirting hard the whole time, the sexual tension a tangible third party. They had moved on to Cuba Libres; she was certainly sitting on his lap by that point. Lauren and Anja and everyone else at the party had far receded in her mind.

She'd been the one to suggest doing tequila body shots. It was very 1990s frat party, but she'd been so obliterated, she hadn't cared. She remembered how he'd kept her gaze as he'd slowly licked the salt off the exposed skin of her chest. That glitter in his eye as he'd come for the wedge of lime clamped between her teeth. He hadn't stopped with the lime, which had dropped between them. For one brief, gloating moment, she'd thought that tequila body shots, tequila shots of any kind, would not be possible with Adam. Then she'd succumbed to the heady taste of salt, tequila and lime on Diogo's mouth.

"Excuse me," said Emma, suddenly lurching out of the makeup artist's chair. The makeup artist, sensing what Emma needed, raised a hand, her cobalt blue-tipped fingers forming an arrow in the direction of the ladies' room.

The acids in Emma's belly were churning. Emma spewed into the toilet just in time. She retched again and again until she felt hollow inside. At the sink, she rinsed her mouth and wiped the sour taste from her mouth while trying not to disturb the painstakingly applied makeup.

They must have left the party soon after that. Diogo had a room in the hotel. She remembered being pressed against the mirrored elevator wall. Holding hands and stumbling giddily down a long corridor. A cool white bed. Hard skin. The abrasiveness of a five o'clock shadow roughly applied to delicate parts of her body. Her arms splayed out above her, Diogo's hands handcuffs on her wrists as his big body moved above her.

Emma rubbed her tender wrists.

Picking up and putting on her strewn clothing. Sinking into the backseat of a taxi. Dialing Annalisa's number. Hanging up with a curse and a click. Clattering up the stairs, not caring if she woke Adam. Crawling into her own bed.

∿

FINALLY HER TRANSFORMATION WAS COMPLETE. Outwardly she looked like the belle of the ball; Emma wished she felt the same inside.

She was slow, unconvincing, even if she had no lines. In the first scene she was dancing in the arms of a handsome tuxedoed gentleman. Her co-star was easy on the eyes, danced well, and tried to engage her in small talk between takes. She wasn't interested.

She thought of Ryan. Was there a chance he might find out about her rather public indiscretion of the night before? Would this affect his reputation? Had she just broken some sort of unspoken contract? If she had, maybe it wouldn't be such a bad thing. Maybe it would be better if this whole relationship was out in the open. She pretended about so much in her life, it was almost more than she could take right now.

"C'mon, wake up," her co-star snapped. Had he been trying to hit on her and was he now upset that she'd ignored him?

In the next scene she had to look stricken as the clock struck midnight. Then she was supposed to run down the terrace steps into, what, post-production would be a swirl of mist, losing a shoe on the steps as she went. She felt wooden. Stupid. Messing up repeatedly. They had to do retake after retake. The director kept yelling at her, speaking to her as if she were mentally challenged. The crew was losing their patience with her, too.

"You're not supposed to look like you're being tortured, Emma. We need to see surprise on your face!"

She looked tortured because she was. The beaded strapless

ballgown seemed to get heavier and more uncomfortable by the second, the clear "glass" high-heeled slippers were too tight, the pointy vamp squashing her toes together.

How do actors do this, wondered Emma, her eyes smarting. She supposed, for a start, they didn't stay out all night and drink themselves to oblivion the night before. (Or they had a lot more practice than she did.)

Her co-star, Brett, was seriously getting on her nerves now, rolling his eyes, muttering under his breath. He wasn't very good looking at all, now that she thought of it.

Finally she was released. Another hour was spent undoing the makeup and hair. After the short night and the long day, she felt exhaustion seeping into her very core. She hadn't been able to stomach anything all day, and now she was famished. On her way home, she saw a Popeye's next door to a Krispy Kreme donut shop. The smell of fried chicken and sugar drew her in like opium. She inhaled her fried chicken, mashed potatoes, gravy and coleslaw, washed down with Coke and two light-as-air glazed donuts. Almost immediately afterward, Emma felt bloated, sick and gross. She pictured each fat calorie going to her hips and thighs. At home, she passed out and slept.

CHAPTER FORTY

When Emma awoke the next day, the heat of the day was already upon her. It was a quarter to eleven. She locked up her apartment and was walking downstairs when she saw Adam's door open and close. Hailey, dressed in her waitress blacks, stepped out and began to descend the stairs.

"Hailey!" called Emma.

"Oh hi, Emma." Hailey stopped at the bottom of the flight of stairs.

"What are you doing here?" Emma asked. "Were you looking for me?"

"I was at Adam's," said Hailey, appearing to be engrossed in the pattern of the tiles on the floor. Oh no, thought Emma. Hailey couldn't even meet her eyes.

"Look, Hailey," said Emma. "I'm really sorry about your interview. I know I'd said I'd help you prepare, but in all the other stuff that was going on, I forgot."

"It's okay, Emma, really. It's over now." Hailey's eyes were still cast down.

"That must have been horrible for you, Hailey. I'm truly sorry."

"Don't stress about it, Emma. It wasn't really that bad. I'm sure I overreacted when I told Adam about it."

Despite Hailey's words, Emma doubted Hailey had shrugged it off. Or forgiven her for breaking her promise. At least Adam had been there for her, thought Emma, glad that Hailey and Adam had become friends.

"Anyway," added Hailey, "I don't think it would have been the right job for me."

Of course it wouldn't have been, Emma realized. It had been what she'd wanted for Hailey, not what Hailey had actually wanted.

"How are things? Are you heading to work?" asked Emma, wanting to make things right between them.

"Yes, yes, I am. I'm working lunch and dinner tonight."

"Cool, maybe I'll stop in later. I hope you can forgive me and we can spend more time together."

The old Hailey would have gushed, "I would love that! Of course I forgive you. I could never be upset with you, you know that!"

This Hailey only nodded her head and scurried away.

IT WAS another one of those days. After a relative cool spell, the temperature and humidity level had been climbing until it was near unbearable. Emma dropped her grocery bags on the kitchen floor and peeled off her soaking tank top and shorts. It was as if she'd just come back from a jog. In just her underwear, she gulped down a glass of iced green tea and put away the perishables in the refrigerator.

Refreshed from her shower, the relative coolness of her air-conditioned apartment and a light lunch, Emma looked through her inbox, trying to find any desirable new leads that she hadn't followed up on. But there was nothing.

A few weeks ago, it had felt as though she could pick and choose the offers. Had they all dried up? No, the truth was, there had only been a handful of good ones; the rest had just been chaff.

She did a search of herself online, something that had become a daily habit. Nothing new. In light of the other night, no news was good news, thought Emma. But she needed more visibility, good visibility, another surge of publicity.

She would call Ryan. They could go for dinner somewhere. Somewhere where people would be sure to recognize them.

Adam's words about her becoming more shallow and self-centered buzzed into her head. Was this what he was talking about? And what if Adam was right and this was her 15 minutes? What then? She could continue blogging, of course; she'd already doubled her readership since the premiere. But blogging wasn't going to make her famous or give her the kind of visibility she was craving. She could leverage all the publicity and try to get a book deal, perhaps. But it seemed like so much effort, and she wasn't sure that's what she even wanted. She'd started the blog to do something after walking out of Luxe, but could she truly say she was passionate about it?

She felt as she had after Annalisa's wedding: lost, not sure where to go from here. No, she didn't feel passionate about it anymore. Or was she just too weak to stick to any one thing? Too uncommitted or flaky? Emma hated these questions and the ensuing doubts that sometimes robbed her of her self-assurance. She envied people like Annalisa, for her passion for the law, and Ryan's for acting and Juliette's for music. She envied those who just knew what they needed to do with their lives and were pursuing it single-mindedly. This left her with the Chloes of the world.

Emma felt a heaviness, a drain on her energy that had less to do with the day's humidity than with her own thoughts.

CHAPTER FORTY-ONE

The moment she stepped outside the building, Emma was assaulted by the humidity, raucous voices and aroma of grilling meat.

It was the following afternoon and from all indications, Chloe's birthday bash was in full swing. Emma headed to the small slab of concrete and long, narrow strip of lawn behind their building. Smoke billowed out from a black sphere on legs. People in various states of undress milled around the garden, beer bottle or red plastic Solo cup in hand. A large child's blow-up pool sat in the middle of the lawn. In an itty-bitty bikini and oversized sunglasses Chloe presided.

She spotted Adam right away. Had she been searching for him? He looked relaxed in a T-shirt and shorts drinking from a bottle of Becks. She went to him.

"Want something to drink?" he asked.

Emma shook her head. She didn't think she could stomach it. "Have you been here long?" she finally asked. With the fight between them, she didn't know what else to say.

"No, just 10 minutes or so."

God, this was awkward. Was she the one who needed to apologize? She didn't know anymore. No, he was the one who started it. The one who, out of the blue, decides to leave her and move out, without even consulting her, and then blamed her for being unavailable.

She was almost relieved to see Juliette and waved her over.

"Hi Juliette," said Emma, noticing that Juliette looked dazed and unfocused, like someone shell-shocked.

Adam said, "Can I get something for you, Juliette? A drink, food? There seems to be some chicken skewers coming off the grill that look tasty."

"No, thank you, Adam. That's kind of you, but I won't be staying much longer."

Just then, Chloe made her way over. "Knightley, I'm so glad you're here!" she said, greeting Adam with a kiss that landed practically on his lips and a press of her breasts against his chest.

Knightley, indeed!

With her front still to Adam and her backside to Emma, Chloe waved a hand in acknowledgment and said, "Emma, too." Chloe finally turned away from Adam to admonish Juliette. "Did I hear something about not staying much longer? I won't hear of it! It's my birthday, and no one is going to leave early. Not until the cake, at least. I got it from Magnolia Bakery—I only get the best—a flourless chocolate cake. I'm so glad I risked a barbecue. In L.A., I always had a pool party and barbecue for my birthday. Of course, we had a real pool, an infinity pool, in fact, with the most amazing view of the Valley. But I think my idea to get the kiddie blow-up pool was inspired, don't you think? Everyone said it's going to rain today, but so far so good. Please help yourselves to food and meat, there's plenty. Where's Ryan? Lots of people here are really stoked to be meeting him! Definitely try the punch, it's my own creation, Chloe's Citrus Cooler. But don't let the name fool you, it's strong! Juliette, come with me." Chloe grabbed Juliette's arm. "There's someone I want to introduce you to. He's single, wealthy, and really appreciates classical music."

"How can she say they look natural?" demanded Emma, thankful for something to say. "They are gravity defying!"

Adam laughed, but it sounded strained. "No, they certainly didn't feel natural. They didn't squash against my chest in a normal way."

"Poor Juliette," continued Emma. "I guess now that Chloe's done her a favor, she feels indebted to her and has become her little minion."

"Oh, I don't think Juliette is as weak as that. I think she goes along, partly to be polite or because it's more effort not to, but she'll be strong-willed when she needs to be," said Adam, looking at Juliette's retreating form for a moment before returning his eyes to Emma.

"Listen, Emma—" Adam began, angling his head and body toward Emma as he did so.

I accept, thought Emma. We both said hateful things the other night. Despite what I said, I don't want you out of my life.

"I don't mean to pry, but is everything okay with you and Ryan?"

Where was this coming from? Had Adam heard about the utterly wanton way she'd behaved with a man who wasn't Ryan? Why should any of this matter to him, anyway? Was he going to lecture her again on her behavior? Ooh, she was definitely taking back everything she was about to say to him.

"Ryan and I? Everything's fine, great," said Emma, throwing in a little laugh for good measure. "Why?"

"You know how I always thought there was something off or secretive about him?"

"Yes," nodded Emma. Adam must have figured out that Ryan was gay. Had Ryan made a pass at Adam? Lots of women found Adam attractive. Certainly a gay guy would just as easily be dazzled by those deep, warm brown eyes, that smile, the great, solid body. Not to mention that Adam was a truly good guy. And smart and successful.

"I just don't want him to hurt you and . . . "

Adam seemed so hesitant, Emma's heart softened. She wanted, needed them to be friends again. Maybe she would even apologize first.

"I've been noticing somewhat suspicious behavior between Juliette and Ryan that makes me wonder if there's something between them."

"Juliette and Ryan!" Okay, this she hadn't expected at all. Emma laughed, thinking about Ryan's secret. "That's the most ludicrous thing I've ever heard. Whatever gave you that idea?"

"It's just a certain way they seem to act around one another when they think no one is watching. As though they know each other better than they pretend to. And this morning, when I was jogging, I saw Juliette coming down the street from Ryan's hotel."

"You think Juliette spent the night at Ryan's hotel? That's funny, Adam! I'm not the only one who can be accused of having an overactive imagination."

Adam seemed uncertain now, defensive. "What's your explanation for why she was hanging around the Meatpacking District at 8 a.m.?" he asked.

"Juliette's always been an early waker. She was probably out for a walk. Or she wanted to escape from that cramped apartment and her aunt. Or maybe she had a one-night stand with some random guy who's staying there. But I can assure you there is nothing whatsoever between Juliette and Ryan." To press home the message without giving away Ryan's secret, Emma added, "I was with him last night."

CHAPTER FORTY-TWO

E mma's shaky mood took a nosedive. How *dare* Adam stalk off like that? When she'd come to the party primarily to see him! To restore the fragile shards of their friendship. She'd even been on the verge of apologizing.

Did she have a sign on her forehead that read "Not worth it"? Or perhaps it said "Exit" with a big arrow pointing off her head. Why did everyone leave her? All the damn fucking time? What had she expected, anyway?

Emma breathed in deeply and chanted to herself, "I don't care what Adam thinks. I don't care that he hates me. I don't care that he's moving out."

She continued to take her calming breaths until she felt strong arms wrap around her waist and herself being spun around. Ryan. From the corner of her eyes she saw how her yelp of surprise had caught Adam's attention and how he, and several of the other guests, had seen the way Ryan had planted a kiss on her lips.

Ha, thought Emma, let that be proof to you, Adam Knightley, that Ryan is interested only in me. Even if he's gay and we're just in a fake relationship. Her convoluted thoughts made her head ache.

Emma had had dinner with Ryan the previous night, it was true, but it hadn't been quite what she had led Adam to think.

They'd ended up at Pastis across the street from Ryan's hotel, both too tired to make more of an effort to go anywhere else. For Emma, it was just the kind of low-key but hip place where celebrities might be spotted, so it was fine for her purposes. Besides, Ryan was a friend. Possibly her only friend at the moment, so she'd been grateful that he'd been available to meet her at all.

But he'd been in a sour mood. Complaining about how ready he was to get back in front of the camera. How he couldn't wait until shooting on his new movie in Berlin started at the end of the month. And what a shame it was that acting had to come with the actor as personality part of it and the problems it presented.

A skinny guy with bad skin and a beanie chose that moment to approach their table and tell Ryan how much he'd enjoyed *Between the Lines*. Ryan had smiled reluctantly for a picture then pulled his flat cap lower on his head.

"There are very successful actors who seem to manage to stay out of the limelight, aren't there?" asked Emma.

"Yes, I suppose to an extent you're able to. But it's not easy. Because in this industry, success seems to go hand-in-hand with fame and fame seems to go hand-in-hand with a lack of a private life," Ryan scoured his face with one hand. He looked miserable. "So the more successful I get, the more I'm screwed."

Isn't that what Adam had been trying to tell her the other night, too?

"But you must enjoy some of it?"

He shrugged. "I might have at one point. I mean part of me can't believe how well things are going and can't believe that I'm whinging about it. I have plenty of mates, you know, from acting school and from when we were doing bit parts on the stage, who would kill to be in my shoes right now. But I think being famous makes it much harder to make simple, everyday choices. For example, if I wanted to date someone normal, it would be hard on . . . this person. Take what happened with Juliette. I wouldn't want that to happen again, you know, to someone I was seeing."

Emma had nodded, thinking about Ryan's secret, about how this must be doubly hard for him, having to hide his private life behind a highly public smoke screen.

Toward the end of dinner, Ryan's phone had pinged. He'd checked it and tapped something back.

"Want to do something else after this?" Emma had asked.

"No, I'm exhausted," replied Ryan. "But thanks for suggesting dinner and listening to me moan. I'm properly full and ready for an early night."

Today, it seemed, a good night's rest had done wonders for his mood, as his exuberant kiss had proved. Yet, the more Emma talked to him, the more she realized he was acting manic. His eyes were unfocused, darting around. Following his eyes, she saw that Juliette was nowhere to be seen. Adam was talking to a pair of girls in bikinis who were blatantly flirting with him. Zak and his bandmates were setting up their equipment. And Chloe and her friends were splashing in the pool.

Just then Belinda appeared around the side of the building hauling Juliette behind her.

"Hi Ryan, hi Emma! So good to see you two. Guess who I found upstairs? I had just gotten up—you know I was on the night shift at the hospital last night—and there was Juliette sneaking into her room. I said to her, 'Why aren't you at the party with all your friends? I bet they haven't even sung Happy Birthday yet.' Her excuse? Not being much of a drinker and a bad's night sleep. But I said to Juliette, 'You're only young once. You can sleep all the time when you're Grandma's age. But you, Juliette, you need to go out there and mingle. Your friends are there, Emma and Adam, Chloe and Zak and Ryan,' I told her.

'They'll wonder why you're not there. You should be down there with the young people, not sitting in your room by yourself on a beautiful, hot summer day.' So I hurried up and got dressed and told her, 'I'm going to come down with you myself.'"

During Belinda's speech, Juliette had looked wan and her eyes darted from Ryan to Emma to Belinda before settling somewhere above Emma's shoulder.

Belinda droned on about the party, how it wasn't every day that someone her age gets invited to parties. But haven't we had some great ones recently? The premiere and the recital and how we must really pin Adam down today for a date for his goodbye party while we're all here together.

On cue, Chloe, who thankfully had slipped on a coverup over her bikini, was coming over with one arm around Zak's waist and the other around Adam's. "Everyone in the house all gathered here together, how great is that?" she said.

"Except for Mother," pointed out Belinda. Everyone ignored her.

"Time for a group shot," said Chloe, indicating to Zak that he should pour shots from the squat rounded bottle he was holding in which gold flakes swam in a clear liquid.

"I don't drink, thanks. Happy birthday, by the way! This looks like a fantastic party. Thanks for having me, Chloe. I feel so honored. Don't worry, I won't stay long, I'm sure you don't want little old me tagging along, but don't mind if I do have some of the food, it smells delicious and I haven't really eaten anything all day," chattered Belinda while Zak poured.

Juliette, Emma was surprised, reached for the first shot. Everyone else dutifully reached for a plastic cup, even Emma, figuring that not drinking could raise a few eyebrows. Besides, she really needed a drink right about now.

With a defiant glitter in her eyes, Juliette raised her cup and said, "To us," before downing its contents. The others followed suit with a chorus of "To Chloe," "Happy Birthday," "To me," and

"Cheers." Juliette, coughing and spluttering, resisted Ryan's attempt to pat her back.

"Juliette, have you shared your news yet?" asked Chloe. "No? Shall I do the honors? I have been responsible for getting Juliette a job as a nanny and piano teacher! The 8-year-old is a little child prodigy, so I'm told, and needs someone like Juliette who can teach and coach and practice with her every day. The parents are determined that she will attend Juilliard and be a star one day. They also have 2-year-old twins, so while the girl is at school, Juliette will be able to help with the two little boys. They're a real handful, apparently. It's in Seattle. The mom is the sister of a friend of mine. The dad has a very senior position at Microsoft. A very respectable, well-to-do family. It won't be glamorous in the same way as working for Hollywood stars, but I'm told they have a very spacious, beautiful home right on the lake. I'm sure Juliette will be very comfortable there."

Belinda clapped a hand over her mouth. "I don't know if I should cry or celebrate!" she exclaimed. "Oh Juliette! Mother and I would absolutely hate to lose you and so soon after you've arrived. It feels like it was only yesterday. We have gotten so used to having you here, you playing the piano every day, it's like the old days. At the same time, this sounds like a real opportunity. And we knew we couldn't keep you with us forever, as much as we'd love to—"

Blahdy Juliette blahdy blah!

Emma turned to Juliette. "They are going to hire you without even meeting you?"

"Or does your reputation precede you?" quipped Ryan. Juliette sent him a withering look. Adam raised an eyebrow at Emma. She ignored him.

"They felt that if Juliette was good enough for Blake and Genevieve's kids, they would be good enough for theirs. They have Juliette's letter of reference, of course. I arranged a Skype call between them and Juliette, naturally. They called Juliette yesterday to offer her the job."

"When would you start?" asked Adam.

"Beginning of October," replied Juliette.

"Oh, this is fast!" gasped Belinda. "We'll have to have a goodbye party for you, too! Oh Juliette, how we shall miss you. I miss you already and you're still here. This is wonderful, but so sad for us all!"

"Can I get anyone a drink or something?" asked Ryan. Juliette said nothing. Zak and Adam both held up the beers they had in their hands. Emma shook her head. "Emma, my love, are you sure? You look like you could use something to cool you off, looking as hot as you do." Ryan moved closer to Emma, put an arm around her waist. Emma laughed, surprised by Ryan's words and action.

"I do, do I? It's because when you're near, I'm on fire," she flirted back, smiling broadly into his face, not sure what had come over her, knowing that they were being watched.

"Give me a woman of fire and passion over a cold one any day! Emma, I fancy paying a visit to your brilliant roof-deck again. Perhaps we can disappear for a little while and check out the view from above. I'm sure no one will miss us."

"Oh no you don't, you lovebirds!" chided Chloe. "Don't mean to put a damper on things, but you can't leave before we've had cake; and Ryan, you promised you would meet some of my guests!—Where are you trying to sneak off to, Juliette?—After that Ryan, you and Emma can do whatever you want. Zak and I went up there once—Oops, sorry Emma, it was just too tempting!—and did some, y'know, *star gazing*. Ha ha ha. I can highly recommend it!" Chloe winked. Zak slapped Chloe playfully on the ass.

Emma's face reddened, as much from indignation as embarrassment. Ryan's behavior was uncalled for and throwing her off balance. And why the hell was Adam glowering at her as though she'd done something wrong?

Belinda, leave it to her, jumped right in: "Ah, star gazing! I do love looking at the stars. It's just a shame it's so hard to see them from this city. What was it like in, L.A., Juliette? Could you see the stars at night?"

"Belinda," laughed Emma, "have you any idea how funny you are? If you got a penny for every time a joke went over your head, a penny for every time you inadvertently made a joke, and a penny for being the butt of a joke, you'd be so rich you could afford not to live off of my family's charity. Anyway, they weren't talking about star gazing, they were fucking up there. You do know what that is, don't you?"

Emma could almost see the words as they flew out of her mouth. She'd wanted to stop them, but they seemed to leave of their own accord, and once they were out, they were unrecoverable. She hazarded a gaze at Belinda, who looked stricken. Then slowly, Belinda's features loosened as they readjusted into a smile, then a frown. Then with a nervous titter, Belinda mumbled:

"Was that meant to be a joke? Oh, I guess I wouldn't know now, would I? I see. But I'm not sure I understand the point that Emma was trying to make. Was she telling me that I'm a silly old lady? Or was she trying to say I'm just a charity case? Or that I'm the one that everyone laughs at because the things I say aren't as funny as I think they are. Oh, I don't quite get it, so I guess, yes, it must have been a joke. Wasn't it, Emma? A joke. Yet another one that I didn't get. Yes, it must have been a joke. A very clever one, that was. You are too, too clever, Emma. I am very grateful, you know, for your granddad and dad's kindness. Every single day. Yes, Juliette? Yes, you could see the stars from the Dixon's house. Because they were in the hills and there weren't many houses close together. Not so bright like here. Yes, that would make sense. Yes, and I see, of course, *those kinds of stars*. Oh, that was quite funny, wasn't it? Emma was right. She's always right about everything."

Emma had the feeling of watching herself as if from a distance. Ryan kept his arm around her as he whispered something into her ear. She laughed, the sound unnaturally loud and obnoxious to her own ears. She was reminded of Lauren.

"Belinda, the potato salad is very good. Chloe said you made it. It's delicious with the German sausages. Shall I get you a plate?" Adam offered Belinda his arm.

"Has the potato salad been a hit? I sure hope so. I would love some sausages. That sounds like exactly what I would like right now. Thank you, Adam, you are too kind."

The group began dispersing. Chloe took possession of Ryan. Adam led Belinda toward the food tables. With both Chloe and Belinda occupied, Juliette took the opportunity to skitter away. Zak, seeing who he was left with, had simply stated, "Got to help the guys set up," and walked away. Emma stood alone. Good riddance to you all, she thought, pressing her lips together. Emma walked over to the drinks table and ladled herself a cup of punch. She sipped it. Watching the revelers and their juvenile antics only increased her irritation; her mood worsened.

She went upstairs to her deck. Ryan was right about one thing: no one would miss *her*. It was quiet here, the sound of laughter and voices floating up like Mila's bubbles, many popping before they could reach her.

Sitting on the sofa, looking up at the sky, she heard footsteps behind her. Had Ryan escaped from Chloe's clutches so quickly?

"There won't be any stars tonight," she said without turning around. "It's going to rain soon."

"Before you say anything you might regret . . . it's me, not your lover boy."

"Adam."

"Emma, I just wanted to say—"

Emma braced herself for another one of Adam's lectures. She

could already hear it: *Emma, what the hell got into you? How could you be so cruel? It is my duty, since no one else is doing it, to point out when you're behaving badly. And that was you at your worst. Belinda deserves your respect, not your contempt. Pointing out that she was living off of your family's charity—that was uncalled for. Emma, who used to make sure you ate healthily when you had finals to study for? And bring you medicine and chicken noodle soup when you were sick? She cares about you, Emma. And you made her look like an old fool in front of people she respected.*

She would deserve every word. What she'd said to Belinda had been humiliating on so many levels, and she was ashamed, really and truly ashamed.

"—goodbye."

"Goodbye?" What did Adam mean by that?

"I thought you would want to know, so I don't get accused of not telling you anything: I'm away on business the next week and a half. I'll be moving out right after I get back."

"Oh." But this can't be it. This can't be all he wanted to say to her? "What, no lecture? No telling me how badly I behaved?"

Adam sighed. After a long while he said, "What's the point?"

Emma drew in a sharp gasp of breath. He could have punched her and it would have hurt less. *What's the point?*

Tears of shock and shame and pain rolled down her face. He wasn't even going to waste his breath on her.

She sipped the air with a shuddering breath. She expected to hear him retreat, but it sounded like he wasn't moving. She couldn't turn around, didn't want him to see how the tears streaked her face. *Don't go,* she wanted to say. *What am I going to do when you're no longer there to watch over me?* she wanted to say. *Thank you for having been in my life,* she wanted to say. *I'll miss you.* But she didn't say any of those things. Because it wouldn't mean anything to him. Anymore. It was too little, too late.

Guitar chords and "Check, check," rose from the garden. She stood up and walked to the edge of the roof, looked down. She listened to Zak introducing his next song, a dedication to the birthday girl. Emma recognized the words from "Muse." Despite herself, a smile quirked at her lips. When she turned around, Adam was gone. She wrapped her arms around herself, feeling the chill in the air. When the sky opened and the plump drops began to fall, Emma went back to her apartment.

CHAPTER FORTY-THREE

The bouncy chirping of her phone on the coffee table woke Emma; she must have fallen asleep on her sofa. The rain was still falling. She felt exhausted. Sucked dry. Her heart hurt. The twilight was disorienting.

"Hello?"

"Emma, Emma," she heard Isabel's voice, frantic. "It's Dad."

"What, Isabel? What's happened?" In the background Felix was crying.

"Dad's in the hospital. We're at a friend's place in Carroll Gardens. We can swing by and pick you up. In about 20 minutes?"

"Yes, I'll be ready. What happened? Is he . . . okay?"

"His heart. It's critical, I think. I'll call again when we're around the corner."

Emma took out her weekender bag and threw in a couple of changes of clothing and her toiletry and makeup bags. Her laptop and chargers. She slipped on a light anorak and put her handbag next to the weekend bag and waited on the sofa for her phone to ring.

What the hell was taking them so long? thought Emma,

looking at her watch. It had only been 15 minutes since Isabel's call. It didn't matter, they could still be too late.

Too late. Too late. Too late. The thought haunted Emma. She couldn't escape its relentless taunting: Too late. Too late. Too late.

Too late to repair the damage to her and her father's relationship.

Too late to tell her father she loved him.

Too late to say she was sorry.

The phone rang, startling Emma. "Hello? On the corner of Hudson? Okay, see you soon."

Emma raced down the stairs as quietly as she could, not wanting anyone to hear her. The sidewalk was black, the air cool and steamy at the same time. Only a drizzle remained from the downpour from earlier. From the sidewalk, she could see that Chloe's guests were making their way back out from the basement apartment to the garden. Emma pulled up the hood of her jacket and ran to Garrett's car. She tossed her bag in the trunk and squeezed herself into the space between Mila and Felix's car seats, buckling herself up as the car sped through the night.

THEY WERE in the glaringly bright waiting room of the hospital. To Emma and Isabel's immense relief, their father's condition had stabilized.

"It might be best if I explain a few things before you see Morley," said the bald, paunchy man, who Emma knew to be Roger Bankhead, her father's longtime second-in-command and the company's leader since Morley's retirement. He'd been significantly less bald and less paunchy the last time she'd seen him years ago.

"I spoke with Morley this afternoon. I told him I'm resigning."

"You can't! He completely relies on you," said Emma.

Roger took a sip from his vending machine coffee. "That's not the worst of it. The business has been doing badly. Much worse than even he realized."

"How bad is it?" asked Isabel.

Roger looked from Isabel to Emma, then down at the paper cup in his hands. "Bankruptcy, possibly."

Emma gasped. "Worth Papers bankrupt! That's not possible!"

"I'm afraid that it may have come to that. It's been very challenging times," said Roger, explaining that no one was buying cards and stationery nowadays because of the Internet, e-mail and text messages. That the company couldn't keep going as it had been, and how reluctant Morley had always been to make any of the changes necessary to take the business into the 21st century. "Our largest account, Macy's, decided last week not to stock Worth Papers anymore. Without them, the company's practically ruined!" Roger's shoulders slumped. "I'm sorry."

EMMA WAS SHOCKED to see how weak and withered her father looked.

At least he'd pulled through. It wasn't too late; things would be okay.

After all the necessary words had been said, Morley turned his head from Emma to Isabel. "You've heard from Roger about Worth Papers, haven't you? I'm so sorry, girls! I'm so ashamed. Your poor granddad. He'll be turning over in his grave to know what a mess of things I've made."

"No, Dad," said Emma, squeezing his hand. "You have nothing to be ashamed of. You did the best you could."

"No," Morley said. "You don't know everything. I, I . . . hated the company. When my older brother died—that was shortly before you were born, Emma—and then your granddad a few years later, the burden of the company fell on me. I resented that. I wasn't the businessman either of them was; I was an artist. I hadn't been groomed for the role; didn't have a whit of interest. I tried, I really did . . . " Morley couldn't go on. He was winded and he sounded broken.

"Shh, it's okay, Dad," said Isabel. "You don't have to say more."

"Thanks, Isabel . . . but I need to tell you . . . both. Need to talk. Say everything . . . "

Silently they sat as Morley recovered himself.

"I couldn't cope," he continued. "Numbers, logistics, strategies. I didn't know what I was doing. That's why I spent so much time in the office, Emma, time away from you. I was trying to grasp it all, to take my responsibilities seriously. Oh, but how I hated it! I stumbled along, made lots of bad choices. Tried to act like I knew what I was doing to hide my shame and frustration. But it didn't work. People saw through me, and I lost their respect . . . "

Tears streaked Emma's face. How had she not known? He'd never been much of a talker, sure, but she'd thought all his working late into the night and going in on weekends was because he would rather be at work than with her.

Morley turned his face to the ceiling, closed his eyes. He was so still for so long, Emma thought he'd fallen asleep or . . .

"Daddy," said Emma, jostling him, panic edging the word she hadn't used since she was a child. His eyes opened and he turned his head back toward her.

Thank God, she breathed. "But why didn't you want *me* to help?" She had to know this one thing.

"I was ashamed, Emma. I didn't want you to see how incompetent your father was. I didn't want you to lose respect for me, too. To hear what people were saying behind my back.

"I never pressured you or Isabel into the family business because that had been my fate. And I didn't want that for you. I wanted you to choose your own way, to choose your own life. To do what you loved, not what was forced on you."

"Oh, Dad! I had no idea." Emma blotted his wet face with a tissue. "I thought you just didn't want me around."

"It was never, never that, Emma," said her father, looking hard into her eyes, so she would understand. Emma grabbed another tissue to staunch her own tears. Had Emma been less self-involved, would she have realized how unhappy her father had been?

Her father continued to explain about how much worse things had gotten, owing largely to competition and technology. "I finally couldn't manage it, so I handed off more and more to Roger. We had to restructure and reallocate assets."

"I would have helped. I wanted to, planned to when I graduated," said Emma. He'd cut back on her monthly allowance at that time, too. She'd believed he was being unfair, but she realized now it was probably due to financial considerations.

"I know you did, Emma. But you thought it was the same company it was when you were a little girl and your granddaddy was still in charge. It wasn't like that anymore. I didn't want to saddle you with that right when you had your whole life and so many opportunities before you."

Emma's heart squeezed. Her father had done that for her? And all this time, she'd begrudged him for it. Had blamed him for not believing in her. For not caring enough for her.

"It wasn't because you didn't think I was good enough?"

"No, Emma! Is that what you thought? I'm sorry if it was. You have so much to offer, so much life. In that way you remind me of your mother. I didn't want to hold you back. I didn't want you to feel trapped as your mother had. I admit I didn't handle it well. I pushed you away when I should have told you the truth. I'm ashamed of myself and of what you must think of me. I've ruined your life, your futures!"

Again, Morley shut his eyes.

"No Dad, you haven't ruined our lives at all," Isabel said. She and Garrett were fine, she told him. And with Garrett in finance, he would be able to help find a solution for the company.

"Shh. We don't blame you, we're just happy you're okay," added Emma. "The last thing you need is to apologize to me. I should be the one apologizing for shutting you out, taking it all personally. I was caught up in my own life, my little non-important life. We can figure out the company's problems later. Like Isabel said, Garrett will take care of it. I'll stay with you, don't worry, I'll help. We'll figure it out together."

Back at Hartfield, after bidding an exhausted-looking Isabel good night, Emma sat on her bed, sober and wide awake. At least her father was okay. When she'd thought she'd lost him, she'd realized just how much he'd always meant to her, how much blame and resentment she'd carried, how many wasted years lay between them. After his revelations, the extent of her ungratefulness ate at her, making her feel ashamed. But it wasn't too late, and she vowed she would be a better daughter.

Still unable to sleep, she tried calling Annalisa, but it went to voicemail. She thought about calling Adam. She cradled her phone in her hand, his name highlighted. She had only to press the green call button to hear his voice. But what would she say to him? Anyway, he didn't want to hear her voice or be burdened with her problems. *What's the point?* He would surely hear the news from Garrett at some point or other, and he could call her then. Or not. She snapped her phone close and put it down.

CHAPTER FORTY-FOUR

After breakfast, Emma found a few boxes of her old books and toys and brought them down to see what might be suitable for Mila and Felix to enjoy. As she went through the boxes with Mila, Emma felt the nostalgia of seeing a long-forgotten favorite book or a toy. She found her favorite rag dolls with their yarn hair and calico dresses and aprons.

"I played with them when I was a little girl like you," said Emma. "This one, with the brown hair, she's called Hazel, and this one, with the yellow hair, is Lottie LouLou."

"What did you play?" asked Mila.

"We had tea parties. We went on adventures. We played house; I pretended they were my little girls."

"Who was the daddy?"

"Most of the time there wasn't a daddy. Sometimes I made my teddy bear be the daddy."

"What else did you play, Auntie Em?"

"We played work." Emma smiled at the recollection. She remembered sitting on her grandfather's lap in the evenings peppering him with hundreds of questions about what he did every day. He told her how exciting it was to run a business and make all the decisions and watch it grow. He would take her on visits to the mill and the factory and the warehouse and point out what everything was, how it worked, and what it was used for. He would introduce her to employees, and proudly say that she was going to be in charge of Worth Papers one day. Emma had asked, "Is that like being the queen?" And her grandfather had laughed his booming laugh and his eyes had twinkled and he had said yes, yes, it was exactly like that, and if she wanted to be the queen of Worth Papers one day she could be. "I was the Queen of Worth Papers, and Lottie LouLou and Hazel worked for me. I told them what to do. Sometimes if they didn't behave or do what I told them to do, I would say they were fired. If they were good workers, I gave them gold stars."

She found a box containing a collection of assorted notecards. She had gotten into the habit of saving one each of her favorites. Looking through them now with Mila, Emma delighted in seeing Mila's eyes light up at the pretty designs or the way she fingered the butterfly glittering with jeweled foil colors, the delicately embossed gold starfish or the fairies in their bulb dresses flitting around the blossoms.

After lunch, Emma went to the hospital to see her father. The talk yesterday had been cathartic, and not only for her, she was sure. Just one conversation, and so many secrets and long-held resentment had been aired.

Maybe there was something about hospital beds.

Although she didn't want to burden him more, she needed to understand about her mother.

"Tell me about my mother," said Emma.

"She was beautiful, young, full of life. That was what I saw when I met her in Milan. You remind me of her at that time."

Emma was surprised; she didn't know her parents had met in Italy. How little she knew about the past or had wanted to know. Her father told her about living in Florence after his separation from Isabel's mom. He'd been painting and was full of passion and excitement for the future. But then he'd gotten the call that his older brother had been killed in an accident. On the way home, he'd passed through Milan, where he'd met Emma's mother, Diane. A poor, Iowan farm girl, she'd been discovered by a modeling agency and had been shipped to Milan to walk the runaways. Morley had fallen for her instantly, perhaps because she was so full of life and hope when his life was suddenly full of sorrow and darkness. He convinced her to go to New York with him.

They had lived in Emma's apartment, something else which Emma hadn't realized; she'd always thought they'd lived at Hartfield. While her father was working, Emma's mother was loving the New York life, the parties, the wealth she suddenly had access to. And then she got pregnant.

"She was so young, only 19, and I was twice her age. She was having fun, she was getting some modeling work. A baby would change all that. But I made her have you. I blackmailed her with money to stay. It was already clear we weren't good for each other, but I didn't want to admit the failure. I thought she would change, that having you would change everything. I never regretted it for a moment, Emma."

Diane had resented the baby, the responsibility. "She was self-centered and narcissistic. I was unavailable and depressed. She would abandon you to neighbors, babysitters and go out. Disco, drinking, drugs. It was the late '70s. She tried to stick it out, but I guess we both knew it wasn't going to work. I was working up here in Highbury; she wouldn't give up her lifestyle to live at Hartfield, plus she and your grandfather didn't get along. It was for the best when she finally left, Emma. I'm surprised she stayed as long as she did."

"But I remember being cradled and hugged and sung to. I have memories of being not much smaller than Mila and feeling happy. Picnics in the park with you and her."

Morley closed his eyes. When he opened them again, they

held a faraway look. "Usually Belinda Bates and her mother watched you when your mom went out. If you have happy memories, it was probably because of them. Sometimes on the weekends, Belinda and I took you to the park and picnicked. Maybe that's what you remembered."

Belinda had babysat her! It was memories of Belinda holding her, of Belinda and her father and her together that she had cherished?

Emma's mind reeled from everything her father had told her.

CHAPTER FORTY-FIVE

E mma returned from the hospital in time to catch some late afternoon sunshine. Barefoot, she ran around the lawn chasing after Mila or being chased. They picked raspberries and stuffed them into their mouths, enjoying the bursts of tartly sweet flavor.

Emma couldn't imagine Isabel leaving Mila. Why couldn't she have had a mother who'd loved her? Who'd wanted to share moments like this with her? But she'd had moments like this, Emma reminded herself, but Belinda had been the one to chase her and pick raspberries with her.

While Mila had a tea party with Hazel and Lottie LouLou, Emma joined Garrett and Felix on a picnic blanket and asked, "How bad do you think it is?"

Garrett understood. "Without all the reports and financial information, I don't know. Roger mentioned there were liquidity problems and without Macy's, it sounds like operations will need to be reduced, that means layoffs and selling off or renting out the presses and warehouse space. Selling Worth Papers outright might be the best option—"

"Selling Worth Papers! But it's Granddad's legacy. It's tied to our family—the name, this place," said Emma squeezing Felix, who had crawled over to her.

"I know, Emma. Isabel said the same thing. But without anyone to oversee it, to fix the major problems, bring it into the 21st century—Roger is right: Stationery is a hard sell in the digital age—"

"But it's not dead! I love stationery. Just not always the old-fashioned stuff that Worth Papers still makes. But people are still getting married, everyone still sends out paper wedding invitations."

"But it doesn't mean Worth Papers isn't suffering from digital. And competition. If Worth Papers is to survive, either within the family or bought up by an outside entity, it'll need new products that will tempt a modern audience, a new business model that will complement digital, something. I'll know more tomorrow, after my meeting with Roger and some of the senior staff. I can give you a debriefing afterward."

That evening over dinner, Mila asked, "Where's Uncle Adam? Why isn't he here?"

Emma felt his absence as well. It was normal within this family constellation for him to be present, she told herself.

"He's away on a business trip," she told Mila.

"Speaking of Adam, what do you think of his new apartment? It's swanky, isn't it? A total steal. I'm certain his realtor friend will be making sure the favor's returned," said Garrett with a wink.

Emma's ears perked up, but she tried to appear nonchalant. "Actually, I don't know much about it. Just that it's in Tribeca. We haven't had much opportunity to talk lately."

"I guess you'll have even less opportunity to talk after he moves. Considering your love-hate relationship, that might not be a bad thing," added Isabel.

How could her sister and brother-in-law be so insensitive?

"Is Uncle Adam moving? Are you moving with him, Auntie

Emma? You have to, you know, if you're going to get married one day. Will I get to be the flower girl?"

Garrett and Isabel exchanged glances and laughed in the way that parents do when they think their child has said something either very clever or very funny or both. Thank goodness, thought Emma, otherwise they'd notice how red her cheeks were. To her relief, her cell phone began to ring.

"Excuse me," said Emma with a glance at her phone. "It's Annalisa and we've been playing phone tag for days. Thanks for making dinner, Iz, I'll help clean up later."

"Hi, Ans! So glad you called back," Emma said, as she shut her bedroom door behind her.

"Emma, finally! Is your dad okay? What happened?"

Emma gave a briefing of the events of the last days.

Annalisa explained why she'd been trying to get a hold of Emma the week before—a stupid misunderstanding between her and Tom that had caused her to become insecure and jealous. "I thought once we were married and living together, those doubts would go away, but apparently not. Anyway, things are all good again."

Emma apologized for her very rude, drunken, middle-of-the-night call.

"It's okay, Emma. Tom was a bit peeved, since it woke him, too, but it was no biggie. But you said something about meeting someone. What about Ryan?"

"I said something about meeting someone? Oh, yes, I think I remember vaguely now. It was just a one-night stand."

"'Just a one-night stand'? Emma, this is you we're talking about here. You don't do 'just a one-night stand.' Who was he? Someone hot?"

"Yes, very. A soccer player."

"Really? Tom's hugely into soccer, I've even watched some of the World Cup with him; see what married life does to you? What team does he play for?"

"I can't remember; the Boston team, I think. His name's Diogo, he's from Portugal and he played in the World Cup."

"Diogo. Wait! Emma, don't tell me you hooked up with Diogo Cruz, the guy whose pregnant wife has filed for divorce over cheating and domestic violence charges! He also has a toddler."

"No way, you're kidding!" said Emma, unconsciously rubbing her wrist. "It can't be him, can it?"

"Tall, dark and handsome?"

"Yes. Oh God!"

"Can you get online, Emma? Go search for Diogo Cruz. He's been in the news for weeks. How could you have missed it?"

"I don't know!" said Emma, typing the name into her laptop. "You know I don't follow sports."

"But it's getting into the gossip magazines now, partly because of how hot he is. He was in that spread of soccer players in their undies that Annie Lebowitz shot for *Vanity Fair*."

"Oh no, it is him," said Emma, looking at the pictures on her screen. She clicked a headline that mentioned cheating and divorce. She skimmed through the article with a dull sense of dread. At least the article had downplayed the physical abuse charges. "But others at the party would have recognized him. They would have told me."

"Who were you with?"

"Well, Sasha of course, was there; she invited me. And Lauren; she would've known who he was. Oh, no, Lauren! Shit, shit, shit!"

"When does *In the Know* hit newsstands?"

"Tomorrow morning."

CHAPTER FORTY-SIX

At least Emma was prepared, which was more than she could've said for Juliette when the Blake-nanny scandal broke. At least she was tucked up here in Hartfield, relatively safe from the paparazzi.

On the cover were Tom Cruise and Katie Holmes. Emma's relief was short-lived as she spotted the headshots of Diogo and Ryan along the side of the magazine. A tiny round picture of her face was inset between them above the bright yellow words: "Diogo vs. Ryan." Beneath that: "Bad boy Diogo scores again!" She flipped the magazine open and there she was on Diogo's lap. There he was licking her chest. A third photo caught them embracing in the elevator before the elevator doors had slid shut. There was no mistaking what those pictures suggested, and for once, thought Emma wryly, they were right.

Her blatant hedonism was there for all the world to see. She cringed at the thought of Adam seeing those pictures, though why she would she wasn't quite sure. Probably if she'd listened to him that night and stayed in, none of this would have happened.

There was another picture of Diogo with his arms around a woman with a bump and a cute little girl—his wife and daughter.

And there was a picture of Ryan and her from Friday night at Pastis; he was rubbing his eyes and looked woeful and hopeless.

The story read that Casanova Diogo couldn't keep his cock in his soccer shorts or his hands off any attractive woman, his latest conquest being Emma Worth. Apparently, they were two of a kind, she being a lying cheat, telling friends that everything was wonderful between her and Ryan on the same night that she was caught in the act with Diogo. Ryan's publicist confirmed that Emma and Ryan were not together, had only briefly dated, and that Emma had only ever used Ryan for the publicity.

Emma looked at the pictures and reread the article, fuming. How had this happened? They'd made her sound like a despicable woman with no morals, someone who used people for her own gains.

Suddenly, the full impact of how Juliette must have felt hit Emma.

The worst part of it, thought Emma, was that on some level, she deserved it. This was her payback for what she'd done to Juliette. And this was Lauren's payback; Emma had been betrayed by Lauren before, and it was her own stupid fault for letting it happen again. And had someone warned her about Diogo, would it have made a difference? She'd been so upset by the fight with Adam, compounded by the encounter with Lauren and Anja, that she'd gotten drunk as quickly as possible. Completely forgetting about Ryan, she'd named her mission and had her heart set on Diogo; she doubted anyone's warning would have deterred her by that point. She'd only have laughed it off as jealousy and been more determined to get into Diogo's bed.

And what did it mean for her reputation? The article had already implied that *Worth It* fans would see what a fake and immoral person she was, definitely not the kind of person to look up to as a role model.

"What's up?" Isabel asked, coming into the kitchen.

Emma passed the magazine, opened up to the offending

pages, to her sister. Isabel looked at the pictures and skimmed the article, shaking her head. "Oh wow, oh wow, Emma. I'm sorry, this is horrible! What's the real story?"

Emma sighed. "I had no idea who he was; I was drunk and okay, I slept with him. But that's all."

"What about Ryan?" Isabel asked.

"There's nothing between Ryan and I, never was. It was just a publicity stunt. He's a friend. They've actually made it sound way more exciting than it really is."

"So it's true that you used him?"

"No!" said Emma. Yet, even Isabel believed her of stooping so low. What would the rest of the world think? "No, it wasn't like that at all. I really liked him. When he asked me to the premiere, I was hoping something would happen. It was only afterward that he revealed it was his publicist's idea."

Still, it didn't mean that Ryan would forgive her. Or should. They'd had an agreement, however casual it was, and she'd made him look like a cuckolded fool. Emma dropped her head in her hands.

"What are you going to do?"

"I don't know. What can I do? I suppose just wait for it to blow over. I'm just glad I'm up here, away from the city, away from it all."

"Me too," Isabel said, handing back the magazine. She gave Emma a hug and went to the cupboards to get bowls and cereal. "It's so peaceful here. Mila and Felix are really enjoying the gardens and all the space. And Mila is loving her kindergarten."

"I'm glad, Isabel; I'm glad you're here with me. And I'm enjoying having the kids around. Dad will love it too when he gets out of the hospital. And Isabel, sorry for being so selfish before and only thinking about myself and my problems."

After Isabel left to give the kids their breakfast, Emma poured herself a mug of coffee and went onto the terrace to be alone with her thoughts. Adam had warned her that if she continued to go down this career path and court media attention, everything she did would be scrutinized and everyone would know who she was sleeping with. Well, it seemed his predictions had come true.

Now she just needed to fortify herself for the fallout that was certain to follow.

CHAPTER FORTY-SEVEN

First the national diamond chain synonymous with engagement rings called to say they were pulling the ads featuring Emma; the scandal Emma was embroiled in was not compatible with their message.

Emma had expected as much, still the call was devastating.

Then Amalia called to chew Emma out about her behavior. "I thought you had promise, Emma, that you knew how to play the game. I couldn't have been more wrong."

"How could you make me sound as though I was the one using Ryan when it was the other way around?" retaliated Emma.

"I had to salvage Ryan's reputation somehow. But it was what it was, Emma: an exchange of interests, an agreement. Don't act as though you didn't benefit from being linked with Ryan. Ryan told me after the premiere that it was your idea to keep pretending you're together. So don't be so quick to cast blame."

Could Amalia be right? Did Emma simply use people for her own gains and blame others?

"As far as the public is concerned, you and Ryan were dating," Amalia continued. "So you had no right to go around practically fucking someone else in public. At least wait until you get into the hotel room. And next time, make sure you know who's lap you end up in!"

"Thanks for the tip, Amalia. I'll keep it in mind for next time," said Emma and stabbed the disconnect button.

At least Hailey's call to warn her of the news, in case she didn't already know, was the one balm to a day full of rejection. After Emma told Hailey about her father and being at Hartfield, Hailey had offered to pack some extra clothes for Emma or take care of anything Emma needed. It seemed she'd forgiven Emma, and Emma was grateful for a friend like Hailey. In fact, she was grateful for all the friends she could get.

The bad news kept coming: The Enchanted team had found the footage for the commercial unusable and was going to scrap the whole campaign. They also refused to pay Emma for her work because she had broken the contract by showing up on set drunk. She was lucky, the legal department argued, that they weren't going to sue her for sunken costs and damages. Emma was certain they were giving her the ax because of the scandal.

Several sponsors and advertisers also wanted to sever ties with *Worth It*. Intrepid reporters and bloggers asked her for exclusives to explain her side of the story.

Ryan still hadn't called, which probably meant he was too disgusted or upset with her to speak to her.

Emma hadn't thought the day could get any worse, but she'd been wrong. Yet again.

"The situation is pretty dire," said Garrett later that night, while Isabel was putting Mila to bed. "Things have been going downhill for a long time. There have been year-on-year losses on top of low company morale because employees feel they have no leader to steer a ship that's headed straight for the rocks. Everyone's jumping ship before it sinks, so some of the best, longest-serving and most loyal employees have left or are looking for other opportunities. Who can blame them really."

As a result, explained Garrett, there'd been delays in vendor payments and late shipments. Customer service was suffering. Roger and her father, he said, were like the blind leading the blind—Roger being an operations guy, already running at his limit, and neither a leader or very courageous.

Emma swallowed, guilt flooding her. She shouldn't have let the situation get as bad as it had. She should have, yet again, listened to Adam and tried to better gauge the company's state of affairs. Not taken her father's rejection so personally. "What are we going to do now?"

"I'm in touch with an outside auditor to assess the financial damage and find out how much Worth Papers is currently worth. Once we know this, we can either try to sell Worth Papers at a steep loss—"

"Sell the company? We can't do that!"

"I'm sorry, Emma, but it seems like there are few other options, if any at all. We can try to sell off some property, for example, your building—"

"Sell the building, oh no!"

Emma pictured Belinda Bates and her mother out on the street, and her heart ached.

"I know that's not pleasant to hear, it's your home—"

"I'm not concerned for me," said Emma. "It's Belinda and poor Mrs. Bates I'm worried about. Where will they go? Where will they live? They won't be able to afford the rent anywhere in the city. They'd have to live far out in the boroughs. Belinda will have to commute ages to work and she works such long, irregular hours at the hospital. Mrs. Bates will be alone all the time in some new neighborhood where they won't know a soul!"

"That's very considerate of you, Emma. I'm sure we can come up with some solution for them."

"But couldn't we sell something else?"

"There's just Hartfield, and frankly, Hartfield won't be worth half as much as what we can get for your building, considering the location and potential rental income," said Garrett. With the money from the building, they could pay off the debts and still potentially sell the company at a profit. "But it may not be easy to find a buyer in this climate; a stationery company is not likely to do well."

"And if we don't sell? The building or the company? What about filing for bankruptcy?"

Garrett explained that it wasn't an option because Morley still owned Hartfield and Emma's building. Their only chance, he said, is if they could get someone to invest millions and find someone capable, dedicated, and forward-thinking to turn the company around. "But it's not like that's going to happen. When your dad's better, I'll explain the situation and make him come to a decision. But we need to act fast. Before another major distributor pulls out or the company loses more money."

After everything, Emma felt nothing. It was as if it were all happening to someone else with her watching from afar, unable to connect. Numb and exhausted, Emma fell asleep and dreamt.

CHAPTER FORTY-EIGHT

S he was a contestant on some convoluted version of *Who Wants to be a Millionaire?* Adam was the host. Belinda was trapped in what looked to be a giant birdcage on the stage. Her dad was strapped down to a giant printing press. Her goal was to answer three questions correctly. For the first correct answer, she would free Belinda. For the next correct answer, she could stop the machine from crushing her father. And if she managed to do both and answer the last question, she would win the key to the kingdom of Worth Papers and she would be crowned the queen.

Jeering her from the sidelines were Chloe and Zak, Lauren and Amalia. Cheering her on were Hailey, Isabel, Garett and Annalisa. Adam asked the first question: "Which of these popular '80s and '90s movies best describes Emma Worth: A.) *Fame*, B.) *Pretty Woman*, C.) *Clueless*, D.) *Girls Just Want to Have Fun*. After some deliberation, thinking about all she'd learned lately, Emma hazarded C. Belinda Bates was freed. "What is Emma Worth's biggest flaw?" was the next question. Her choices were: A.) She thinks too well of herself; B.) she only sees what she wants to see and doesn't see what's right in front of her eyes; C.) she uses people for her own gains; D.) all of the above. She started to say C, but was stopped by Adam's frown; she could see Isabel and Annalisa's mouths moving, trying to tell her the correct answer, but she couldn't hear it above the hissing and booing and calls of "slut" and "home-wrecker" coming from the audience. Finally, she answered D. Adam's face lit up and her father was saved. The third and final question was the hardest. It was: "What became of Emma Worth?" She looked at the four choices and had no idea. She felt herself sweat. She asked for 50-50 and her choices narrowed down to A.) She saved Worth Papers, or C.) She died penniless and alone.

She saw Hailey biting her fingernails and Lauren's taunting face. She used her lifeline and asked Isabel for help. Isabel told her it was A. She told Adam her final answer was A. He smiled then, a warm radiant smile that felt like sunshine and warmed her whole body. The crowd disappeared; it was just her and Adam on stage, and he was handing her a dragonfly-shaped key.

But before he could reach her, Ryan and Diogo leapt onto the stage. Caught in a tug of war, Emma was being pulled by Ryan into a spotlight with fans and flashbulbs waiting, while Diogo was trying to pull her into his bed. Adam glared at her, sunshine replaced by darkness and coldness. She shivered, and shouted, "Stop!"

The word jolted her awake.

Her heart thumping, her breath ragged, Emma sucked at the cool, early morning air, and let it out slowly until she had managed to calm down. The house was silent; a thin glowing streak shone in the blue-black sky. She pulled on an old cardigan of her dad's and wrapped it tightly around herself, trying to find the warmth she'd dreamt about.

It was time to think about her future.

The Enchanted shoot and what Ryan had said over dinner at Pastis only reiterated that being a celebrity was nowhere near as glitzy as it looked in the media. For someone like Ryan, with talent and a passion for acting, his private life was what he sacrificed for his art. For her, with no passion for acting, no talent for posing in front of a camera, it was just a fool's errand.

After the premiere, she had been hailed as the next style icon and been adored. Now she was vilified as a liar, cheater, homewrecker and slut, and the repercussions would continue to come. If this was what being famous meant, then she wanted no part of it.

Her 15 minutes were over. Perhaps she had another three minutes to go, but it would be infamy rather than fame.

And her blog? Even if her reputation survived this, Emma's heart wasn't in it. It didn't feel right to be telling young women how to behave when she was getting it all wrong, all the time. She'd written about how important image was. And look at her image now.

In the end, the image she curated for the world didn't matter. It didn't matter what the public thought. Because her family and friends would see through it. And their opinion was the only one that counted because, without them, she'd have nobody.

She'd forgiven her father and the past, and she would make a fresh start with him. She would be a better sister to Isabel and a good aunt to her niece and nephew. She would be a better friend to Hailey. If her friendship with Adam was still salvageable, she would try her best to listen to what he had to say; he'd only ever had her best interest at heart. And she would be kinder to Belinda and try to save the building for her and Mrs. Bate's sake.

And suddenly, it was as if the spotlight that had blinded her and led her astray had been switched off, and she could see clearly.

All this time, since that rift with her father, she'd been trying to figure out what to do with her life, to find her passion and her purpose.

And here it was, right in front of her eyes. She'd forgotten about wanting to be the queen of Worth Papers & Stationery, about playing work with her rag dolls, about those visits to the company site with her grandfather. At NYU, she'd imagined how what she was studying would help her when she eventually headed up the company. She had expected it as her due, which was why, when her father had refused to let her complete her final project on Worth Papers, when he wouldn't even listen to her plans to come work for the company after she graduated, it had been such a blow. He'd told her it wasn't going to happen, so she should just accept it and get a job in fashion or a similar field.

That had shattered the self-worth she'd worked so hard through high school and college to build. She'd begun to act like the image-conscious, shallow, self-centered young woman her father expected of her; perhaps that would finally make him proud of her.

But now she knew the truth: He'd only been trying to save her from his and her mother's fate. The thing was, she wasn't them. She wanted to be involved with the company, needed and craved it; it was in her blood.

This was what she wanted, and this was her one and only chance to make it a possibility. This was her chance to save Worth Papers & Stationery, for her father and Belinda and herself and all the employees who depended upon it for their livelihoods.

It wasn't going to be easy; she had so little practical experience. But she could do this; she felt it in her bones. She would move back to Hartfield and do her damnedest to turn the company around.

CHAPTER FORTY-NINE

Because she was going to have some convincing to do, Emma didn't share her decision about Worth Papers right away. She needed to be able to make a strong business case for herself first. And for that, she would need time to prepare. Yet, already, her mind was churning out ideas.

Over breakfast, she asked for Isabel's professional opinion, asked why she thought people weren't buying Worth products anymore.

Isabel told her the designs were outdated, the trend in design having gone toward a different aesthetic. Given a choice, she said, between a box of Worth cards or one with a fresh modern spin, most young people would go for the latter, even if the quality was worse.

"So with new designs, could Worth Stationery be more competitive?"

"Mila, please keep your milk in the bowl; your cereal bowl is not a splash pool. Sorry, Emma, yes, realistically, I don't see why not. But it would take a lot more than fresh designs to get the company back on its feet."

"What other trends are you seeing now in design? I mean in terms of digital and technology?" asked Emma.

With only three interruptions from Mila and Felix, Isabel explained that digital technology was making customized photo cards and personalized greeting cards cheap and easy to produce.

Emma laughed and covered her face with her hands to play peek-a-boo with Felix, enjoying his gurgling laughter when she removed her hands.

"You seem very chipper this morning, considering that you're an infamous home-wrecker and about to be thrown out of your building," observed Isabel as she spooned oatmeal into Felix's mouth.

"I am, aren't I?" said Emma, practically giggling. "I've been doing some soul searching and coming to some conclusions. I'll let you know more, but I'm going to spend the rest of the morning in Dad's study before I go see him this afternoon."

After breakfast, Emma wrote down what Isabel had said and brainstormed ideas and began to research the competition online. Before arriving at the hospital, she made a pit stop at the bookstore and purchased several business-related books. That night, she perused the books and tried to understand the different problems facing Worth Papers. The next day, Emma did a SWOT analysis—identifying Worth Papers' strengths and weaknesses, opportunities and threats—until it was time for her and Isabel to go pick up their father from the hospital.

As soon as they were in the car, Isabel said, "Okay, Emma, what's going on? You're acting all giddy like you're in love. And you've been locked away in Dad's study for two days."

After making Isabel swear not to say anything for another day or two, Emma told Isabel that she intended to make the company profitable again.

"But how?"

"I'm not totally sure yet, but I've got some ideas. I still have to do a lot of work, and we need to know exactly where Worth

Papers stands financially, but the thing is, Isabel, I believe in it; for the first time, I feel invested, not like with the blog or whatever else I've done before. It just feels right."

"Are you sure, Emma? It would be tons of work, little free time, a lot of stress and responsibilities. And from what Garrett says, there's no guarantee that it's even possible."

"I know, Isabel. I've thought about it all. Yes, it feels daunting, and I'm going to need a lot of help, including yours. Would you be interested in shaping the design aesthetic and creative direction of the company? I know you're capable."

By the time they arrived at the hospital, Isabel was fully on board. Emma's energy and enthusiasm had rubbed off, especially when Emma started to tell Isabel about her idea to provide a customizable online card service, with modern designer templates for wedding invitations and photo templates for save the dates, thank you cards, baby announcements, and Christmas cards. The latter would be printed on premium card stock with tasteful patterns, personalized message, or extra photos on the back, differentiating them from the competition, who simply printed the cards on flimsy photo paper with the Fujifilm or Kodak watermark on the back.

"We'll collaborate with well-known graphic designers, illustrators, fashion designers," Emma explained. The idea, Emma said, was to create premium, customized designer stationery that people would be happy to pay more for. At the same time, using digital printing technology, they would be able to keep costs down while providing high-quality designs.

～

THE NEXT EVENING, after Morley and the children were settled in bed for the night, Emma told Garrett her plans for Worth Papers. As backup, she provided a plotted grid showing where Worth Papers stood among the competition and one that showed Worth

Papers' strengths and weaknesses and the opportunities and threats. She revealed an outline of the strategic marketing plan of the new direction Worth Papers would embark on to take advantage of new opportunities. Isabel chimed in her support and showed the mockups Emma had asked her to create.

Garrett expressed doubt and played devil's advocate for a while. Having prepared for it, Emma was able to respond to his suppositions and doubts with informed, well-thought-through answers.

"I'm impressed," Garrett finally said as Emma let out her breath. "Adam's the businessman, of course, so he'd have the insights; you'll probably want to run it by him, but you've convinced me, Emma. Though I do have to warn you, I'm not the one that needs convincing, nor your Dad; it's the employees that really need to be on board. And they're not necessarily going to be an easy sell."

Emma nodded, knowing this was just the beginning. No, it wouldn't be easy, and maybe she was naive enough to think she could do it. But for the first time in a long time, she felt the thrill of success that came, not from making a lucky guess or calling on a connection, not for looking a certain way or being someone's date, but from real effort.

It was decided that, starting Monday if Morley had no objections, Emma would effectively be in charge and start meeting with senior staff to get a full grasp of the situation. The auditor would come back with initial reports on Wednesday. Garrett would remain as financial consultant and sounding board in the beginning. In the meantime, Isabel would do an assessment of Worth Paper products to see which lines and styles would need to be discontinued and which could be tweaked.

The next morning, Emma, with Garrett and Isabel's support, told Morley of her plans for the company going forward.

Her nervousness about needing to convince her father was unfounded. Once he saw that Emma was serious and really wanted to take on the challenge, he gratefully agreed. "It wasn't right of me to try to tell you what to do, Emma, to shape what you did with your life. You're yourself, not me, not your mother; I realize now that you have that spark that your granddad and your uncle Robert had had, and it was wrong of me to try to deny that, to try to deny you their legacy. I just hope I'm not too late."

CHAPTER FIFTY

Ryan had suggested a divey Brazilian bar and restaurant in the East Village. Emma walked in out of the brightness of a setting sun and adjusted her eyes to the dim interior. Ryan's text had been cryptic, only saying that he would be grateful if Emma could meet him; that it was important. Curious and slightly nervous, Emma scanned the room for him.

Standing up from a back booth, Ryan greeted her with his arms wide and planted a big, loud kiss on her cheek.

Emma hadn't known what to expect, but after all the bad things that had happened to her lately and Amalia's call, she'd braced herself for Ryan's anger or disgust.

"Gotten into any new scandals lately?" Ryan teased.

But maybe she was going to get off lightly. Maybe her luck was changing? She could only hope.

"Not that I know of. But the night's still young," said Emma matching his tone.

Ryan guffawed and Emma smiled. This was more like it; she ordered a caipirinha and felt herself relaxing.

"I'm a little offended you don't look more miserable," joked Emma. "I did break your heart."

"Ha," said Ryan before his tone turned serious. "How have you been dealing with it all, anyway? Juliette says she hasn't seen you around all week."

Emma quickly caught Ryan up on events since Chloe's party.

"So while the scandal was quite a blow," Emma concluded, "in light of everything else, I couldn't really dwell on it, which was a good thing. It helped me see, probably faster and more clearly, that I was just some pathetic wannabe, blinded by the spotlight."

Saying it like this, Emma was astonished by just what a shallow, starstruck fool she'd been. No wonder Adam had gotten so upset with her.

"It still doesn't give Amalia the right to treat you as she did. I fired her, you know."

"You did? Because of me?"

"Partially," Ryan answered. "I didn't get into this industry to be some publicist's puppet. I've learned the hard way that you can't always avoid playing the game, but as much as I can get away with it, I'll try to avoid it, and try to live my life on my own terms. I'm sick of the lies and pretending. I'm ready to come clean . . . about everything."

"Oh," said Emma, "you mean you're going to come out of the closet?"

Ryan spluttered on his beer and slapped his chest to clear his air passage. "Oh God, Emma. I'd nearly forgotten about that. Like I said, I'm done with all these lies and secrets."

"But . . . ? You mean . . . ?"

His blue eyes danced. "I'm not gay. Never was."

"But why did you tell me . . . ?"

"Emma, I never told you I was gay. You assumed I was," said Ryan.

Emma thought back to the night of the premiere. She'd tried to seduce a jumpy Ryan; he clearly hadn't been interested. So what had she done? She'd concluded it was because he was into guys. She'd made up her mind that he wasn't attracted to women to protect her ego. Emma shook her head, unable to believe how self-absorbed she was. Now that she was starting to see with blinders removed, what else had she been wrong about?

"But if you're not gay, then why . . . ?" Emma stopped and took a long sip of her drink to try to cool the burning in her cheeks.

"Why wasn't I interested in sleeping with you?" he finished for her.

Emma nodded, not looking up. Had her ego always been this fragile? Did she fear rejection so much that she had to make false assumptions? Was this a legacy from having a narcissistic mother who had never wanted her? Or believing her father was rejecting her when he only wanted to protect her?

"Emma, lack of attraction wasn't the problem. The thing is, there's someone else."

Emma's head shot up. "What! Who?"

"That's the reason I asked you to meet me tonight," said Ryan. "To tell you in person—I owe you that much—before you read about it in *In the Know* or hear about it from Belinda or someone."

"Uh-oh, I'm not sure I can take any more scandals or surprises," said Emma, only half-jokingly.

"Me neither," said Ryan.

"So? The suspense is killing me. Who have you been dating? An actress? Someone famous? Is she married or something?"

"It's Juliette."

"Juliette!"

"You're surprised? I was certain you'd sussed out that we were secretly dating."

"Juliette," repeated Emma. "Wow, I had no idea whatsoever!" Yes, she'd been wrong about that, too.

"We tried to hide it. As far as we know, no one's guessed our secret."

"Except Adam," said Emma, remembering what he'd told her at Chloe's party. "But how? When? Why keep it a secret?"

They'd met in France at the wrap party for *Between the Lines*,

Ryan told her. "We got to talking and there was this amazing chemistry. Most of the cast and crew were done but Blake and I had a few more scenes to shoot in Paris. So I convinced Juliette to come out with me one night in Paris. We just really connected. It was like Ethan Hawke and Julie Delpy in *Before Sunrise*."

"And then what happened?"

Juliette and the Dixon-Lanes returned to L.A.. A year later Ryan was cast in *Episode* and moved to L.A.. At an industry event, he ran into Blake, who invited him to his 50th birthday party.

"When I saw Juliette again and heard her play and sing, I fell for her all over again. This time, I wasn't going to let her slip through my fingers. We started dating, but Juliette insisted on keeping it a secret. She said she didn't want Blake and Genevieve to know. I think it was because she didn't think it was going to work out between us. She was also terrified of the media and being in the spotlight; you know how private she is. I still had a girlfriend in England. It was more or less over, but neither of us had made it official, so I initially agreed to Juliette's plan. And because of both our schedules, it worked out."

Eventually, Ryan said, they decided that he and Juliette would go away together while *Episode* was on hiatus, Blake and Genevieve having agreed to give Juliette the summer off. During the summer, they would make their relationship public and Juliette would give her notice. She'd then join Ryan in Berlin before they headed back to L.A. together, where Juliette would set up as a piano teacher.

"Because of the timing of *Between the Lines'* release and Juliette's gran's stroke, we ended up in New York. I was naive and didn't know I would need a publicist and all the other things that went with being in a summer blockbuster. When Amalia learned about Juliette, she asked us to keep our relationship secret until after the premiere because she felt I needed to be seen with someone who was more comfortable in the spotlight."

"So you got me to be your date for the premiere, then let me think you were gay to spare my feelings because you were secretly dating Juliette," said Emma, her face burning red.

Ryan nodded, looking sheepish.

"You asshole!" hissed Emma. How she'd flirted with Ryan the night they'd had dinner with Juliette and Adam! How she'd tried to seduce him after the premiere! How obnoxiously they'd flirted at Chloe's party in front of everyone! "Did you and Juliette laugh at me behind my back?"

Ryan shook his head vehemently. "Of course not, Emma. You've every right to despise me. I acted like a total arse, and I'm sorry. I'm ashamed of putting you and Juliette through all that heartache because of some stupid Hollywood image Amalia was trying to create for me. We did such a good job of pretending, you and me, that Juliette even started getting jealous."

"Poor Juliette! After all she'd been through!" said Emma. "And it was *you* who gave Juliette the piano and the necklace?"

Ryan nodded. "When you started with the secret-admirer thing, I had to throw you off the scent, so I made up that thing about Blake and Juliette. That was low, I know, but at the time it was just a bit of fun. I didn't think you would tell anyone else, let alone someone who worked for a gossip magazine," said Ryan.

Emma opened her mouth to tell Ryan off. To make him feel bad for trying to put the blame on her. But she'd been as complicit as Ryan, hadn't she? She'd been the one who'd insisted on meddling in Juliette's business, wondering why she was in New York, not believing that the piano was a present from Blake and Genevieve, and pushing the secret-admirer angle. Telling Lauren was just the inevitable next step.

Her flare of anger at Ryan burned out. "But when the gossip broke, why didn't you and Juliette just come clean then? The premiere was over by then."

"That's what I wanted to do. But Juliette said it would only bring more media attention. It would turn into this love triangle between Juliette, Blake and I, and everyone would want to know more about—"

"—this paragon who'd managed to snare two of Hollywood's sexiest stars," finished Emma.

"Yeah. She couldn't imagine more media attention or having people digging even deeper into her past than they already had."

"So what's changed now? I thought Juliette was going to Seattle."

"She was; we broke up the night before Chloe's party when she told me she was taking the job. I tried everything to get her to change her mind. It was the hardest, most bittersweet night of my life. Which was why I was so obnoxious at the party. Trying to spite Juliette and make her jealous. I'm sorry Emma, for using you like that. Again. But something I said must have gotten through. After Chloe's party, Juliette said she'd reconsidered and hoped it wasn't too late."

"Wow, that's . . . romantic," said Emma. "Do Belinda and the others know?"

"Juliette's telling her aunt as we speak, so everyone should know by now, too. Of course, she had to break it to the family in Seattle and to Chloe, who's not speaking to her now."

"It figures," said Emma, laughing.

"Does this mean you forgive me?" asked Ryan, giving her his cutest puppy dog look.

"I'll have to think it over," said Emma, not quite able to suppress a smile. "But I do feel I owe Juliette another apology."

"Then let's go back to Belinda's and you can tell Juliette yourself."

CHAPTER FIFTY-ONE

The mood at Belinda's apartment was jubilant. Emma was grateful for the warm welcome, grateful to be included in the family celebration.

All these years, Emma realized, she'd regarded Juliette with a mix of pity and jealousy.

She'd always felt superior to Juliette because the Worths were rich and important, and the Bates were beholden to them. She'd felt socially superior to Juliette because she had connections, and Juliette had few to no friends. And she'd been confident that, in any contest with Juliette, barring a musical one, Emma would always come out on top. For these reasons, Emma had always pitied Juliette.

At the same time, Emma had been jealous of Juliette's beauty, Juliette's musical talent, and perhaps some inner depth Juliette possessed that Emma lacked. As perverse as it sounded, Emma had even been jealous that Juliette's parents had died. Juliette didn't have to wonder what was so awful and unlovable about her that her own mother would abandon her and her father would push her away; lucky Juliette could simply be secure in her parents' perfect, eternal love. And, Emma realized, she'd been jealous because Juliette had Belinda, a parental figure who loved her unconditionally and was proud of everything she did.

She remembered, too, how jealous she'd been when she'd thought that Adam was interested in Juliette. Had it been true, it would have been far more devastating to Emma than tonight's revelation. She shoved the thought aside.

Congratulating and hugging Juliette now, Emma found it was like hugging a friend, an equal.

"What changed your mind?" she asked Juliette, once all the embarrassed explanations and apologies were out of the way.

"About Ryan? My mother followed my dad to Montreal and Paris, but she'd never learned to speak French well, didn't work, and didn't feel like she fitted in. I didn't want to be like that, following Ryan around like a weight, being hounded by paparazzi, not having a private life, my own life. But my mother had a depressive personality, so maybe she wouldn't have been happy anywhere. In the end, I realized I wasn't my mother and I needed to take my own risks in life. I mean, what's the worst that could happen? I've survived my parents' death, so I'd survive if things didn't work out with Ryan. I'd already survived a gossip magazine scandal, and I'd survive another one."

How little she'd understood Juliette! Emma regretted that she hadn't made more of an effort to get to know her.

Belinda, as could be expected, was beside herself with happiness for Juliette, clucking around like a mother hen while she served champagne and snacks.

Seeing Juliette and Ryan together, Emma felt a small pang of envy. She left them alone to go find Belinda, who was bustling around the kitchen.

Time for more apologizing.

"Belinda," Emma said, "could you find it in your heart to forgive me for the nasty things I said to you last week? It was completely unjustified, and I am truly, sincerely sorry."

"Oh, that," said Belinda, reddening, flapping her hands. "It was nothing. Nothing at all. I'd forgotten all about it. You had every right, I can be . . . I can be—I guess with all the jabbering—pretty annoying. I'm sure I deserved everything you said. It's my fault. I'm sure I drove you to it."

"No, Belinda," said Emma, laying a gentle hand on Belinda's arm to still it. "It was completely undeserved. I had other stuff on my mind; I took it out on you. I'm sorry."

Emma then told Belinda about her father's heart attack. She patiently answered all of Belinda's questions about her dad's care and his diet and exercise and listened to Belinda's repeated best wishes about her father's speedy recovery.

"Would you like to visit him sometime?" Emma asked on a whim, seeing Belinda's genuine concern, aware now that her father and Belinda had been acquainted once upon a time, had even been friends, perhaps. She thought of Adam. "I could drive you out to Hartfield."

Belinda was silent as she considered the offer. "Yes, perhaps, if your dad doesn't mind. Yes, I would like that, Emma. But only if it's not too much trouble, of course. Hartfield is so beautiful. What a privilege it was to go there as a guest at Annalisa's wedding."

"Why didn't you ever tell me that my parents lived here? That you'd taken care of me as a baby?" After asking the questions, Emma remembered that it had been her own assumption that her parents had always lived at Hartfield; she'd never bothered to ask.

"Emma, it was a very, very long time ago, ancient history," said Belinda, taking off and wiping her glasses.

Emma was surprised; here was one topic that Belinda didn't care to speak about.

Emma did not reveal the plight of Worth Papers, not wanting to worry Belinda unnecessarily. But she did inform Belinda it was likely she would be based out of Hartfield for the next couple of weeks at least, using her father's recovery as an excuse.

"What a wonderful daughter you are, Emma. I know your

father will appreciate it. He loves you so much; I never knew a father to love a child as much as he loved you."

Emma's heart clenched. She gave Belinda a grateful smile and a hug.

"Oh Emma," said Belinda, clearly surprised by the gesture, a thin film of sheen in her eyes. "In all this excitement, I nearly forgot to tell you that Adam told me he wouldn't have time for a goodbye party."

Emma's pulse quickened at the mention of Adam. The whole evening, she'd felt his absence as keenly as if he'd been there.

"I still can't get over the fact that he's actually leaving here. With you being away at Hartfield and him moving out next Friday, not to mention losing Juliette and Ryan on Monday, it sure will be lonely here," said Belinda, wiping at her eyes. "But what a wonderful summer we've had, I keep on telling Mother. What a privilege it was to have had Juliette for the summer and to get to know Ryan. When Mother starts to get sad, I say, 'Look on the bright side, Mother,' and I tell her exactly what I just told you," said Belinda with a sniff.

Emma's heart went out to Belinda and her mother, who had held and cared for her when her own mother hadn't wanted to. It reiterated for Emma why it was so important for her to save the company and save her building, and she promised herself she would make a special effort to see the Bates, even when she was living at Hartfield.

"When does Adam get back from his business trip?" Emma asked. She was certain it was Wednesday, but she wanted to make sure.

"Not until Wednesday, I believe. I'm pretty sure that's what he said. Or was it Thursday? No, definitely Wednesday because he said he would need Thursday to catch up with work and pack because the movers come on Friday. That bit I do remember for sure."

With all the secrets out in the open, all the false assumptions and accusations cleared up, Emma felt lighter than she had in months.

Now it was only Adam she needed to speak with. Adam with whom she needed to make things right.

Yes, on Wednesday night, after the meeting with the auditors in Highbury, she'd come back here and apologize to Adam. She'd patch up their relationship and make sure they were back to being on good terms when he left the building.

After feeling like she had emotionally matured by about 20 years in the last week, Emma wondered if she was finally ready to honestly examine her relationship with Adam. To see if she could risk opening her heart to something more.

CHAPTER FIFTY-TWO

Hailey hadn't been available for Saturday brunch but said she could meet Emma for a coffee before her dinner shift at Café Bisou started.

It was probably a good thing, thought Emma, as she spent the morning preparing for her Worth Papers debut on Monday. Then, clasping a list of boutiques and stationery stores on Madison and Fifth Avenues, Emma went uptown to do some research before catching up with Hailey.

Later that afternoon, when Hailey walked into the café they'd agreed upon, Emma immediately noticed how well Hailey looked. Wearing a figure-flattering dress Emma had never seen before, her curls bouncy and shiny, Hailey looked happy and confident. And she'd managed that with no help from me, Emma couldn't help noting.

"And you, Hailey? How have you been?" asked Emma after catching Hailey up on her decision about Worth Papers and the big news about Juliette and Ryan.

"I've been good, Emma. Really, really good," said Hailey, shining with an inner radiance, the same radiance Emma had spotted in Juliette last night: the glow of love.

"I'm so glad to hear that!" said Emma, truly happy for her friend. "What—or should I say who's—brought this about?"

"Is it that obvious?" asked Hailey, blushing and smiling. "Well, it's all because of Adam—"

"Adam!" exclaimed Emma. It felt like something inside her had shattered.

Images—some remembered, some imagined—flooded Emma's mind's eye: Adam escorting Hailey home from her launch party. Adam and Hailey leaving the premiere together—she'd thought he was with Juliette, but she'd picked the wrong woman. Hailey crying on Adam's shoulder after her botched interview. And most damning of all, Hailey leaving Adam's apartment last Friday morning, dressed for work; she'd spent the night with Adam.

Outwardly Emma held her face poker straight. But inside her systems had gone haywire: Her heart was palpitating wildly, irregularly. Nerves sent tingles throughout her body so every inch of her was hyperaware. The bottom had fallen out from her stomach. And her lungs weren't working; she couldn't seem to get enough air, and her breath kept catching in her throat.

"Yes, he's the most caring, sweet, thoughtful guy, isn't he?"

Emma could only nod, not trusting her voice.

Since getting to know Hailey better, Adam had definitely taken an interest in her, always asking Emma about her, speaking highly of her, and admonishing Emma about what he considered to be Emma's meddling in Hailey's life. Emma had assumed any interest he had in Hailey was relative to Emma, was some extension of his friendship with Emma. Yet, she'd been wrong. Again. He'd acted solely based on personal interest. *In Hailey.*

"I didn't want you to know, Emma, because I didn't think you would approve. I asked Adam to keep it quiet because—"

The trilling of Hailey's cell phone stopped Hailey mid-sentence. To Emma it sounded like the dull, repetitive warning of an emergency alarm, the one that had gone off inside her and was causing all the chaos in her body.

"It's Helene," said Hailey, looking at her screen. She pressed the accept button. "Hi, Helene, what's up?"

Half a minute later, Hailey hung up. "Sorry, Emma. Molly, another server, is sick and can't come in today. Helene's asked me to come in an hour early to cover for her. That means I've got to go now. I hope that's okay."

"Of course," said Emma, faking her best light-hearted tone and pasting on her brightest smile.

As soon as Hailey rushed out, Emma let her face fall and her body sag.

What she'd begun to examine last night in bed—turned around in her head as if it were some unknown creature's egg in her hands—were her feelings for Adam. She hadn't known whether something would hatch from it, and if so, what it would be. She'd only known it was delicate and had the potential to be something precious, so she would need to treat it with care.

Well, now she knew what was inside that egg. But it wasn't going to have a chance to hatch. She was too late.

Emma staggered outside, like a drunk from a bar.

Aimlessly she walked along the thronged sidewalk, bumping into people, unseeing of what was around her, only seeing the truth inside her: She *needed* Adam. He was the one person who'd always been there for her, had been there nearly her whole time in the city. He was the one who pointed out when she was behaving badly, who wanted to help her be a better person. He was the one whose approval she always sought, whose opinion mattered the most.

All this time, she'd taken him for granted. On some female level, she'd known he found her attractive and had reveled in it and kept the knowledge in her back pocket like an emergency credit card to be pulled out when she saw something amazing that she had to have in a shop window. She'd enjoyed the privileged place she had in his life. For she had been confident—in the way only a woman whose heart wasn't compromised could be—that she was special to him and that he'd never been truly serious about any of the women he'd dated. She'd been satisfied with their set-up because she didn't think she could take it if he'd gotten to know her—the most intimate, vulnerable essence of her—and found her wanting and unlovable, the way her mother had.

Tears blurred Emma's eyes. The sharp corner of a possessed shopper's boxy Barneys New York bag jabbed her in the thigh. Well, Emma, she told herself, swiping at her eyes. You're too damned late. Adam was irrefutably in love with Hailey. Irrefutably because he was too much of a gentleman to consciously toy with a woman's feelings, certainly not someone like Hailey's.

Hailey had stolen the thing Emma wanted right out from under Emma's nose before Emma had had a chance to reach into her back pocket and whip out that credit card.

But Adam was not some possession like this year's must-have designer bag; he was one of a kind. Nor had Hailey stolen him; she had won him fair and square.

Sure, the old Emma wouldn't have given up without a fight. May even have tried to tussle with Hailey, confident in her superiority. But now she wasn't so sure she was better than Hailey.

More importantly, she couldn't do that to Hailey. Hailey was her friend; one of the few she had. What was it that Adam had said? That Hailey had drawn the short end of the straw in their friendship, that Hailey was too good for her? He was right, and she had no intention of betraying Hailey again by competing with her for Adam's affection. She had already been responsible for giving Hailey one broken heart; she didn't want to be responsible for breaking it again. Even if Adam couldn't love her, he could be proud of her for being selfless, for staying out of people's business, and for being a better friend to Hailey.

Yes, she'd lost to Hailey of all people. Hailey! The David to her Goliath, the tortoise to her hare.

She'd lost the most important contest of her life.

She'd lost because she'd been too afraid to enter the ring.

She'd lost before she'd realized what the prize was.

She'd lost Adam.

And there was not one damned thing she could do about it.

All she could do was root for her friends from the sidelines.

CHAPTER FIFTY-THREE

On Tuesday, Emma pulled up at Hartfield after another soul-crushing day at work.

What had given her the idea that she could run Worth Papers & Stationery? It was definitely nothing like playing work with Hazel and Lottie LouLou, that was for damn sure.

She'd encountered employees at all levels who were sullen, unwilling to help, distrustful, condescending and disrespectful.

Oh my God, they'd been disrespectful. On Monday, when she'd been given a tour of the warehouse by the warehouse director, a group of male employees had had a copy of last week's *In the Know* open before them as they'd slid their eyes knowingly over her body. She heard one say, "I'd bang that!"

If it wasn't catcalling or whistles, it had been dirty, lascivious looks. And she was certain a senior manager had grabbed her ass when they'd walked into the elevator together.

Others had shown their disgust with her hoity-toity Manhattan heiress lifestyle and blamed her for the company's financial and other problems.

How naive she'd been! She hadn't expected any of this. She'd imagined that the employees would welcome her with open arms, like some savior or the prodigal daughter come home, and kiss her feet, not spit on the floor right next to her feet, as a factory worker had done today.

And that was all on top of trying to decipher the company's jargon, hierarchy, structure, finances, values, supply chain, goals, strategies, and, and, and.

Tonight, she was going to tell her dad and Isabel and Garrett that she was backing out of Worth Papers. She had bitten off way more than she could chew; she was going to have to leave with her tail between her legs.

She got out of her dad's car and tried to put the workday behind her, at least for a few hours. Breathing deeply to clear her head, she opened the door to Hartfield.

Immediately she sensed that something was different.

From the family room came Mila's lively chatter and screams of "giddyap," as well as Isabel and Morley's voices and Felix's gurgling noises. There was another voice, too, a deep, familiar male voice.

Could it be? Emma's heart lurched into her throat. But he wasn't due back until tomorrow. What was he doing here, at Hartfield, anyway? Emma wanted to run into the family room to confirm Adam's presence with her own eyes. Instead she went to the foyer mirror, combed her fingers through her hair and made herself walk steadily toward the room. At the doorway, she watched the domestic scene for a moment unnoticed. Adam was crawling on the floor giving Mila a ride.

How had she looked at Adam all these days and weeks and months and years with indifference when just gazing at him now made her heart swell? How broad his shoulders were. How long and muscular his limbs were. How strong his jaw was. She could swear he was the most gorgeous, manly creature she'd ever laid eyes on.

Mila spotted her first. "Auntie Em, Auntie Em, look who's here!"

Still on all fours, Adam raised his eyes to hers. They were liquid and warm and brown, with flecks of gold in them. His soft brown hair was as tousled as ever. She longed to run her fingers through it. She noticed the flash of his teeth and wondered what it would feel like to have them nibbling her. His lips were full and beautifully shaped. Had she never noticed that before? She imagined them on hers. Her mouth parted and a small gasp made by the intake of her breath escaped.

Mila had dismounted and Adam stood up. Emma wanted to launch herself into his arms, but that privilege was no longer hers. She wasn't a little girl like Mila or even a college coed who could get away with such behavior, nor was she Hailey.

"Yes, I can see," she said walking slowly toward Adam, wondering if everyone could see the way her legs were shaking like a foal taking its first steps. She stopped in front of him, her chest rising and falling. His hand cupped her shoulder as he leaned in and planted a peck on her temple. She closed her eyes and breathed in the sensual, spicy, woodsy smell of him. "I didn't think you'd be back from Singapore until tomorrow."

"I came here as soon as I heard," he said.

"We've caught him up on all the events here," explained Isabel. "Dad's health, the situation with Worth Papers, and Dad's told him about your plans for the company."

"I know you probably would've wanted to tell Adam yourself, but I couldn't help myself. I'm so proud of you, Emma."

Emma pressed her lips together, pride at her father's words mingled with the shame that she couldn't live up to them.

"I'm completely blown away, Emma," said Adam, looking at her with such warmth and intensity that she wanted to burst into tears, but whether they would be tears of joy or sadness she couldn't say.

"You think it's a good idea?" she finally asked. "Do you think I could do it?"

It suddenly occurred to her that if Adam said she could do it, she wouldn't quit. She'd go back tomorrow and the next day and the next, determined to prove she was worthy of his belief in her, determined to win all of her employees' grudging respect, however hard she had to work for it.

"Emma, I've always believed in you," he said.

That was all the motivation she needed. She would throw her whole being into this because so many people were counting on her and she would not fail them. Or Adam. Or herself.

"I'd really like to stretch my legs after the long flight," Adam said. "Emma, would you join me for a walk around the grounds?"

"Better not. It looks like rain," Morley said.

"And dinner will be ready soon," added Isabel. "You will be staying for dinner, won't you, Adam?"

"Oh please do, Uncle Adam!" chimed in Mila.

"We won't be long," Adam said, "and yes, Isabel, I'd love to stay. Thank you for the invitation."

They had not seen each other since that horrible evening on her roof. So much had been left unsaid. And so much had happened in the meantime. Emma didn't know where to start, so she just walked beside him, aware of the energy crackling between them.

"Your dad says you're going to be staying here for awhile?"

She wanted to tell him that without him in their building, it wouldn't be home anymore. That she always thought she loved her apartment and her building and her neighborhood. But what she actually loved—who she actually loved—was her neighbor. That it would have been more painful to stay, to be reminded of him every day.

"Yes, Dad needs me, and Worth Papers is here. I need to be here, away from distractions," she ended up saying.

"Emma, I also heard about Ryan and Juliette. Hailey told me."

At the mention of Hailey's name, Emma's face darkened, reminded as she was of the one person who stood between her and Adam. Of course Hailey and Adam would have spoken. Of course, despite his busy week, despite being away on business, he'd have time to speak to the woman he loved.

HE COULDN'T MISS the way Emma's face had clouded over at his mention of Ryan and Juliette.

When Hailey had told him that Ryan and Juliette were a couple and that Emma's dad had had a heart attack, Adam could only think about getting to Emma. He imagined the blow for Emma of learning about her dad and then finding out her lover had thrown her over for someone else. And not just for anyone else, for Juliette, who he knew Emma was secretly jealous of. He still had meetings and a dinner scheduled, but he'd canceled them all, saying there'd been a family emergency. He'd gone straight to Changi Airport looking for the next flight back.

"I'm really sorry, Emma," he said, running a hand up and down her bare arm. "I could punch his lights out just thinking about how he treated you!"

He had known from the night at Maison Dalat, when he'd seen Emma with Ryan, that Ryan couldn't be trusted. Not with Emma's feelings, anyway.

Emma shrugged. "Ryan told me everything. But you'd guessed all along, hadn't you? You tried to tell me, but I laughed it off as impossible."

"I was only trying to warn you. I thought he was trying to play you both."

"We all do things for love sometimes that may seem wrong to others, especially by those who end up getting hurt. But I get why he did what he did."

"That's big of you, Emma. I know how much it must hurt right now, but time will heal these wounds."

He'd rushed here, if he were honest, in hope. That now that Ryan was out of the picture, he might have a chance.

He'd wanted to catch her, hold her, soothe her, as he had the night she'd broken up with Jeremy. But this time he wouldn't jump the gun. He would give her the space to get over her feelings for Ryan, then he would court her and let Emma know exactly how he felt about her. He owed himself that. If she rejected him, he would never try again.

Emma stopped. "Wait, you think I'm in pain because he chose Juliette over me?"

"Aren't you?" Adam's brow knitted together.

"No, I was never in love with Ryan!" Emma said, a little smile tugging at her perfect lips.

"You weren't?" asked Adam, trying to make sense of this. "But it certainly appeared that way."

Emma looked away as she said, "I guess you could say we used each other for our own reasons, but it's been over for a while."

Adam could very well imagine exactly how Ryan had used Emma, and it did not sit well with him one single bit. But no, that was beside the point. The point was, she wasn't hurt, hadn't been in love with Ryan. Which meant . . . maybe he didn't have to wait —because he couldn't wait, not where Emma was concerned. He was known for his coolness and control in business, but with Emma . . .

$\sim$

ADAM'S FOREHEAD SMOOTHENED. "So you're happy for him and Juliette? No hard feelings?"

"Yes, I'm happy for him and Juliette. I hope they have a long-lasting, successful relationship."

"Oh, Emma," Adam said, a ghost of a sigh. She could feel Adam looking at her. She stared at his mouth. She saw it opening, then closing, then opening again.

"So your heart's safe?" he finally got out. That was an inside joke from a long time ago, something she would ask him after a night out, to see if anyone he'd met had caught his interest.

If you want to know the truth, Adam, it's not. You have it and you're capable of ripping it to shreds or flinging it away. But you can't know the truth. I'm not going to do that to Hailey.

Instead, to deflect from having to answer the question, Emma said, "Is yours?"

"Funny you should ask," Adam said, looking at her, his forehead scrunched up again. "As a matter of fact, it isn't. I—"

"Please, don't!" Emma didn't want to hear Adam confirm that he was together with Hailey. Maybe if he didn't confirm it, there was still hope for her. Feeling her eyes brim, she fled toward the orchard.

"But Emma . . . " he said, trying to grab her hand.

"Don't Adam, I don't want to know," she said, shaking his hand away, increasing her pace.

"But I—Dammit!" There was a loud clap. Thunder perhaps? Or had Adam just slapped a tree? "Fine, whatever, if that's what you want."

Emma chewed on her bottom lip. It had been important for Adam to tell her. Maybe it was meant as a confession because, as Hailey had said, they hadn't thought Emma would approve. Well, whether she approved of their relationship or not was irrelevant. But his friendship wasn't. She turned back to face him. "I'm sorry. I shouldn't have stopped you and walked away. As a friend, I want to hear what you have to say."

"Fuck, Emma! Don't you see? That's the problem. I don't want you as just my friend. I want more, so much more!"

Emma stopped breathing. Her cheeks tingled. Had she heard correctly? Could it be? She looked at him, saw the anguish on his face, the way he tried to avert his eyes. She couldn't stand to see him hurting. She lifted a hand to caress his cheek. She hoped all the warmth and tenderness and love that threatened to burst from her heart would be reflected in her eyes.

Her chest heaved up and down as she waited for a reaction. His eyes seemed to gain the gleam of understanding. He tucked a lock of hair behind her ear. She parted her lips, all thoughts of Hailey or anyone else gone. It was just her and Adam surrounded by rows of apple-dotted trees. His fingers grazed the side of her face, then his thumb traced, oh so softly, the contours of her bottom lip. It was the most sensual thing she'd ever experienced. She felt kindling deep down inside her catch fire. She'd never wanted anything so badly as she wanted Adam to kiss her right now. Her face tipped up, her breath was coming faster and harder. The fire inside her was building, spreading. Helpless, she flicked her tongue across the broad expanse of his thumb.

It seemed to jolt something inside him, for lightning quick, before she'd had time to gasp, there was no more distance between them. Her mouth, her breasts, her belly, her pelvis were flush against his firm length, as if they were a pair of strongly attracted magnets that had sprung together, unable to resist a force stronger than themselves.

She filled her hands with his hair, her nose with the delicious, woodsy scent of him, her mouth with his greedy tongue. It was more than she could take, and it still wasn't enough. It was only more fuel for the flames.

Even the rain that started to fall on them could not douse it.

CHAPTER FIFTY-FOUR

Adam unlocked his door and pushed it open for Emma to enter. He followed her in, slammed the door shut and backed her up against the door. His mouth found hers in the dark, while his hand found her breast. "Definitely perfect just as they are," he murmured against her smile.

After the most tortuous dinner and drive home he'd ever experienced, he had the woman he wanted exactly where and how he wanted her. Well, almost.

Calm down, Adam. You've dreamed about this moment for so long, don't get ahead of yourself.

He tore his mouth away, turned on the light, and led her to the couch. "What would you like to drink?" he asked.

Emma slid down onto the leather couch, crossed her legs and smiled, her eyelids hooded. Was that an open invitation or was she always so sexy?

"A red I think. Something full-bodied."

He went to the kitchen and rummaged through the drawers, looking for candles. He wasn't a candles kind of guy, but he wanted the mood just right for their first time together. He finally found a couple of tealights, something to put them in, and a matchbook from a small Italian trattoria Brooke had liked. It took three strikes before he could get the match to blaze. Lowering the match toward the wick in the first cup, he noticed how his hand was shaking. The flame licked his finger. "Ouch," he said, dropping the match and bringing his finger to his mouth.

Adam cursed himself, embarrassed. He couldn't remember the last time he'd been nervous with a woman.

"Here let me," said Emma, who'd come up next to him. She'd reached for the matchbook and at the same time she'd taken his burnt finger and enveloped her warm mouth around it.

Adam gulped, floored by desire.

When the rain had started, he'd wanted to continue kissing Emma. He hadn't ever wanted to stop, but for decency's sake, he'd had to. Once back at the house he never got a chance to get Emma alone.

They'd sat next to each other at the table, which in retrospect hadn't been such a good idea; he couldn't have repeated a single thing the others had said to him over dinner. All his awareness had been reserved for Emma, whose arm kept brushing his. Or had it been his arm brushing hers? Emma, whose hand had found its way onto his lap at one point and had drawn patterns on his thigh. Emma, whose hand he'd caught in his, whose palm and wrist he'd stroked with his thumb while he appeared to be absorbed in something her father was saying to him.

The candles lit and glasses of wine poured, he lowered the lights, put on some Ella Fitzgerald and sat down next to Emma.

While they'd been kissing in the orchard, words hadn't been necessary. Over dinner, words hadn't been possible. In his rental car—Emma, to his relief and titillation, had asked for a ride back to her apartment "to take care of a few things"—words had not seemed appropriate. Instead they had made small talk about neutral subjects: Annalisa, Mila, work.

And now, he felt, words should be spoken, declarations made, clarifications given. At the same time, they'd reached this point and he was afraid. Less by the intensity of his own feelings, which were scary enough, but by the fear that this was just sex for her, that he was just a rebound from Ryan, some poor substitute.

By finding that out now, he wouldn't be able to go through with it.

With this.

His mouth zoomed in on hers and tasted the 100-dollar-bottle of wine on her lips, which were worth every penny.

He wouldn't be able to—she'd put a hand up his shirt—feel her hands exploring his whole throbbing body.

He started to inch up her top. She raised her arms, and he lifted off the scrap of turquoise silk and drank in the perfectly shaped orbs that rose and fell with her breath, the hints of dusty pink tips visible through the dainty black lace that encased them.

He wouldn't be able to know whether her breasts were as round and perky as they looked or whether they would hang and sway slightly when released from their lacy nets; he wouldn't know the exact size and color of the peekaboo pink nubs and know how tightly they would pucker between his teeth.

He wouldn't be able to—she was now in his lap—stand up and carry her, with her legs around his waist, to his bed.

He wouldn't be able to do everything he planned to do with her once he got her there.

No, he was too far gone by this point to stop.

Screw taking it slowly. Screw talking—there would be time for that later. Besides, he was certain he'd read all he'd needed to know in the look she'd given him out there in the orchard. And now he would show her everything that was hammering away in his heart.

∽

THEY SLEPT ENTWINED until sunlight filled the room. Their sleep had been interrupted once by a mutual desire to revisit the pleasure of the first encounter and explore the promise of what future encounters may hold.

"Thank you," Adam said when their eyes seemed to flutter open at the same time the next day.

"For what?" she murmured languidly.

"For being you, for fulfilling and surpassing all the illicit fantasies I've had of you over the years, for making me feel incredible."

"Is that all?" she smiled as his mouth found hers.

"If you want more, I'm sure it could be arranged," he said, rolling her onto her back.

"For someone who's nearly 40, your stamina is impressive."

"I think that comment deserves a spanking."

CHAPTER FIFTY-FIVE

Showered and dressed, Adam carried two steaming mugs upstairs to Emma's apartment. He'd made her cappuccino exactly as she liked it: strong, not too hot, with a sprinkling of chocolate powder on top. He let himself in and set the mugs on her kitchen counter. He heard her in the shower and imagined her soaping herself all over. He had to quickly squelch the mental image before his desire started to rise again. At this rate, he'd never get any work done. He picked up his mug and went to sit on her couch while he waited.

On the coffee table was a rolled-up magazine. It seemed out of place there on the tidy glass surface; the thick fashion magazines and coffee table books were stacked neatly on the lower rack of the coffee table visible through the glass top. He took a sip from his mug then unrolled the magazine. It was an issue of *In the Know*. He was about to put it down when a bit of red caught his eyes—Emma's hair. A tiny picture of Emma was inset between some Lothario type and Ryan. Cocksure after their morning romp, amused at what this was going to be about, he opened the magazine and it fell open on photos of Emma, *his Emma*, with some other guy!

He dropped the magazine as though it'd burnt him. He ran a hand through his hair, trying to catch his breath. He picked up the magazine again. Emma looked exactly as she had last night: the head thrown back, the hooded eyelids, the look of desire that had robbed him of his senses. *But she was with some other guy!*

Adam's breath tore out of him in ragged puffs; his chest hurt. He checked the issue date, not wanting to jump to conclusions. Nope, it was recent. Adam dropped his face into his hands, scrubbed it in his palms. Was she in love with this fucking soccer player? Was that why she couldn't say if her heart was "safe" yesterday? Or was this guy only someone she was fucking . . . as she had *him?* The thought that what they'd just shared—which had meant the entire world to him—might have been something casual for Emma wrenched something loose inside him. He remembered the moment he'd realized that Caroline hadn't been faithful to him. He couldn't face that again. Not with *Emma*, who he loved more than even he'd admitted to himself. Who else was she screwing? No, he didn't want to know. He would not go there; he wouldn't torture himself as he'd done with Caroline—

"Adam, I was thinking, I could—" Emma walked out of the bathroom, a towel around her nakedness. She stopped when she saw what was in his hand. "Shit."

"Shit is right," he bit out. "When were you going to tell me you were seeing someone else, Emma? I thought, I thought we were . . . Never mind! What was last night? Am I just a fuck buddy to you?"

Emma tittered. "Lauren said you'd make a good fuck buddy."

The laughter and words were like a poisoned arrow. He remembered that same laughter after her breakup with Jeremy—when she'd pushed him away after he'd confessed he cared for her. His worst fear was confirmed. And he had nobody to blame but himself.

∾

Fuck! Fuck! Fuck! That stupid fucking laugh of hers! Horrified and ashamed, Emma wished, more than anything, that she could take back what had come out of her mouth. She started to say something else, but suddenly shirked back. Out of the corner of her eye, she'd seen Adam's arm rise, had instinctively thought he was going to give her a massive backhand.

The rolled-up magazine shot across the room and hit the back wall with a thud. Emma felt as if she'd been hit.

"What the fuck, Adam!" she screamed, taking out her horror and humiliation on him, then regretting it immediately.

"You're a fine one to talk!" He was across her apartment, his hand on the doorknob.

"Wait, Adam!" she yelled as the door jerked open then slammed shut. He was gone. She fell against the door, then slid onto the floor.

Stunned, she just sat there.

As if she needed any more emotional upheaval at the moment!

She wasn't even in a *relationship* with Adam, and she'd already fucked it up. This was too damned hard. Was this self-loathing and heart-wrenching pain even worth it?

But then she remembered what it had been like to be with him. It'd felt, it'd felt . . . There were no words to describe the wonder of it.

The hot tears coursed down her face; she dashed them away with her hands, the edge of her towel.

She could go to him now and tell him he'd gotten it all wrong. There was nothing between her and Diogo; it was *him* she loved. There was only him.

But what if he didn't believe her? But why shouldn't he? And anyway, what was the deal with him and Hailey? A wave of guilt rushed over Emma at the thought of Hailey, but she thrust it aside. What right had he to, without even knowing the whole story, jump to conclusions? When he was likely doing the same thing he was accusing her of doing? And shouldn't he be the one to apologize to her for just storming out of here like that?

No, she couldn't let him believe that what he'd seen in the magazine had meant anything to her, certainly not compared to what they'd shared last night. Dressed, her heart pounding, she ran downstairs. She knocked, but he didn't answer. She began to pound on his door, desperate to see his face, to explain. The door stayed shut; he wasn't in the apartment.

Emma cursed herself for dithering as long as she had. Why hadn't she gone after him right after he'd left? Stupid, stupid, stupid!

Back upstairs she picked up her cell phone, called him. It rang, rang, rang, rang, rang, then she heard his voice. His voicemail message. She tried again and again before giving up.

Utterly despondent, Emma sat there for she didn't know how long. Until she realized she needed to get back to Highbury for the meeting with the auditors; she couldn't be late.

This was just a little misunderstanding, she told herself. He'll calm down eventually and she'll be able to explain. If Adam wasn't going to answer her calls, she could at least send him a quick message.

Just a one-night stand. Didn't mean anything. Let me explain.

She'd done all she could; now the ball was in his court.

Now she had other things to worry about. She needed to be clear-headed for the meeting. She needed to be a professional.

Emma took out her suitcase and threw things inside, grabbed a cream cheese-smeared bagel and Vitamin Water from the bagel shop, and made her way to Grand Central Station for the train to Highbury-on-Hudson.

∾

THE WORDS on the screen glared tauntingly back at him.

Had he been so blinded by love all these years that he hadn't noticed what a spoiled little bitch she was? He'd always defended her actions and apologized to her when he'd felt he'd gone too far in his reprimanding of her wild and willful ways.

And now she'd used him. In the most excruciating way possible. She'd kissed him and let him do things to her he'd fantasized about doing for years. She'd responded, oh how she'd responded, there was no mistaking the signs.

Yet . . .

Now she was telling him last night hadn't meant anything; it was just a one-night stand.

She'd played him all right.

He could not believe his own stupidity. That he'd let this happen to himself. There was a reason he hadn't made a move on Emma all these years; a reason why he was moving out of the building. It was called self-preservation. And now he'd fucked it all up.

She'd probably just slept with him so she could compare notes with Lauren or something. Or maybe she felt sorry for him and his pathetic, long-unrequited crush on her and decided she'd sacrifice one night to him with an emphasis on "as your friend."

Well, he'd had enough of Emma Worth and her itch scratching or notch adding or whatever the fuck last night was to her. He was thankful that he wouldn't have to see her again, barring the occasional family event.

And he certainly had no desire to hear what sort of explanation she was going to give to excuse her inexcusable behavior.

"Adam, sorry to interrupt your thoughts," said Hailey, "but you haven't answered my question."

He set his cell phone down on his desk and ran his palm over his face. "Sorry, Hailey, my mind was elsewhere. What did you want to ask me again?"

"The software developer candidate Jason Liu called to ask

whether there was a decision on the hiring for that position. Shall I go ahead and schedule a second interview with him?"

"Yes, Hailey. Yes, please do that, I'd hate to lose him. You have my calendar, just check when Rob can join, too. End of next week would be great if you can get him in then."

"Thanks, Adam." Hailey turned to go, then she turned back. "Are you okay? You don't look so well. Are you feeling sick?"

"You could call it that. My stomach is turning and I've got a bad taste in my mouth. It must have been something filthy and foul I ate last night, but I'm hoping I'll get over it soon."

Hailey looked puzzled at his odd choice of words. "You should go home and get some rest then. You're likely jet-lagged, too. Anyway we weren't expecting you this week at all."

"You're right, I might head home early. Try to shake this thing and get a start on the moving . . . "

After Hailey was long out of earshot, he added, " . . . on."

CHAPTER FIFTY-SIX

"How did it go on Wednesday?" Annalisa's voice came through Emma's phone.

"Fine."

"How was the auditor's report? Anything surprising or was it what you'd predicted?"

"It was, um, what we were, um, expecting. Actually, it, was, uh . . ."

"Emma, what's up with you?" demanded Annalisa.

"Don't know," said Emma, rubbing the back of her neck. "My head's exploding with all these figures and business terms."

"Are you having second thoughts?"

"More like fifth thoughts," muttered Emma. "It's over-whelming to say the least. But things are ironing themselves out." Emma shook her head and bit her lips to stymie the tears from springing into her eyes.

Again.

In the last three days, she hadn't heard a peep from Adam, no matter how many times she'd checked her phone.

On Wednesday, she'd gone into Worth Papers curious about what the auditors had to say and eager for the distraction.

Knowing where the company stood financially was a crucial step in her current fact-gathering and getting-to-understand-it-all stage.

The results, in terms of capital, hadn't been quite as bad as feared. The report pointed to clear problem areas, which corroborated with her SWOT analysis. She'd already identified ways they could streamline processes and mitigate weaknesses, in particular replacing some of the older presses with digital ones. This meshed with the plans to bring the company into the 21st century and make it competitive through customizable offerings.

Although many employees were still rude; she made sure no one got away with disrespectful behavior. The next time the senior manager had tried to grab her ass, she'd looked him straight in the eye and hissed, "Please take your filthy hand off my ass. Sexual harassment is not tolerated here. If you try that one more time—with me or anyone else in the company—it'll be your balls in my hand."

Oh, she could be no-nonsense. And in her current mood, nobody wanted to mess with her.

At the same time, she made sure those who needed to be heard and had solid arguments got an audience with her. She would need all the support she could get.

Slowly, she could tell, she was gaining respect.

All of it had given her the confidence to go on, to ignore for a few minutes or hours the thing that she couldn't forget.

Over dinner, she'd pick at her food and tried to act normal with her family. But as soon as she'd shut the door to her room, she would take off her cheerful, brave mask and give in to her mental exhaustion and emotional turbulence.

She felt like a collection of battered body parts after an accident: bruised eyes, busted-up head, crushed chest, lacerated heart.

She couldn't count the number of times she'd reached for her phone and cradled it, willing it to ring. Maybe he was just busy catching up at the office and getting ready to move, she told herself unconvincingly.

"You know, Adam should be in his new place now," said Emma into the phone, needing to bring him up, to say his name.

"Oh right. That went by fast. It's like an end of an era with him leaving the building. When are you going to see the new place?"

Emma couldn't stop the sob from escaping her.

"Emma Worth! What the hell is going on? You tell me right now! It's not something to do with Adam, is it?"

Emma nodded into the phone.

"You're not—you haven't—don't tell me . . . *you and Adam?*"

At that moment, Emma missed her best friend almost as much as she missed Adam. Annalisa could read what was in her heart, even without words, even sight unseen, 3,000 miles over the phone.

"When did this happen? What's wrong? 'Cause you're obviously not crying for joy right now."

The words spilled out: The misery of realizing that Adam and Hailey had to be seeing each other. The shock of finally understanding what was in her heart. How it'd felt to see him at Hartfield. His declaration that he wanted to be more than friends. She glossed over the more intimate details and fast forwarded to the horrible morning after.

"Holy shit," said Annalisa, letting out a deep breath. "You and Adam, together! Who would've thought? I should be surprised, I *am* surprised, but at the same time, it's not surprising at all. It seems to make perfect sense. You're in love, Emma! I never thought I'd see the day."

"You've obviously not listened to a word I've said. We're obviously not together, which is why I feel so shitty. Obviously."

"Obviously, it's just a little misunderstanding that needs clearing up."

"I seriously doubt that. I told him that Diogo was just a stupid one-night stand."

"And what did he say?"

"Nothing, he still hasn't responded to my text message. It's been complete radio silence."

"Wait, back up here, Emma. You told him over text message? You mean you haven't actually spoken to him in person about this?"

"No. He never gave me the chance to."

"What exactly happened after he left?"

Emma explained about going to his apartment and trying to call him.

"Finally I texted him, wrote that it wasn't what it seemed in the magazine and to let me explain."

"And you haven't heard anything from him since?"

"No, not a peep. Oh Ans! What am I going to do? What if he never calls? I feel like someone's drilled a hole in my chest. I can't eat a thing. I keep thinking, what if the amazing night we had together is the only night I'm ever going to have with him?" wailed Emma.

"I'm so sorry, Emma. I totally get what you're feeling; it was the same when Tom and I broke up that time. But I just can't imagine that Adam wouldn't have responded unless he doesn't believe you? Or . . . ? Can you go back and read me exactly what you texted him."

Emma did as she was told.

"Fuck, Emma! Don't you see?"

"What?"

"He thinks you're saying that *he, Adam,* was the one-night stand; that the night you two spent together didn't mean anything to you!"

Emma's heart stopped. "No!" she cried in horror. But reading the words again—the words that to her could only ever be about Diogo, and never, ever in a million years be about Adam—and thinking about them from Adam's point of view, in the context of their last encounter, and her breath was knocked out of her. "Oh shit! Poor Adam!"

～

EMMA FOUND the nearest parking lot and parked her dad's car. She had asked Garrett for Adam's address and had driven—too fast—to his new apartment. She walked down the street and looked for his building, praying he was in. She barely paid attention to the neighborhood and exterior of the building, just wanted to get to Adam as soon as possible. A well-dressed couple was coming out of the building; she ran to catch the door before it closed. Inside, she punched the elevator call button and watched the numbers impatiently. He was on the top, the eighth floor. What if he didn't want to see her, wouldn't let her explain? What if he wasn't alone?

Finally she was in front of what should be his door. She collected herself, smoothed down her hair and knocked. She knocked again. Then she heard footfalls. The door opened and there was his beloved face. It was unshaven; the cheekbones appeared sharper than the last time she'd seen him. The skin under his eyes was dark. She caught a whiff of scotch on his breath when he muttered, "Oh, it's you."

She suddenly felt shy, uncertain.

"What? Have you come back for more? I thought it was just a *one-night* stand." Adam took a sip from the tumbler of amber liquid he was holding. "Or did you want to make sure you were the first one to christen my new place—last one out, first one in —us being such good *friends* and all?"

Adam walked back into his apartment and sank down onto his couch, the leather creaking.

Emma closed the door behind her, navigated around the strewn pieces of furniture and boxes and sat down next to him.

She wanted to ask for a sip of his drink to moisten her dry mouth and burn away the stickiness in her throat. But what she had to say was more urgent.

She slowly released her breath. Then in a gush, she explained what Annalisa had made her realize about the text message, her words tumbling over each other. "I came right away. I couldn't let you go on thinking I didn't care," she finished. Then on a whisper she added, "I love you, Adam."

He turned his head to look at her. "What did you say?"

"I love you," said Emma, louder, reaching a tentative hand toward his face, needing to touch him, needing him to know the truth. "I couldn't have you continue hating me without knowing how I really felt."

His hand covered the hand on his cheek. He set his tumbler on the floor and then took her face in his hands, drew it to him until their lips met. Her stomach did a backflip. Her heart dropped between her legs. She tasted whiskey on his mouth and wanted to drink him in.

He pulled away. "I could never hate you, Emma. God knows I've tried. Even when I was sure you'd used and discarded me, I only hated myself because I still couldn't stop loving you."

"You love me?" asked Emma.

"I've loved you probably since the night I met you. But it was only when I began to feel so jealous seeing you with Ryan that I couldn't take it anymore. It's why I had to move out, Emma."

"And it was because of that horrid fight we had and finding out that you were moving out that I got wasted and slept with Diogo. It didn't mean anything, I swear. It was nothing like what we had the other night. Nothing at all like that."

"Shh, Emma, my Emma, you don't have to say more," and he silenced her with another kiss.

CHAPTER FIFTY-SEVEN

They spent the whole next day in Adam's apartment, with the exception of one brief trip to the corner bodega to pick up supplies. They made love and ate from takeout containers and talked.

Everything that needed to be said was communicated: Explanation about motives. Clarification about misunderstandings. Confessions that dated back years. Mutual wonder and delight at this new stage of their relationship.

The fullness, after so much emptiness, was almost too much, too beautiful, too excruciating for Emma to take.

On Sunday morning, Emma told Adam that after breakfast she would head to her place and then back to Highbury. Although she didn't want to leave him, although he tried hard to convince her otherwise, she told him she needed to prepare a few things for work and return the car. She also teased him that he wouldn't get any unpacking done if she was around; he conceded her that point by showing her just how unproductive a day, in terms of unpacking, it would be if they stayed together in the apartment again.

Fingers entwined, they walked to her car after breakfasting at a local café. Adam gave Emma a lingering kiss against the car door, a caress on the cheek, and a wave as she drove off.

Emma let herself into her apartment, looking forward to having a little time alone with her feelings. To hold the perfect fragile thing that was now hers—not unlike a newly hatched baby bird—and examine it unassailed by the sensations and stimulations being with Adam caused, however counterintuitive that sounded.

There was also someone she needed to see: Hailey.

Adam had revealed that Hailey was working for him as a part-time paid intern. When he'd spoken with Hailey after her disastrous interview, he'd wrested out of her that she might be interested in personnel and recruitment. That explained why Hailey had been at Adam's apartment the other morning and why he'd called her from Singapore.

Emma had felt a new wave of emotion for the thoughtful, generous, altogether wonderful man she was head over heels in love with and who loved her back. Awash with joy, pride, relief, love, lust, and yes, also guilt—for he'd been a far better friend to Hailey than she herself had been—she had vowed not to let Hailey down again.

As she waited for 3 p.m., when Hailey's shift would end, Emma logged into her computer. She scrolled through her e-mails. Anything to do with interest in her as the face or figure of this or that, any requests to interview her, she declined or deleted.

She wrote a quick post announcing that she would be putting *Worth It* on hold. She'd decided not to entirely shutter it because the blog could be useful, with a change of focus, in her new enterprise.

She e-mailed her sponsors and partners and those interested in working with *Worth It*, explaining the decision.

Satisfied with her efforts, Emma had the feeling that she was closing a volume of her life and beginning a new and more fulfilling one; a life in which she had a purpose and the love of her life by her side.

Just before leaving her apartment she got a text message. From Adam. She read it, smiled, sighed and felt a jolt of desire before tapping back a reply that she hoped would have the same effect on him. Her smile broad, she pocketed the phone and went to meet Hailey.

~

"You what?" Hailey asked.

"I thought there was something between you and Adam." Emma blushed.

No more secrets. No more stupid misunderstandings. No more false assumptions. That was her new motto, even if that meant admitting all the ways she'd messed up.

"But he's *old*," said Hailey, giggling "and my *boss*. He's more like my uncle."

Talk about off the mark.

"He's only 38!" said Emma, smiling to think what Adam would think to hear her defending his old age for once.

Emma sighed and leaned back against the cushy headrest, enjoying the warmth of the water around her feet, the sensual touch of the rose petals against her skin as they skimmed the surface, and the scent they released.

This was seriously relaxing. As was clearing the air with Hailey.

"Why did you feel that you couldn't tell me you were doing an internship with Adam?" Emma asked.

"I thought you wouldn't approve of me wanting to do HR. I thought you'd think it wasn't glamorous like doing marketing for a big beauty or fashion name."

"Oh Hailey," said Emma, touching the back of Hailey's hand, "I wouldn't have dissuaded you from pursuing working in HR. I would have . . . " Emma faltered.

She would have done exactly that. She would have persuaded Hailey that a career as an HR manager was all wrong for her, that she could do better than that. Just as she'd persuaded Hailey that programmer Rob was all wrong for her and that lead-singer-in-a-band Zak was interested in her. How right Adam had been. She'd meddled and wronged Hailey again and again. She'd never actually listened to Hailey's wishes. She'd tried to control her and dress her and make her do what Emma wanted, just as she had done as a little girl with Lottie LouLou and Hazel.

"You're absolutely right, Hailey. If you'd told me, I would have tried to dissuade you for exactly the reasons you named. You were right not to tell me. I'm so sorry, Hailey, for messing up your life; I thought I was helping, I thought I was doing it for you when I was really doing it for me and my own stupid vanity and self-gratification."

Once Adam had told her about the internship, Emma had figured out that Rob must have been the "who" that was making Hailey so happy, and Hailey confirmed it.

Hailey expressed delight and relief that Emma not only knew about Rob, but wholeheartedly approved and was genuinely happy for her.

Hailey also told Emma she suspected Adam had set them up, offering Rob and her two tickets to a Yankees game he said he couldn't make. "Rob's a big baseball fan; I've never been to a game before. We went and had so much fun, we've been hanging out ever since."

Did Mr. Anti-matchmaker Knightley have a hand in getting Hailey and Rob together? Emma couldn't wait to tease him about it.

CHAPTER FIFTY-EIGHT

"Why are we putting an extra plate there next to you, Auntie Em?"

"Didn't your mom tell you? Uncle Adam's coming for dinner. He may even stay all weekend."

"Yippee! Uncle Adam's coming! That's the best news. I can't wait to show him my school."

Emma grinned at her niece's enthusiasm, but she was just as excited to see Adam as Mila was. Wednesday morning was definitely too long ago. Naughtily, she wondered when it would be seemly for them to sneak off for some alone time. Then she wondered, selfishly, whether she'd have to share him with the rest of the family this weekend.

When the doorbell rang, Mila ran to open the door, closely followed by Emma. Adam stood there behind a large bouquet of dahlias and garden roses.

"Hi," Emma said shyly.

"Hi yourself. These are for you," he said, passing her the bouquet and stealing a kiss before dropping to his haunches and giving Mila a tweak on the nose.

While Emma put the flowers in a vase, Adam listened to Mila's excited chatter about her kindergarten class. By this time, Isabel had come downstairs with a freshly bathed and pajamaed Felix and Morley had also joined them in the large, modern kitchen.

"Garrett's just called and is on his way," announced Isabel, then turning to her brother-in-law said, "Hey Adam. Nice to have you join us tonight."

Adam gave Isabel a hug and took Felix from her. He breathed in Felix's baby scent. Emma couldn't take her eyes off of them. Then he went to Morley and extended a hand, "Evening, sir. Thanks for having me. I trust you're feeling well?"

Morley patted him on the arm. "Oh yes. I feel well, never better. And no need to 'sir' me, 'Morley' is fine."

"Is it true that you're going to stay here all weekend, Uncle Adam?" piped up Mila.

"Yes, if you want me to," said Adam to Mila.

"Yippee! But where will you sleep? I know! You can share my new bunk bed with me. I'll even let you have the top."

Emma quickly said, "We'll figure it out after dinner. There's plenty of room here."

By then, our family will know about Adam and I. The thought filled her with nervous excitement.

"Hello, where's everyone?" Garrett appeared in the kitchen.

After taking Felix from Adam, Garrett said, "How's the new bachelor pad, bro? You haven't unpacked yet, have you? Which explains why you're here."

"You're right. I haven't touched anything. It doesn't feel at all like home yet."

"It's no surprise to me why it wouldn't feel like home," said Morley, "Emma's not there. You would have done better to stay put in the old apartment. As it is, she's been running back there every other night."

"It was only Tuesday night," Emma protested.

At the same time Isabel said, "I'm sure that's not what Adam meant. He's just got to get familiar with the new neighborhood."

"What was the problem there, anyway?" continued Morley. "Was the rent too high? For family we could've lowered it."

Everyone laughed. "It had nothing to do with the rent or apartment, Morley. I loved it there. But it was time that I moved on and bought my own place."

"It doesn't hurt that Adam got an offer he couldn't refuse, eh?" said Garrett, winking and nudging Adam in the ribs with his elbow. "Have you asked your cute realtor out yet?"

"No, and I don't intend to, and never did. I only have eyes for one woman." With that pronouncement, he stared so unabashedly and long at Emma that she flushed with pleasure and the others couldn't help but understand.

Isabel clasped a hand to her mouth and gasped. "You two? You're . . . together?"

In confirmation, Adam took two steps over to stand next to Emma and placed his arm around her waist, drawing her to him. Emma nodded, her heart full.

"Well I'll be damned! You sneaky devil! How long have you been keeping this under wraps? I should have known considering you didn't come out to visit us in Park Slope as often as you've trekked up here in half the time."

"This definitely calls for a celebration. I believe there's a bottle of Veuve Cliquot in the fridge," said Isabel.

"Does this mean you now love each other the way mommies and daddies do?" Mila wanted to know.

EPILOGUE

Two years later

Emma's eyes swept around Hartfield, which was dressed up in all its festive glory. The robin's egg-blue place cards and menus at each setting were from Worth Papers' new wedding-day stationery line and looked exquisite. The colorful, hand-folded paper cranes—they hadn't quite managed 1,000, but who's counting?—were charming.

"Dad, what a wonderful day," Emma sighed.

"That makes a father very happy to hear," said Morley, squeezing Emma tightly as the song ended. "Thank you for the dance."

"I wouldn't have missed the father-daughter dance with you today for anything. Now go find Isabel," said Emma giving him a playful push as she watched couples reassembling on the dance floor as the band struck up a lively rendition of Glenn Miller's "In the Mood."

As her toes tapped along, Emma's eyes were drawn to Ryan and Belinda. Ryan was leading Belinda to the catchy swing beat and to Emma's surprise, Belinda was following along, throwing in some fancy footwork of her own.

"I didn't know Belinda was such a good dancer," Emma remarked to Juliette, who had come up to stand next to her.

"Apparently, back in the day, my mom and Aunt Belinda loved to go dancing," said Juliette.

"She looks radiant, doesn't she?" said Emma.

"Yes, I couldn't agree more. It's good to see she's gained back all her weight since Grandma's passing."

Emma nodded. "And how are you Juliette?" she asked.

Juliette told Emma that she and Ryan would be going to Australia for Ryan's next film. Ryan would go first and Juliette would join him a few weeks later when her students went on summer break.

"Do you mind all the traveling?" Emma asked.

"No, I love it," replied Juliette, telling Emma that she thrived on the time away and being able to explore the sights and discover different cultures. "All of that unleashes my creativity and I'm able to compose. It's such a change from L.A., where our lives are pretty routine with *Episode* and my teaching—though of course that will change next year when *Episode* concludes and we move to London. Ryan's really itching to be back on the stage."

"That sounds wonderful. By the way, the pictures of you and Ryan from the Oscars—Wow!"

"Thanks." Juliette blushed. "Once I got over my fear of the cameras, my fear of everything in general, and stopped taking myself so seriously, life's become a lot more fun. I guess being with Ryan doesn't hurt."

"No, I can't imagine it would," said Emma as Ryan dipped Belinda and the room exploded in applause.

"And you, Emma?" asked Juliette, when the applause had subsided. "You seem much more grounded these days."

"You mean less of a snobby, self-satisfied know-it-all?"

laughed Emma. "Well, work certainly keeps me humble. Every day's a challenge, but it makes seeing Worth Papers getting back on its feet that much more rewarding. I couldn't imagine doing anything else."

"Back on its feet and into designer shoes, you mean," said Juliette. "The designs are so modern and tasteful."

"Isabel's a fabulous creative director. The aesthetics is all her."

"I'll have to congratulate her, then. Everyone we know in L.A. is using Worth Papers for their invitations and cards. You know how they love those pictures of themselves and their children! Speaking of, I got a Christmas card from Chloe; it was her and her new boyfriend dressed up as sexy Santa and Mrs. Claus," said Juliette, her eyes twinkling with humor.

Emma was reminded of the wedding invitation—*not* printed by Worth Papers—she'd received from Lauren. Emma doubted Lauren actually wanted her to attend; she'd just wanted to show off that she'd finally snared someone. And was beating Emma to the altar.

"Am I glad to see you two!" In a sudden whirl of blue, Annalisa had descended on them, clutching a half-filled champagne flute. "Give me some cover, will you? I just want to snag a couple of sips of champagne without Tom and my mom getting apoplectic. It's not like a little champagne in the third trimester is going to do any damage." Annalisa drained her glass. "Now I'm going to dash before someone takes a picture of the blue whale next to you two svelte mermaids."

"That's Annalisa for you," said Emma, laughing.

While Juliette got pulled onto the dance floor by Ryan, Emma watched Rob and Hailey dance by. She still couldn't believe she'd ever tried to break them apart or dismissed Rob as being somehow unworthy. Worth Papers & Stationery's CTO for the past two years, Rob had been the company's digital transformation genius, guru and mastermind. If it hadn't been for him,

Emma honestly didn't think the company would have survived. Rob was also a friend and surprisingly fun to have around. Emma recalled last weekend, when the Worth-Knightley clan had gathered at her and Adam's apartment to fold paper cranes for the wedding. After a while, Adam and Garrett had given up on the folding and fired up the barbecue on the spacious corner balcony, and Rob had pulled out his guitar. They'd all ended up having a great time singing, folding, drinking, eating, joking and watching the sun go down over the Hudson River. They'd also toasted Hailey's new job as an HR manager in a tech company.

Emma's gaze shifted to where Adam was dancing—a second dance—with a beautiful young lady.

In a tulle and lace flower-girl dress, Mila was beaming as brightly as the bride.

"Mind if I cut in?" Emma asked her niece.

"Of course not, Aunt Emma. I showed Uncle Adam a few moves so don't be surprised if he starts showing off."

Emma and Adam exchanged smiles. She fit herself into Adam's strong, familiar arms. It felt like home.

"What's that look for?" Adam asked.

"What, you don't recognize it? I was thinking how well you clean up," teased Emma. "In fact, you look good enough to eat. Meow."

Adam's laughter filled Emma up.

"So I guess this is happily ever after?" asked Adam.

"I thought this was where the hard work begins," said Emma.

"I think the bride and groom have suffered long enough to get to this point. They deserve a happily ever after."

"Adam, I swear: You've gone all mushy and romantic on me."

"I can't help it; you have that effect on me, Emma, my Emma."

"My dad and Belinda do make a good couple, don't they? For all my talk of matchmaking, I didn't see that one coming at all. But I'm so thrilled for them. They're like changed people. I'm sure they'll be very happy together."

"I fully agree. And I can't wait until it's our turn," Adam said, raising their joined hands so that the emerald and diamond engagement ring on Emma's finger winked at them, "so I can make you officially mine."

"And you, mine, Adam Knightley."

THE END

DEAR READER

Thank you for choosing to read *Emma and the City* over all the other books you could have read and for making it this far, which hopefully means you enjoyed the book.

Maybe you even loved it and are feeling warm and fuzzy right about now? If so, then my job is complete.

Now I have one small ask: If you did enjoy the book or know others who would, please recommend *Emma and the City* to your friends and followers. And leave a review at Amazon, Goodreads and/or the store where you purchased it. This will really aid in the success of the book and help me connect with readers who might like *Emma and the City*.

Want more *Emma and the City* or to see what else I'm working on? Visit me at www.AmyHilliges.com and sign up for my mailing list. I'd also love to hear your thoughts. What did you love or hate about *Emma and the City*? Would you like to see a prequel, sequel or another Austen adaptation? Let me know!

Thanks again for your support. You rock!

XO Amy Hilliges

ACKNOWLEDGMENTS

So many people to thank, so little space.

First, we wouldn't be here without Jane Austen, who wrote such a brilliant and timeless novel and has spawned such incredible fandom and interest in her novels and their numerous adaptations and spin-offs.

A shout out to all the writers in Zurich, Switzerland and beyond who I've met, connected with or learned from in the last three years. Your knowledge, experience, enthusiasm, feedback and friendship have been invaluable in giving me the confidence and motivation to write and publish this book! Good luck to you on your own writing journeys.

My wonderful editor Cate Hogan helped me turn a decent manuscript into something stronger, more original, more emotional, more dramatic, more surprising and just so much better. You should thank her, too.

To my early reader Claire Doble, our coffees and lunches to discuss writing and life and your enthusiastic response to my manuscript were really necessary and appreciated.

To my Vis-à-Vis buddy Denise Pellissier, our weekly chats

and working sessions and your help and cheerleading have really kept me going. Haven't we come a long way?

Thank you to my beta readers, Austen-fan Jacquie Prindle and my sister, Jenny Ko, for your time and valuable feedback.

Where would we be without our friends and neighbors? Thank you to Cecile Rietmann-Edwards and Rebecca Witt for things like *Clueless* viewings, coming up with fictional names, helping me edit my blurb, working sessions, jogs, trips, and lots of coffee, tea and wine.

A big kiss to my husband for believing in me, supporting me, reading drafts, watching the boys, and listening to me talk endlessly about *Emma and the City*, even when it was the last thing you wanted to do.

Hugs, kisses and maybe a Lego set each to M & K for understanding that I couldn't always be there for you or be as engaged as I would have liked to have been because I had to work.

To my cousins Sandy and Craig for giving me input about piano delivery and tuning, and anyone else who's helped me with the creation and publication of *Emma and the City*.

To my mom, brother and in-laws for your love, support and babysitting.

And thanks to my friends and acquaintances all over the world who've been so eager to hear about my writing and excited to read my book.

Finally, a well-deserved pat on the back (with a side of cream) to me for accomplishing something I set out to do, something that's been a dream of mine for more than 30 years. Hopefully this is the first step to me living my dream for at least another 30 years!

Cheers, thanks and love to you all!

ABOUT THE AUTHOR

Amy Hilliges always wanted to be a writer when she grew up. Finally, at 40, after years being paid to write professionally, she decided she was grown up enough to become a "real writer." *Emma and the City* is the result.

An American expat, Amy lives in Zurich, Switzerland, with her German husband and their two UK-born sons.

Find out more about Amy and her work at:
WWW.AMYHILLIGES.COM

Contact Amy at:
AUTHOR@AMYHILLIGES.COM

CPSIA information can be obtained
at www.ICGtesting.com
Printed in the USA
LVHW030614270420
654496LV00005B/1205